I0612130

THE TRAIL OF THE
CLOVEN HOOF

THE TRAIL OF THE CLOVEN HOOF

Arlton Eadie

RAMBLE HOUSE

ISBN 13: 978-1-60543-414-8

ISBN 10: 1-60543-414-0

Cover Art: Gavin L. O'Keefe
Preparation: Fender Tucker

DANCING TUATARA PRESS #7

THE TRAIL OF ARLTON EADIE

Most consider the early 1930s to be the "golden age" of Weird Tales, and with good reason . . . Lovecraft, Smith, and Howard were at the height of their literary prowess and other mainstays of the magazine such as C.L. Moore, Seabury Quinn, August Derleth, and Paul Ernst (to name but a few) were doing some of their best work. Despite this, the 1930s were also a difficult time for the magazine as this decade saw the loss of several key contributors beginning with Henry S. Whitehead's passing in 1932 and followed by the deaths of Lovecraft, Howard, Pendarves, and Arlton Eadie later in the decade . . . Wait, who was that last name?

Arlton Eadie is mostly forgotten today, but he holds a unique place in the annals of weird fiction. *Weird Tales* throughout its lengthy run remained very much a US-centric publication, with few authors from across the pond appearing regularly. Sure, there were scattered appearances by the ghost story greats like Benson and Wakefield, and even a couple of pieces by the Belgian master of the weird tale, Jean Ray (under his John Flanders byline); but for the main, there wasn't really much of a UK presence, with the exception of G.G. Pendarves and Arlton Eadie.

Both Eadie and Pendarves appeared regularly in *Weird Tales* as well as the UK equivalent, *Hutchinson's Mystery Magazine*. Tragically, both authors were among the number of major contributors who passed away during the 1930s. Ms. Pendarves was rather elderly and had begun writing quite late in life; Eadie was only fifty-one and in just over a decade was well on his way to establishing himself as a major voice in weird and mystery fiction on both sides of the Atlantic.

Not a great deal is known of Eadie's personal life; he was a lifelong resident of Lancing, and began selling fiction professionally in 1927 at the age of 41 and in the next ten years produced some dozen novels and nearly two-dozen shorter works, all of considerable merit. Unlike most authors who suffer through a painful apprenticeship, Eadie started at a high level of craftsmanship and grew from there. While he was known in the US solely as an author of weird fiction, the fact of the matter is that Eadie was comfortable in a number of genres including straightforward mysteries, romantic adventure, and even dabbling in science fiction.

What has always struck me as odd was that all of Eadie's fiction that I read was never less than good and often excellent with the exception of his longest work ... The novel that I refer to I first encountered as a teenager when I purchased the 1934-1936 run of *Weird Tales* from a First Fandom member who happened to be a neighbor. I had previously obtained a few issues from 1932 and 1933 from the same source and having read "The Siren of the Snakes", "The Devil's Tower", and "The Nameless Mummy" I had formed a very favorable opinion of this Arlton Eadie fellow and the fact that there was a whole novel by Eadie contained in this run was almost as important to me as the presence of a number of Smith, Moore, and Howard stories.

Sadly, my enthusiasm was quashed after reading the novel. Even allowing for it being broken up for serialization the story seemed clumsy, the tight pacing that was present in the other stories was absent, so too was the careful plotting and story development. The chapters seemed to lurch drunkenly into each other as though written on the fly. In short, what should have been a book-length masterpiece (based on what I had read previously) was a crushing disappointment.

Yes, the novel that I've so thoroughly trashed in the preceding paragraphs is the book that you hold in your hands. But before you fire off an indignant e-mail or pen the most poisoned of letters to either Fender Tucker or myself complaining of being duped out of your hard earned $20 or $40 as the case may be, allow me to elaborate ...

The book that you hold in your hands isn't exactly the one that I've reviled above. In fact, it's a horse (or centaur) of a different colour entirely. Some years ago I became aware of the book publication of Eadie's novel *The Carnival of Death*, another piece that had been published in serial form in *Weird Tales*. Subsequent poking around revealed that Skeffington's had published a book version of *The Trail of the Cloven Hoof* in 1935; and that began a decade or so of wondering ... Could it be that an author at the height of powers churned out such a clumsy work as what I had read in *Weird Tales*? Or, was it more likely that the sometimes-heavy editorial hand of Farnsworth Wright had effected a hatchet job on Eadie's novel? After years of searching, I finally had my answer last year when an Australian bookseller turned up a copy of the book.

I'm delighted to report that the book you hold in your hands is everything that one might expect a novel by Arlton Eadie to be.

Deftly plotted with the pacing that keeps the pages turning but allows for a leisurely mulling over the clues presented by the author. The pacing is true to the British mystery yarn and not the slambang staccato pace of the American pulp detective tales, but certainly not so slow-paced as to require the excising of some *ten thousand words*! Yes, the reason for the clumsiness of the *Weird Tales* version is easily explained by the ham-fisted editing done by Farnsworth Wright.

As no one seems to have copies of any of Eadie's correspondence, it's unknown whether or not he complained bitterly to colleagues, as did Clark Ashton Smith, or if he simply tolerated the mangling of his prose, secure in the knowledge that his preferred text was preserved for posterity in hardcover format.

In any event the present volume displays Eadie's considerable skill and is the first of what we hope will be several volumes collecting all of his weird and mystery fiction. Rest assured, we are aggressively searching for the book version of *The Carnival of Death*, and assembling at least two volumes of his collected short fiction. In the interim, we will be releasing one of his mystery novels, *The Crimson Query* in the next few months. Now, enjoy *The Trail of the Cloven Hoof* as it was meant to be read, returned to print after nearly seventy-five years!

John Pelan
December 2009

THE TRAIL OF THE
CLOVEN HOOF

CHAPTER I

VAGUE AND MUFFLED, the sound of a shot floated to Hugh Trenchard's ears through the veil of mist which, white and luminous in the moonlight, hung over the desolate moor. He paused in his stride and stood listening, a puzzled expression on his rather good-looking features.

"If the weather were clear, I should say it was some enthusiastic sportsman putting in a bit of night gunning," he muttered to himself. "But that's absurd! Why, it's impossible to see more than a few yards in any direction, and—"

Plop! . . . Plop! . . . "Help!"

The faint shout that followed the next two rapid shots showed unmistakably that something more serious than sport was afoot, and Trenchard without a moment's hesitation quitted the meandering sheep-track, along which he had been carefully picking his way, and began to scramble down the heather-clad hillside. Well enough he knew the difficulty of locating the direction whence the sounds had come; and he was not unmindful, either, of the risk he ran in blundering thus blindly through a part of Exmoor that was quite unknown to him. But for the moment he was only concerned with the possibility of finding a treacherous, impassable quagmire at the bottom of the valley which wound at the base of the steep beacon he was now descending; his one comfort was the indubitable fact that the sounds could not have come from any great distance, otherwise they would not have reached him through the blanket of fog.

In a few minutes he had reached the foot of the slope, to find himself confronted with a dense thicket of undergrowth. He paused for an instant to listen, but the cries had been succeeded by a deep and sinister silence.

"Ahoy!" he shouted with the full force of his lungs. "Ahoy!"

Hugh Trenchard had not the remotest connection with the sea, but he knew from experience that the deep-throated nautical hail would carry farther than any other shout. Scarcely had it left his lips than, with a loud crashing of the bushes, a huge form loomed vaguely through the mist and swiftly vanished up the valley.

There was a tight-lipped smile on Trenchard's face as he lowered the stout ash walking-stick which he had raised instinctively. It was, he reflected, only one of the wild forest ponies which roam over Exmoor. Yet something must have scared it badly to have sent it careering through the brake in that headlong fashion. Moved by this thought, he turned in the direction whence it had come, and after hurrying a few hundred yards had the satisfaction of seeing a yellowish glow amid the ghostly whiteness of the mist. A few more paces, and he could make out the shape of a door standing open. He broke into a run—only to stop with a jerk as he saw the body of a man lying directly in his path.

A cursory examination showed him that the man still lived, though his head was terribly injured. Apparently it was he who had fired the shots, for when Trenchard lifted him a heavy automatic pistol dropped from his nerveless grasp. Quickly carrying him into the house, Trenchard laid him on the settee and—his repeated calls having brought no response from the silent house— at once filled a basin with water from the kitchen tap and set about rendering first aid. With the sure, deft touch of one trained in the healing art, the young man washed the wound and bandaged it with strips which he tore from a clean bed-sheet that was airing in front of the fire. This accomplished to his satisfaction, he removed the man's outer clothing, carried him upstairs, and put him into the first bed he came across.

Returning to the kitchen, he made a hurried but futile search for a hot-water bottle; in the end he used a large flatiron, which, heated on the fire, wrapped in blankets, and placed at the patient's feet, proved to be a very effective substitute. His quest for stimulants occasioned an even longer search, but finally he found an unopened bottle of brandy—and, incidentally, several other things which gave him plenty of food for thought as he sat by the bedside waiting for the first signs of returning consciousness.

In spite of his youthful appearance, Hugh Trenchard was a full-fledged doctor, having passed his final degree just over a month since. It was as a relaxation from the strain of studying for his examination that he had embarked on his present walking tour through Somerset and Devon, choosing his route as the fancy took him, sleeping at chance-found country inns and village taverns; his mind devoid of all care or plans for the future, content to revel in the wide, heather-clad moors, the wind-swept skies, the smiling pastures and nestling homesteads of the West Country; his soul passing through that curious chrysalis stage, when the irresponsible medical student develops into the staid medical practitioner.

Every doctor is a potential detective; accustomed as he is to deduce the malady from the symptoms, he naturally applies the same mental process to other matters, and Hugh Trenchard was no exception to this rule. As he sat there, his favourite briar pipe gripped between his teeth, his keen grey eyes veiled in thought, his mind was busily probing the mystery into which he had unwittingly stepped.

That the old man had been the victim of a murderous attack there could be no question. That he had feared and prepared for such an attack was equally plain—newly fitted bars on the windows of the house and the perfect armoury of weapons which he had discovered in his search told that much. Yet, if the man had suspected his life to be in danger, why had he remained here, a solitary recluse, in the loneliest part of the moors? And why had he run out into the mist to court the very peril he had guarded himself against so carefully? Had his assailant been a tramp in quest of plunder? Trenchard shook his head slightly as he dismissed the thought; the house, though fairly large, bore no evidences that its owner was in affluent circumstances.

Tilting the shade of the lamp so that its light was deflected on to the pillow, Hugh Trenchard intently examined the face of the injured man. His age might be sixty-five, or slightly more, for his face was deeply lined, and his hair and short, full beard were iron-grey. It was a face of unusual refinement, with the brow of a thinker, a face of the type which one sees often when men of science meet in conclave. Who and what was he?

A faint, long-drawn sigh from the injured man snapped Trenchard's train of thought. Pouring some brandy into a spoon, he contrived, after some trouble, in inducing the now half-conscious man to swallow it, and after a few minutes had the satisfaction of seeing his eyes open and a faint tinge of colour come into the ashy cheeks. His lips moved slightly, and the young doctor bent closer to catch the halting words:

"The Terror of the Moor!" It was a mere whisper, yet the awesome horror that vibrated through it sent a chill through the hearer's blood. "The Terror that walks by night—the foul, cloven-hoofed shape that glides through the darkness, seeking but to destroy! Why does God suffer such fiends to stray from their native hell?"

"Easy there," Hugh said gently, rather amused at the febrile shapes that appeared to be peopling the man's brain.

"I swore that I would destroy it," the man continued, as if he had not heard the other man speak, "but it has destroyed me instead. I would die content if I had rid the earth of this monstrous being; but I have failed—miserably failed—yet another victim of the Terror of the Moor!"

Naturally the young doctor's first thought was that the man was delirious, but a closer examination revealed none of the symptoms consistent with such a theory. The pulse, though feeble, was slow and regular; his skin was cool and moist; his eyes lacked the wild stare which usually accompanies a rambling and incoherent mind. The man seemed to read the thoughts that were passing through Hugh's mind, for he observed, with the ghost of a smile:

"Doubtless you're wondering if my words are the irresponsible ravings of a madman—I am almost inclined to wish that you were right! But I can assure you that the Terror of the Moor is a real, tangible being—solid and substantial enough to have caused this"—and he made a slight gesture toward his bandaged head. "But I will not deny that my mind is a little confused with the blow. Tell me what happened."

Hugh Trenchard shrugged as he shook his head.

"As to that, I fear I am as much in the dark as you appear to be," he replied. "I had lost my way in the mist—thought I was miles away from anywhere—when I heard three shots and a cry for help. I dashed forward and came across you lying unconscious on the ground. I carried you into the house and did my best to bring you round. I am a medical man," he added a little self-consciously, "though I must confess that up to now you are my first patient."

There was a strained, eager look in the old man's eyes as he gazed up into Hugh's face.

"When you hurried to me," he asked slowly, "did you see anything?"

"Why, no."

"Or hear anything?"

"No."

"You're sure of that?" the old man repeated. "You did not see or hear any living thing—*any living thing*, mind you!—coming from the direction of the spot where I was attacked?"

"Well"—Trenchard gave a slight smile as he spoke—"now I come to think of it, there *was* an animal of some sort—one of the

moor ponies, I suppose—which blundered past me in the mist.
Probably it had been scared by your shots."

"Where did this—this moor pony pass you?"

The peculiar emphasis which the old man put on the words
caused Hugh to glance at him sharply. Evidently there was a motive behind all this cross-questioning about a seemingly unimportant incident.

"It was in the little thicket at the bottom of the valley," he replied. "Of course, I cannot absolutely swear that it was a pony.
You must realize that it was dark, misty, and there were bushes
between us. I caught the merest glimpse as it raced past. But I can
tell by your manner that you have an idea that it was a beast of
another kind."

The man on the bed nodded his head grimly.

"You're right, sir! I *have* an idea—a very shrewd idea—that the
thing you saw—the thing which attacked me—was a beast of a
very different kind!"

"Indeed?" Hugh was interested, as well as mystified, by the
strangeness of the old man's words and manner. "Doubtless you
had a nearer view of the thing than I had, if it was within striking
distance of you, and it would be more to the point if I were to ask
you what kind of an animal it was."

Again the man on the bed shook his head.

"Young man," he said impressively, "if I were to answer that
question truthfully you would certify me as a lunatic straight
away. I would suggest that you went and saw for yourself the nature of that beast."

Hugh Trenchard uttered a short laugh.

"The thing—whatever it may have been—is a good many miles
away by now."

"Maybe—but the Sign of the Beast remains!" The injured man
raised himself on his elbow and clutched Trenchard's arm as he
went on: "The ground is marshy in the valley—the trail of that
animal ought to be easy to find. Take a lantern and one of my revolvers—they are all loaded—and go and examine those footprints. Then you will see for yourself the nature of the beast that
passed you in the mist!"

Wild as the words were in themselves, they were uttered with
such an air of deadly earnestness as to impress Trenchard in spite
of his cooler reasoning. Without a word he rose to his feet and descended the stairs to the oak-panelled lower room. It was the work
of a very few moments to unhook the hurricane-lantern from its

peg behind the door, light it, and thrust one of the revolvers into his pocket. Then, drawing back the massive bolts as quietly as possible, he stepped into the mist-shrouded night.

He was far from being unmindful that there was a certain amount of risk attached to his errand, but the old man's half-spoken hints had raised his curiosity to such a pitch as to make every other emotion subservient to it. All the same, he kept one hand on the butt of the weapon in his pocket, and the feel of the smooth, cold metal was very comforting when he had left the house well behind him.

He quickly found the spot—marked by an ominous red patch on the gravel—where he had found the wounded man, and from there he headed blindly for the thicket. The increasing softness of the ground seemed conclusive that he was making in the right direction, and presently he came upon the track of the footprints that he had made when he had approached the house. It was simple matter to follow these, and Trenchard pressed with increased speed.

"Yes—it was here that I changed direction when I saw the light from the open door," he muttered as hurried forward, the lantern held close to the ground. "Here I made a detour to avoid that patch of brambles—and it was here, or somewhere about here, that the pony . . . Heavens above—what's this?"

Crossing his own trail was another line of deeply indented footprints, and at the sight of their queer sinister outline the import of the wounded man's strange words became clear.

"My God!"—the words burst from Trenchard involuntarily. "It is the trail of a cloven foot!"

Scarcely had the words left his lips, when, from somewhere near at hand, there came a mocking, demoniac laugh.

Trenchard's stooping figure straightened up like a released spring. He swung round in the direction of the voice; finger on trigger, every muscle taut.

"Who's there?" he called sharply. "Answer—or I fire!"

He paused for a breathless second, but the silence was broken only by the steady drip of moisture from the boughs overhead.

"Who are you?" he cried again. This time the answer came, in a voice that laid an icy finger on the base of his spine.

"The uncrowned King of the Moor! Be warned how you trespass on my kingdom in case you share the fate of Silas Marle—the meddling fool I have just sent to his last account! Put up your gun, you fool, and go your way. No weapon forged by mortal man can hurt me."

"We'll see about that!" Hugh muttered between his teeth.

As he spoke he threw up the hand which grasped the revolver and aimed in the direction of the voice. He pressed the trigger and a crashing report split the silence of the night. Before the echoes had died away the weapon was struck from his grasp, and almost at the same moment his lantern was shattered and extinguished.

But in the fleeting second he had seen the thing which had reached over his shoulder and disarmed him, and the sight seemed to leave his brain numbed with a nameless horror.

For the thing that had descended with irresistible force on his wrist was a limb which terminated in a cloven hoof.

CHAPTER II

I F, TEN MINUTES PREVIOUSLY, Hugh Trenchard had been asked if he was a believer in things supernatural, his answer would have been a contemptuous smile. It would have taken many hours of strong argument, backed by the sworn testimony of many eyewitnesses, to have convinced him that there are forces in Nature which do not conform to the so-called 'laws' of Natural Science. But in such matters a grain of real experience is worth a ton of theory. His conversion from scepticism to belief was instantaneous and complete.

One cannot accuse a man of being faint-hearted if he steps clear of the track when an express train rushes past; his action is the working of a blind instinct of self-preservation from a thing which cannot be withstood or overcome. Hugh Trenchard was no coward, yet when he found himself unarmed, encompassed by mist and darkness, and confronted by a mysterious being which, though speaking with the voice of a man, had the outward lineaments of a beast, his one thought and desire was to regain the shelter of the house. He turned and ran as he had never run before.

Reaching the garden gate, he paused and glanced behind him, listening. The only sound that reached his ears was the pounding of his own heart. Half ashamed of his panic flight, he completed the remainder of the distance at a walk, but he could not repress a long sigh of relief as he shot the bolts of the stout oak door. Now, at last, he could appreciate the motive that had led the solitary recluse to have the windows fitted with iron bars.

"Well?" There was a sardonic expression on the old man's face as he glanced round as Trenchard entered the bedroom. "There's no need to ask if you saw it—I heard the shot."

Hugh nodded as he seated himself.

"I saw its foot—and felt it, too," he returned grimly, rubbing his bruised wrist. "What in heaven's name is it? It spoke with a human voice, yet it seemed to have the form of a beast of some kind."

"You heard it speak?" cried the other eagerly. "What did it say?"

Hugh Trenchard shrugged.

"Oh, some melodramatic balderdash warning me to sling off unless I wanted to share the fate of Silas Marle. He was referring to you, I presume."

"Yes," said the old man slowly, "he was referring to me."

"You must have tweaked his tail the wrong way—you couldn't have trodden on his corns!" Hugh observed, with a rather shaky laugh at his own attempt at humour. "This satyr, or centaur, or chimera—unnatural history is not my strong point, and, anyway, I didn't stop long enough to make any detailed observations that would assist in classifying the thing—it seems to have taken a mighty big dislike to you. It was evidently labouring under the delusion that it had what is vulgarly termed 'bumped you off'—a silly mistake for Old Nick to make, by the way!"

With a slow gesture of hopelessness Silas Marle allowed his head to sink back on the pillows.

"It was no mistake," he said weakly; "I know I shall never recover."

The young doctor glanced sharply and apprehensively at his patient. In cases of shock the human vitality is at its lowest ebb, and a despondent state of mind might well turn the balance against recovery.

"By George, you'd better not let me hear you say that again!" he said in a tone of jocular severity. "You're my first patient, remember, and you've simply *got* to get well unless you want me to lose all faith in myself. Just you turn over and go to sleep. The sun will be up in an hour or so, and then I'll manage to find my way to the nearest house, where I can send someone to fetch a doctor and to notify the police that a homicidal maniac is roaming around."

"I thought you said you were a doctor," said Marle querulously.

"True," smiled Hugh, "but I'm not in the habit of carrying a stock of drugs about with me. And now I think you've talked quite enough—more than enough in fact—so I'll leave you to yourself."

As he was about to quit the room the old man called him back.

"While you are about it, tell them to send a couple of doctors and a lawyer. I want to make my will, and I don't want any question to arise about my present state of mind. I intend to put certain conditions in my will that will raise doubts as to my sanity unless I get a certificate to the contrary."

"Oh, I'll certify your sanity all right," Hugh assured him, thinking it best to humour his queer whim. But Silas Marle shook his head.

"Your certificate won't do," he said shortly. "I want two independent opinions—you'll see why later on."

"Very well, you shall have them," Hugh replied, quite unruffled by this apparent distrust, and before the other could speak again he closed the door.

A good map is an absolute necessity when tramping a district where moorland tracks and bridle paths form the only means of getting from one place to another, and the Ordnance Survey map carried by Hugh was both large-scaled and up to date. Spreading it on the table, he lifted his pipe and examined it closely.

Starting from the little market town where he had spent the previous night, he traced his day's journey, through the tiny hamlet of Worpledene, and thence across the hilly moors. Fortunately he had a fairly accurate idea of his position when the mist had descended, and, as he had been careful to keep to the same path subsequently, it was only necessary for him to trace the dotted line which represented the footpath on the map to discover his present whereabouts.

"Ah, here we are," he muttered, pausing with the mouthpiece of his pipe hovering over a tiny black rectangle which indicated a house, not far from the small town of Excombe. "This is Silas Marle's house, but he doesn't appear to have any neighbours less than three miles off. Ah, what's this?" His eye was attracted by a house which, judging by the size of the square that indicated its position, must be of considerable importance. "The Excombe Private Sanatorium—that should be the very place! There should not be any difficulty in finding a doctor there—perhaps two. A place like that will probably be connected to Excombe by telephone; or at any rate they will have a car which they will allow me to use in view of the urgency of the case. Yes, unquestionably it would be best to make for there."

He rose to his feet and, drawing back the heavy window curtains, saw with satisfaction that the mist was lifting, while in the east a pale golden glow told that the sun was already above the horizon. He was in the act of snatching up his cap from the old-fashioned oak sideboard, where he had carelessly tossed it on entering, when his gaze fell upon one of the numerous revolvers. He hesitated a moment; then, pausing only to make sure that it was loaded in every chamber, thrust it into his hip pocket.

"May as well take it, seeing there's plenty to spare," he thought. "Judging by the number of his guns, anyone would think Marle was about to start a little war on his own!"

The morning promised to be hot and clear, though as yet the mist still lay like spectral pools in the valleys and depressions untouched by the rays of the rising sun. Locking the door of the house and pocketing the key, Hugh Trenchard stepped out briskly, and some thirty minutes later, on rounding a steep shoulder of the hills, he saw in the distance the Excombe Private Sanatorium. The house itself stood in extensive, well-wooded grounds, and only the roof was visible above the high trees. Encircling the grounds was a very tall stone wall, armed with a triple row of iron spikes. A nearer approach showed that the sole means of entry was by a massive archway guarded by an iron gate, which proved to be locked.

Hugh gave vent to a low whistle of surprise as he noted these facts.

"Some sanatorium!" he commented mentally. "Looks more like a prison!"

He stepped up to the gate and peered through the bars. A small gate-keeper's lodge stood just inside; a carriage drive, its edges overgrown with weeds, curved out of sight among the trees.

Hugh tugged at the bell-pull, and after a very long pause a man emerged from the lodge. He was a huge giant of a man, with harsh, scraggy features which looked as though they had been hewn from tough wood with a blunt axe. Evidently he had been aroused from his slumbers, for his hair was ruffled and a full day's growth of stubble showed on his heavy blue jowl. He wore a kind of uniform of dark-blue cloth, and he was fastening the brass buttons of his tunic as he approached the gate.

"Wotcher want?" he demanded sourly, with an accent that had certainly not been acquired in the West Country.

"Can I see the resident physician? The case is urgent."

The man shook his head.

"This is a private institooshun. We only treats in-patients 'ere."

"But I don't want to consult him about my own health," Hugh answered, ignoring the man's surliness. "There has been a serious accident at a house three miles off—a case of attempted murder, in fact—and it is of the utmost importance that certain drugs should be administered without delay."

"This 'ere is a private institooshun—"

"So you said before," Hugh interrupted sharply. "It is a private institution—of which you are, presumably, the man who attends to the gate. I have had some hospital experience, but this is the first time I've heard an attendant presuming to decide whether one of the doctors shall or shall not attend an urgent case."

"I 'as me orders," the man growled sullenly. "Nobody's allowed inside this gate without a written order."

Repressing his impatience at this stupid delay Hugh produced his card-case.

"If that is so, will you be good enough to take my card to one of the doctors? If you will glance at it, you will see that I, also, am a medical man, and if I have any more incivility from you I shall not fail to report it to the proper quarter."

The man gave a grunt and took the slip of pasteboard. But instead of departing on his errand he stood twiddling it between his fingers. At this the last vestiges of Trenchard's patience vanished.

"Well?" There was an edge to his voice that made the other jump. "What are you waiting for?"

"Don't yer be in such a flamin' hurry, guv'nor. 'Ow can I take this to the doctor when he's not at home?"

The man's very looks betrayed the lie before it was uttered, but Hugh knew that to pursue the subject was useless.

"Very well, then. If that is the case, will you be good enough to allow me the use of your telephone for a few minutes, so that I can ring up another doctor?"

"Sorry, guv'nor, but we don't 'appen to have a 'phone."

Trenchard looked at the speaker in blank surprise; then he shifted his gaze and glanced upward at the double wires which, joining others supported by the usual poles, stretched into the distance.

"I suppose those lines are to dry the washing on?" he asked with contemptuous sarcasm.

"The 'phone's out o' order," snapped the man, and turned his back to terminate the interview.

"Hold on a minute," Hugh called after him. "I'll fix up your 'phone for you if you'll let me in. Can't you understand this may be a matter of life and death?"

The man swung round, his small eyes glinting viciously.

"I'll fix *you* if you don't take yourself off!" he shouted. "For two pins I'd come out there and teach you manners."

Trenchard grinned through the bars cheerfully and provokingly.

"I'm always open to take lessons—or give them," he said sweetly. "Won't you please step out here?"

The man's answer was a string of foul language.

"Just for a minute," Hugh pleaded. "No? Nothing doing in the teaching line? Well, as you won't come outside, I'll come in to you!"

He sprang upward as he spoke and, before the other realized his intention, drew himself up and dropped on the other side. Sheer surprise for a moment held the gate-keeper dumb; then:

"Get out o' this—the way you came—or I'll bash you to jelly!"

"Bash away!" Hugh invited with a grin.

As he spoke he placed himself in an awkward fighting attitude, and his opponent immediately fell into the trap. Sure of an easy victory over one so palpably ignorant of the rudiments of boxing, the man made a wild rush at Hugh, determined to finish him off with one tremendous blow of his flint-hard fist. Hugh, on his part, was equally determined that the contest should be a swift one. Every wasted minute lessened the chances of recovery for the in-jured man he had left in the house on the moor. He was fighting for a human life: he knew it, and resolved to take no chances.

There was a grim smile hovering about the corners of his lips as he awaited the onslaught of the infuriated giant. At the last mo-ment he side-stepped neatly—the great clenched fist shot past within an inch of his head. Before the man could recover, Hugh let him have a smashing left, delivered straight from the shoulder by one who knew how and where to hit—full on the point of his un-shaven chin. It was a blow that had been the deciding factor of more than one inter-university middle-weight championship. The giant swayed for a split second, then crashed to the ground like an uprooted oak, and the fight was finished.

Almost before his adversary's body had reached the ground, Hugh was speeding up the drive toward the house. It lay farther back than he had thought, and the avenue of approach wound among the clumps of trees in a bewildering and—just then—exasperating manner. Actually the time could have been merely a matter of minutes, but it seemed ages before he came in sight of a stark-looking mansion, of a dreary, uninspired style of architecture that proclaimed its mid-Victorian origin as clearly as if the date were blazoned across its pompous frontage. Trenchard had seen many public hospitals, and a few private ones, but never had he seen an institution which wore such an air of desolation. Had it not been for the smoke which rose from the chimneys he would have thought the place derelict, untenanted; for every visible window was closely shuttered, and a deep, unbroken silence prevailed.

"Evidently they don't believe in open-air treatment at *this* place!" the young doctor thought as he approached the front door and rang the bell. As he waited for an answer, his eyes travelled along the double tier of shuttered windows, his mind dimly wondering what kind of a medical man would keep his patients in semi-darkness, for the only daylight that could enter was that which could find its way through a small diamond-shaped aperture cut in the centre of each shutter.

For a full minute he waited thus, then raised his hand to ring again. But ere his finger reached the bell-push his arm dropped to his side and he remained staring in amazement at what he saw.

Through the nearest diamond-shaped aperture a single gleaming eye was regarding him fixedly. The hole was so small that he could only distinguish the eye and a portion of the face, but the little that he saw was sufficient to turn his blood to ice. In the faint shadow cast by the shutter, *the eye was shining with a greenish light!*

Hugh Trenchard's studies had taught him enough comparative anatomy for him to know that it is only the eyes of animals that possess the peculiar glistening layer known as the *tapetum lucidum;* yet the section of face immediately surrounding the eye was grotesquely human. He was just on the point of shifting his position to get a nearer view, when the face was withdrawn with a jerky abruptness which suggested that the thing—whatever it might have been—had been suddenly and forcibly pulled away from the window. At the same moment a shrill, animal-like cry came faintly from within, and, "Good morning, sir," said a smooth voice from the doorway. "To what do I owe the pleasure of this visit?"

Turning with a start, Hugh found himself face to face with a figure which, to one unversed in the procedure of the operating-theatre, might have appeared weird and unearthly.

The man was dressed from head to foot in white: a white cap covered his hair, and his features were invisible beneath the veil of white gauze, which, wound round the lower portion of his face so that the eyes alone were visible, gave him the aspect of an animated corpse.

The man in white noted the start of surprise, for there was a hint of amusement in his voice as he went on:

"I must apologize if my somewhat unusual attire has scared you—"

"Rubbish!" Hugh broke in, stung by the man's manner. "I've worn that rig scores of times."

"Ah, indeed?" A look of speculative interest came into the watching eyes. "And may I again inquire what brings a brother practitioner to my door?"

He listened in silence while Hugh hurriedly explained what had happened, not omitting his encounter with the man at the gate. At the conclusion the man in white made a gesture of annoyance.

"Tut, tut—it is really to be regretted that Dawker tried to keep you out. He is an excellent servant, but stupid—ah yes—hopelessly stupid. It is true that he has strict orders to admit no strangers, but undoubtedly he exceeded them in not making allowances in such an exceptional case. Needless to say, my telephone is entirely at your disposal. I hope you will excuse my not removing this antiseptic mask," he went on, indicating his gauze-swathed features. "When you arrived I was on the point of performing a—ah—a little operation. Be pleased to enter, Doctor Trenchard."

The unknown stood aside deferentially as Hugh stepped across the threshold. As the door closed, then followed the unmistakable click of automatic bolts and with a sudden foreboding of hovering peril, he realize that he was a prisoner in the house of mystery.

CHAPTER III

HUGH TRENCHARD RATHER PRIDED HIMSELF on the soundness of his nerves, yet his first impulse was to turn on his strange guide and force him—at the point of his revolver if milder methods failed—to open the door. But he quickly saw the foolishness of revealing his suspicions at this stage, and he felt that it would be worse than foolish to turn tail after he had gone to so much trouble to gain an entry. Besides, there was the injured man to be considered. If he could but get a 'phone call through to the nearest town, he was quite content to rely on his quick wits and well-trained muscles to make his escape from this sinister 'sanatorium'.

He had not the slightest doubt that the house hid some mystery which, in more senses than one, shunned the light of day. The high walls, the evil-faced gatekeeper, the surgeon with the masked face, the closely shuttered windows—each detail no doubt easily explainable by itself, but taken together they formed a danger signal which it would be madness to ignore.

All this passed through Hugh's mind as he was being conducted down a long corridor which, although it was broad day outside, was illuminated by electric globes set at intervals on the distempered walls.

"You must use a lot of current," he observed, intending thus to lead up to the subject of the darkened rooms. But his guide saved him the trouble.

"Ah yes. Exactly." For the first time Hugh noticed a faint foreign intonation in his voice. "But we have—how do you English express it?—ah yes, we have plenty of current to burn. We have our own generating plant, and it comes in useful for many purposes besides illumination." The eyes which looked out from the blank, gauze-swathed face flashed a keen glance at Hugh as he went on: "Of course you noticed that I keep the windows shuttered, and doubtless, as a medical man, you thought it rather peculiar, eh?"

"It's certainly a bit different from the usual hospital custom," Hugh admitted cautiously. "But I presume you have your reasons."

A soft, almost purring laugh issued from the veiling white gauze.

"Exactly—I have my reasons," the other said slowly. "Some of my patients—many of them, in fact—are ophthalmic cases, where, as you will readily understand, an excess of light may be most injurious. I find it more convenient to exclude the daylight altogether, so as to be able to regulate the degree of illumination at will, and to adapt it to the needs of each particular case."

"Of course," assented Hugh, though he was not deceived for a minute by this glib explanation. "And do you find the results satisfactory?"

Although he had tried to make his voice assume the natural tone in which one medical man might express an interest in another's work, he could not altogether divest it of a faint ring of amused sarcasm. Again the masked man turned and glanced at him.

"Ah yes," he said very softly. "The results are, as you say, quite satisfactory, and some of them are unique. Maybe I shall be able to afford you personal proof of my capabilities in my own particular line."

"I shall be delighted," Hugh murmured conventionally. Try as he might, he could not help an icy shiver passing down his spine at the equivocal offer.

Presently their progress was barred by a small white-painted door, which, from the absence of the usual panels, Hugh assumed to be of iron. The self-styled ophthalmic surgeon unlocked it with a key which he carried, with many others, on a slender steel chain.

"After you, Doctor Trenchard," he said, politely standing aside.

"You keep things well locked up here," the young doctor could not help remarking as he stepped through.

"Naturally," was the suave reply. "The 'phone is in my dispensary, where there are dangerous drugs—'Safe bind, safe find', as your proverb runs."

"That's exactly what my dear old granny used to say," said Hugh gravely. "Proverbs and nursery rhymes were her weakness, bless her kind heart! Her favourite was 'Will you walk into my parlour? said the spider to the fly', but in my young days I could never help wondering how the rhyme would have ended if the innocent little fly had turned out to be a nasty wasp."

The other's answering laugh sounded a trifle forced "Ha, ha, ha! How you English love your leetle joke!"

"Don't we just!" Trenchard's genial grin seemed to stop short of his steady, watchful eyes. "But *practical* jokes are considered bad form nowadays. Where's that telephone?" he added with a quick change of tone. Again his ear had caught the click of a hidden bolt in the door they had just passed through.

"Patience, my friend. The telephone is here—right by my operating-room."

The man in white threw open a door as he spoke and this time he did not invite his guest to precede him. With every muscle braced for quick action Hugh followed; a second later he could have laughed at his grim anticipations.

The room in which he found himself might have appeared extraordinary to a layman, but to one familiar with morphological museums it presented no unusual features. Its general arrangement was that of a small library, but instead of volumes, the shelves were packed with glass jars, each filled with colourless spirit in which floated bleached and horrible-looking anatomical specimens. But the thing which interested Hugh most at that moment was the telephone which stood on the table. Eagerly he advanced to the instrument, but before lifting the receiver he turned to the man in white with a sudden question:

"Might I know the name of the institution from which I am speaking?"

"Tell them that you are at the Excombe Private Sanatorium."

"Speaking by the courtesy of . . .?" Hugh Trenchard paused interrogatively. The man's strange reticence made him more curious than ever to learn his name.

"The name of Dr. Lucien Felger may not be unknown to you?" he asked a trifle pompously.

It was an indirect mode of answering his query, but Hugh merely shook his head.

"I hope you'll forgive my ignorance, but it's quite unknown to me. Do you happen to be registered?"

"Not in this country," was the swift answer. "I graduated at Vienna. Of course, in order to conform with your excellent laws, I cannot appear as the head of this establishment—that position is held by Dr. Nathaniel Mutley."

"Oh, I know *him* all right—at least, by reputation." Hugh thought it was not policy to add that the reputation in question was none too savoury, the doctor having very narrowly escaped having his name struck off the register by the General Medical Council for infamous professional conduct. The fact that such a man occupied an important post served to bring back Hugh's suspicions with redoubled force. Without further words he lifted the receiver and called the Excombe exchange.

"Put me through to the local police station."

Dr. Felger uttered a low laugh.

"Is it really necessary to trouble the police?"

"I think it is," Hugh answered curtly. "A man has been savagely attacked—"

"Granted—but by what?" There was a note of sardonic humour in Felger's voice as he put the question. "It has doubtless escaped your memory that Exmoor is famous for its herds of wild deer, and it is a well-known fact that the stags are apt to become very savage and dangerous to approach at certain seasons of the year. It is scarcely necessary to remind a scientific man like yourself that the red deer belongs to the *Ruminantia* division of the widespread natural order of *Ungulata,* or hoofed animals. They are *Artiodactyl* mammals—in non-scientific language, 'cloven-footed'—and when they are enraged they are in the habit of using their hoofs as well as their antlers. Do you not think it feasible that your friend— his name escapes me for the moment—owes his injuries to some wandering stag which he encountered in the mist?"

Hugh shook his head at this specious explanation.

"You forget that I heard someone boast, in so many words, that he had killed Silas Marle, and threaten me with the same fate."

"Ah, exactly." Felger's slow shrug was an expressive indication of disbelief. "It is curious how one's perceptions can be deceived in moments of strain and excitement. Tell me frankly, Dr. Trenchard, if one of your patients were to tell you the same extraordinary tale, what would *you* think?"

"I should hand the case over to a mental specialist. But please excuse me for a few moments. I've got my connection." He turned and spoke into the receiver.

"Is that the Excombe police station?"

"Yes—sergeant in charge speaking. What's the trouble, sir?" came the answer, very clear and distinct.

"Attempted murder." And Hugh hurriedly gave him the particulars.

"Very good, sir," said the voice when he had finished. "I will send a constable along in the car at once. *Two* doctors, I think you said? And a solicitor? Good! I'll give orders that they are to call at the sanatorium to pick you up."

"Thank you. I will wait here for you. Good-bye."

Trenchard hung up the receiver and turned to the other man.

"That station-sergeant at Excombe appears to be a smart man," Hugh remarked. "He lost no time in getting busy on the case—seemed to take it almost as a matter of course, judging by the few questions that he asked. Apparently he's a Londoner; his accent is certainly not West Country. He said that the police car would pick me up here, so I fear I will have to trespass on your hospitality till it arrives."

Dr. Felger bowed.

"My little institution is honoured by the presence of so astute a member of the medical profession," he declared fulsomely. "Would you care to see my operating-room? It will serve to pass the time. You would? Excellent! Pray excuse me while I see that everything is in order."

With another bow, Dr. Lucien Felger quitted the room and closed the door. A good ten minutes elapsed before he reappeared and beckoned to Hugh.

"This way, Dr. Trenchard."

Glancing at him, Hugh saw that he now wore clamped to his forehead a small but powerful portable electric lamp, such as surgeons are accustomed to use to shed light on the patient while performing delicate operations. It was quite an ordinary article of hospital equipment, yet for some reason the fact that Felger was wearing it outside the operating-room filled his mind with a sense of vague misgiving. Outwardly nonchalant, but in reality alert and watchful, he followed his host down the corridor.

"Here we are.

As he spoke Felger ushered him into a bare, spotlessly white room whose only furnishings were a metal operating-table, another bearing numerous bright instruments and a sterilizing-bath, and a fixed hand-basin surmounted by two silver taps. Felger crossed to the smaller table, took up a phial containing some clear, colourless liquid, and looked at it thoughtfully.

"I think I mentioned that I was about to perform a little operation? It seems that you have timed your arrival—your entirely unsolicited arrival—at a very opportune moment, Dr. Hugh Trenchard. I promised to show you a little of my surgical skill, and so . . ."

Without warning the whole of the lights were suddenly extinguished, leaving the place in a darkness utter and impenetrable. Felger gave a mutter of annoyance.

"Tut, tut! It's really too bad that the generating plant has chosen this moment to break down. However . . ."

There was the click of a turned switch, and the lamp on his forehead flamed into brilliance. Its rays struck full into Hugh's eyes, half blinding him and rendering everything invisible save that dazzling white glow. At the same moment his nostrils caught a whiff of an odour which is never forgotten by those who have experienced it—the sweetly volatile reek of chloroform.

"I should advise you to keep the stopper in that phial, Doctor." Hugh spoke quietly, but there was an edge to his voice like chilled steel. "I might act peculiarly if that stuff gets to my head. I might, for instance, let off the pistol I've got in my pocket, and somebody might get hurt!"

"A loaded pistol?" remonstrated Felger's voice from the darkness. "Dear me! How foolish of you to carry such a dangerous thing about with you!"

Hugh smiled grimly.

"Silly of me, isn't it? But there! I'm always doing silly things. For instance, I had a perfectly crazy idea that the man who answered my 'phone call was not the police-sergeant at Excombe, but the estimable Dawker, speaking from the lodge at the gate of this house. Foolish of me, of course—but I've a good memory for voices, and I recognized his Cockney twang the moment he began speaking. To make sure, however, I put through *another* call while you were out of the room, and it may save you some trouble—to say nothing of a possible stretch of penal servitude, or something worse—if I inform you that my second call got through to the police. They should be here at any minute now, and, if I'm not forthcoming, there'll be some questions asked which will take you the rest of your life to answer. Have you got that, my dear Professor Felger—of Vienna? Then switch on the lights and open that door, or I shall be under the painful necessity of performing a little operation on you—without anaesthetics!"

The beam of light waggled to and fro as Felger shook his head reprovingly.

"Really, sir, your wild words fill me with amazement! Penal servitude? Police? I am absolutely at a loss for words in which to express my regret at having made myself so grossly misunderstood. If I find that my servant has played a little innocent practical joke on you by answering the call himself, he shall most certainly be severely reprimanded."

The lights came on again as he spoke. Hugh uttered a short laugh.

"Your electrician must be a thought-reader—or was it a secret foot-switch that worked the oracle? No, don't speak—another day will do for explanations," he jerked out crisply. "Forward, slow march, the way we came in, is the order of the day. This trigger seems to have a mighty light pull, so if you've got any more practical jokers like friend Dawker on the premises, it'll be healthier for you if they bottle up their humour till I'm outside." He bowed toward the door with the same elaborate gesture which the other had used in entering. "After *you,* Dr. Lucien Felger!"

Slowly and in silence, Hugh carefully keeping step with the man in front, the two traversed the echoing corridors. As Felger unlocked the outer door he turned to Hugh with a pleasant laugh.

"Good day, Doctor. I am charmed to have made your acquaintance. But for the life of me I cannot understand why you have suddenly become so mistrustful of me. Surely it is unnecessary for me to repeat that I was only about to demonstrate to you a minor operation on one of my patients?"

"Quite unnecessary," Hugh agreed with emphasis. As he pocketed his revolver there came the sound of prolonged honking from the direction of the gate. "That'll be the real police-sergeant from Excombe—I wonder if he'll be grateful to your ham-faced gatekeeper for deputizing for him! Au revoir, Professor. I have a feeling in my bones that we'll meet again."

"Assuredly we will—and very soon!"

The hissing vehemence with which the words burst out revealed for the first time the seething volcano of baffled hate which lay beneath the suave urbanity of Professor Lucien Felger.

CHAPTER IV

I T'S A QUEER STORY you've just told me, Mr. Trenchard, and, frankly, I shouldn't feel inclined to place much credence on it—if it was not for the fact that something very similar happened here just over a year ago."

Hugh and Sergeant Jopling, of the Somerset County Constabulary, were seated in the dining-room of Marle's house when the latter volunteered this rather startling piece of information. A cheerful fire of logs crackled in the wide grate; the lamp was lit and the heavy curtains drawn across the diamond-latticed windows. Altogether the room looked much more cheerful than Hugh had thought possible when he had first seen it through the hovering wreaths of mist. Much had happened since their arrival about midday. The two local doctors had examined the injured man, and, although they expressed the opinion, privately, that he was in a very serious condition, they had no hesitation in signing the document which the solicitor drew up, certifying his complete sanity. In order to place the matter beyond dispute, they consented to act as the two necessary witnesses to the will itself.

This was a short document, and a very few minutes sufficed for the legal gentleman to draw it up; whereupon he and one of the doctors had taken their departure, leaving Silas Marle in the care of the other. For some reason that Hugh was unable to fathom, the old man stoutly refused to allow him to undertake his case. It was perhaps only natural that the young doctor should feel slightly piqued at this implied lack of confidence in his professional ability; it was not until some time afterwards that he divined the motive which lay behind this almost churlish refusal.

It came as something of a shock to Hugh to learn that the attack on the old man had been preceded by a similar occurrence. He eagerly pressed Sergeant Jopling for details.

"Yes, sir, very queer it was," said that worthy officer. "I'm rather surprised that Mr. Marle didn't tell you himself, seeing how he's . . ." He stopped in the middle of a sentence and eyed Hugh in a curious manner as he concluded rather hastily: "I meant to say, seeing that you're so friendly."

Trenchard could not help wondering what the sergeant had been about to say at first, but he merely smiled as he shook his head.

"You must remember that Mr. Marle was badly hurt when I first saw him, and he was not in a condition to say much."

Sergeant Jopling stroked his drooping moustache thoughtfully.

"Just so, sir, just so," he agreed. "It were very lucky for him that you happened along just when you did. And—if I may make so bold to say so—it were very lucky for *you,* sir, that the poor man wasn't killed outright."

The young man stared at him in unaffected amazement, and his anger was not less than his surprise.

"Now what exactly do you mean by that?" he asked at length.

The sergeant had a disconcerting habit of gazing up at the ceiling and speaking as though he were addressing some unseen person on the next floor. He did so now as he went on very deliberately.

"I mean, sir, seeing that you were the only person near at the time, and as we only had your unsupported word for what happened, some people—I said *some* people, mind you—might have got the notion into their heads that you had something to do with his injuries, and if there had been a less intelligent officer in charge of the case you might have been charged with killing him—provided, naturally, that he had been killed. Or, conversely, as one may say, with doing him grievous bodily harm if sobeit he was only injured—as the matter stands at present."

Trenchard's hearty laugh made the sergeant's eyes leave their contemplation of the age-blackened rafters and turn on him.

"I suppose you mean that for a roundabout hint that you suspect *me?*" he said, still laughing. "Why, the thing is absurd!"

"Oh, some folks might not think it so absurd. I've taken Marle's depositions, and he cannot swear as to who actually struck him down—which is not surprisin' seeing that it was dark and misty at the time. And—if you'll pardon me saying so, sir—that yarn of yours about a cloven-footed devil would sound a bit thin when told to a hard-headed—I mean a clear-headed British jury."

In spite of himself, Hugh began to lose his temper.

"You can have a look at the footprints, if you like," he retorted stiffly. "Doubtless they're still there."

"I've had a look at 'em," Jopling observed complacently. "What's more, I had the Harbourer of the Staghounds—the man whose duty it is to track and locate a stag before the hounds are brought out—I had him up here and asked his opinion of those hoof-prints. Without a moment's hesitation he said the trail was the slot of an old stag—a 'warrantable' stag as they call it hereabouts, meaning one fit for hunting."

"An old stag?" Hugh repeated. "How old does a stag have to be before he's described thus?"

Jopling stuck his thumbs through his leather belt and leant back in his chair, nothing loth to display his knowledge of the ancient art of venery.

"Well, it's like this, sir. They don't talk of the ages of deer the same as they do of, say, horses—a two-year-old, or a three-year-old, and so forth. A stag is spoken of by his 'points', that is the number of points, or tines, that he carries on his antlers. A stag under a year old has no horns at all; at four years the brow antlers begin to grow. You may not be aware that stags shed their antlers every year, and grow new ones in the spring, and as the animal grows older new points are added—an old stag might carry as many as fifteen. Nick Froude, the Harbourer, can tell the age of a stag by looking at its trail better nor you can tell the age of a female by looking at her face—'specially nowadays since they've taken to having their faces lifted every now and again. In Nick's opinion, the stag that left that slot down in the coombe yonder was the very same beast that attacked and killed old Marle's missus just over a year gone."

Hugh Trenchard started as he grasped the full meaning of the policeman's words.

"So Marle's wife was murdered by that—" he paused, then added, to avoid further argument—"that old stag? Did you have charge of the case?"

A faint smile spread over Jopling's rubicund features.

"Well, you could hardly call it a 'case', sir, seeing as how it was the act of a brute beast. The matter was reported to me, but all I could do was to notify the verderers that a dangerous beast was at large. They put the hounds on its trail, and a pretty dance he led them. Cunning? I tell you that old stag was as cunning as Satan himself! He seemed to know that what he'd done would bring the hounds after him, and the tricks and dodges by which he covered his trail showed an understanding that was almost human. There was not a stream that he didn't wade along for a few hundred yards; he seemed to know that the scent don't lay over water. Finally he took to a newly tarred road, not far from the village of Withypool, of all places, and there, of course, the hounds were at fault. They put some of the 'tufters'—the oldest, most experienced hounds—on each side of the moorland which bordered the road, and let them range free to see if they could pick up the scent again. But the creature must have gone clean through the main street of the village and out the other side, and so got clear away."

"Extraordinary thing for an animal to do which is usually regarded as being extremely shy of human beings," Hugh commented dryly.

"Just so, sir. Usually they make for the high forest lands round about Dure Down, or Dunkery Beacon. It's my belief that the creature was mad."

A mad stag? Trenchard frowned. There was one thing which he could not reconcile with such a simple theory—the voice he had heard that night. Whatever the malign thing was that had struck his pistol from his grasp, it was certainly not a demented deer! But the sergeant's attitude of scoffing disbelief did not encourage him to voice his doubts.

"I gather you might make use of the staghounds on this occasion?" he contented himself with asking.

"Unfortunately there'll be some delay in putting them on the scent." Jopling shook his head ruefully. "There's been an outbreak of foot-and-mouth disease at a dairy farm near the kennels, and the dogs have been shifted to other quarters some distance away. The earliest they can be here is to-morrow morning. The scent will be rather cold by then, but we must hope for the best—and no rain in the night."

But the worthy Jopling's hopes in this respect were doomed to be disappointed. Toward sunset a drizzle set in which rapidly increased into a steady downpour. Hugh listened to it lashing against the leaded casements as he sat before the fire in the library with his ancient-looking, calf-bound volume which he had taken almost at random from the shelves. He was in the middle of deciphering a passage of the quaint, blackletter print when the door opened and Dr. Brewster, the local practitioner who had offered to remain with the injured man, appeared. Hugh laid his book face upward on the table and rose to greet the new-comer.

"Well, how's your patient this evening?" he asked.

Ronald Brewster was considerably older than Hugh. The two had met while 'walking' the same London hospital, and a close friendship had sprung up between them. He was a hefty-looking specimen of manhood, with hair of a shade that it would be gross flattery to call auburn and a face that was remarkable more for its habitual expression of irrepressible good humour than its beauty. He was a noted rugby player, strong as a horse, and, as Hugh well knew by his encounters with him in the boxing-ring, stubborn as a mule where physical endurance was concerned. Taken altogether Hugh could not have picked on a more useful ally in a quest which was more than likely to have a spice of danger in it.

"He's going on fine," he said in answer to his friend's question. "It was touch and go a little while back, but I'll stake my professional reputation—"

"The world-wide reputation you have gained by a year's practice in a one-eye country town!" laughed Hugh.

"—that I'll pull him through."

"Well, Ronnie," said Hugh, with a bow of mock gravity, "if the poor man is really lying at Death's door, I know of nobody more likely to pull him through than yourself!"

Brewster had caught up the nearest cushion with the intention of hurling it at the head of his libelous fellow medico when his eyes fell on the book on the table. He dropped the intended missile and began to turn the age-yellowed pages.

"Hullo, what's this?" he said with a contemptuous grimace, as he read the title-page. *"Ye Boke of Sorcerie, Strainge Demons and Unnatural Monstres.* I must say I like your notion of a little light literature! Are you swotting for a Professorship in the Black Art?"

"Oh no," disclaimed the other. "I'm a mere dabbler as yet. This Silas Marle seems to be a queer bird; his bookcase is simply crammed with ancient tomes which deal with occult subjects. Some of the learned authors are delightfully humorous—though unconsciously so. Just listen to this." He rapidly turned the leaves until he found the place where he had left off, then read aloud:

"But there be Monstres (that ys to saye Creatures whyche conforme nott to ye Manner of their Kynde) broughte forth by ye naturall impure fluxes and humours in ye Air, and in nowise ye Worke of Arte Magike ne Dyvellysshe. Of yse sorte be ye Sheep with twain Heads, Swine with Five Legges, and Twin Children of ye Human Kynde whose Bodyes be Joyned ye one to ye other. When suche appear (ye whyche Godde forbydde) they do prestige Turmoil and Warre, Greate Floodes, Grievous

Drought, Pests, and Famynes, and divers Grievous Calamitity-
ous Evyls—"

"By Jove, the fellow is quite an antediluvian Old Moore!"
ejaculated Ronnie at this point.
"Shut up and listen.

"But there be divers Monstrous Thynges ye whyche walke
ye Earthe (maugre seen by Fewe, Godde be thanked) broughte
forth by Enchantementes and Sorceryes. Yse be yclept Ye Har-
pye, ye whyche be half-maidens, half-byrds of foule and om-
nivorous hunger, the rauversshers of All who dysappeare Without Trayce. And there be Ye Wyvern, whose fore parte be as a
Dragone and hynder parte that of a Serpente (if caughte upon
Sainte Swythen his daye it breatheth Fyre for a full Yeare)—"

"Very useful in ye winter-time, begad!" put in the irrepressible
Ronnie.

"And there be Ye Flitter-Gibbet, ye whyche den devoureth
ye Fatt of Hanged Maulefactors; and Ye Mandragora, ye whyche screameth lyke a woman when dragged from ye Earthe.
And there be Chimera—"

"Most decidedly there be!" Ronnie agreed heartily. "Does the
old liar give the natural history of Ye Jabberwock or Ye Snark ?"
"Shut up I'm just coming to the really interesting Part!"
"Thank heaven for that!" was Ronnie's pious rejoinder.

"But alle yse Thynges are as naught besyde ye Foule and
Namelesse Thynge whyche, fearsome blonde measure,
haunteth ye Desolate Moore of ye Aunctient Kyngdome of
Wessex. Of its aspect no man hathe lyved to telle. It slaythe
wythe Arte and Cunnynge beyonde very belief, nathless it
leaveth ye Cloven Trayle of its Devyl's Foot wheresobeit it
walketh. Onlye by thys Sygne may it be knowne, for ye outer
aspect (by ye whyche it cajoles and deceives its Victyms) is
evere changefulle. There be tymes when it cometh in the guise
of a Holye Clerke; anon it appearethe as a Fair Knight bedight
in costyle velvet and whyte Semite, or trussed in harness cap-à-
pie. Anon (as seemyth best fytted to lure its Victim to hys
Doom) it cometh in the guise of a Maiden, rauvishynge to the

eye and fair withal, who knocketh on ye Casement, be-seechynge entry. But woe to hym that—"

He read no further. Above the sough of the wind and swish of the driving rain there came a light tap on the windows and the sound of a girl's low, sweet voice:

"Please may I come in?" it said.

CHAPTER V

T HE TWO MEN SAT RIGID AND MOTIONLESS, staring at each other across the printed page, and in that breathless moment each seemed to read in the other's eyes a feeling deeper than mere surprise.

Both were of the age when Hamlet's famous and oft-quoted admonition to Horatio has least appeal: 'There are more things in heaven and earth . . . than are dreamt of in your philosophy.' Yet, in spite of youthful scepticism and scientific training, each sat as though he had been turned to stone by the few words uttered by that melodious voice.

Ronnie was the first to recover. He sprang to his feet, uttering a kind of shamefaced laugh.

"I vote we let the lady in," he cried. "If the rest of her is in keeping with her voice, she ought to be a very desirable addition to our party."

Hugh rose from his seat more slowly.

"I think we'd better hold a parley through the window first."

"Scared of bogies?" queried Ronnie with a laugh.

Hugh did not answer immediately. Truth to tell—although he would have smiled at them amid other surroundings—the words of the ancient necromancer had affected him more deeply than he had at first realized. As he had read the quaint, measured phrases aloud, to the accompaniment of the wild, mournful booming of the wind in the wide chimney, with the flickering flame of the lamp sending fantastic shadows dancing on the oak-panelled walls, he had infused into the words a sincerity which almost convinced him of their truth. In spite of his cooler reasoning, he found himself wondering if it were indeed blind chance that had ordained that the alluring voice should make itself heard at the very moment he was describing the terrible qualities of the 'Terror'.

"Going to let the poor girl in?" The voice of Ronnie snapped the spell which seemed to bind Hugh. He shook himself like a man suddenly awakened from sleep.

Of course," he said quickly. "But there's no harm in being a bit cautious. We haven't solved the mystery of the attack on Silas Marle yet, remember, and there may be more dangerous things than spooks hovering around."

He slipped back the ponderous bolts and opened the door a little way. For a moment the rush of wind driven sleet almost blinded him; he sensed rather than actually saw the vague form which advanced with a queer, shambling gait, toward him.

"Heavens, what a time you are! I'm just about all in.

Without pausing to put into operation his carefully thought-out precautions, Hugh flung wide the door and caught the swaying figure in his arms. With a sudden tingling of his spine, he realized that he was clutching something which felt like the furry covering of some beast! In spite of himself he felt a shudder pass through his body as he stood hesitating in the doorway. The voice of his friend roused him with a jerk.

"What are you standing there for, gaping like a stranded codfish?" Ronnie cried. "Have you never seen a girl in a fur coat before? Carry her in here"—he threw open the door of the living-room—"and look sharp about it. The poor girl seems half dead with cold and exposure."

A shaft of lamplight from the open door convinced Hugh that his burden was indeed of the human species, though little of the face was visible between the wide, upturned collar of the coat and the limply drooping brim of the rain-drenched hat. It was only when he had set her gently in the large, leather-covered armchair in front of the fire, and removed the hat and coat, that he glimpsed her features. As he did so, an involuntary exclamation of admiration escaped his lips.

The girl was more than pretty—she was beautiful. Pale and dishevelled though she was, she appeared to have brought a new and wonderful radiance into that sombre room. Her very pallor accentuated rather than marred the sweet, sad profile of her face; her hair, in spite of its dampness, shimmered like a mass of spun gold in the dim rays of the lamp, with here and there a diamond-like sparkle when the light caught a lingering raindrop. Beneath her fur coat she wore what appeared to be an evening frock of silvery gauze, which, although torn in one place at the hem of the skirt, and showing more than one mud-splash, invested her slim figure with such a pale, ethereal radiance that she might have been a pixie that had stolen in from the storm-swept moor. Hugh stared and stared at her as though anxious to imprint her image on his brain before she vanished from his sight, and every moment that he looked he became more and more convinced that she was the most stunning girl he had ever seen.

Meanwhile the impetuous Ronnie had appointed himself physician-in-charge.

"Humph!" he remarked, as he lifted the slender wrist and felt her pulse. "This is a case which calls for a little stimulant. Put some more logs on the fire while I hunt out the brandy."

The instant the door had closed behind his chum, Hugh saw a sudden change come over the hitherto-expressionless face. The long-fringed eyelids abruptly opened, revealing eyes of clearest blue. But it was their peculiar expression rather than their beauty that made Hugh Trenchard stop with a log held in mid air. They had in them nothing of that bewildered look which is natural to one recovering from a swoon; instead he thought he could detect in their depths the wary calculating look of one who had anxiously awaited the moment when they would be alone. He could have staked his life that the girl had been shamming unconsciousness, And the question which came hammering at his brain was "Why?"

But he was not left long in doubt as to the answer. With a quick, sinuous movement the unknown girl sat upright, at the same time slipping her hand into the socket of her coat and pulling out a long envelope.

"Quick!" she whispered, holding it toward him. "Take this, and keep it till I claim it again. Let no one know you have it in your possession—no one, you understand?—and guard it as you would your life. It contains something which means everything! You promise?"

Instinctively Hugh's hand closed on the packet; as he transferred it to his pocket he glimpsed a large red seal impressed with what seemed to be an heraldic crest.

"I promise," he said softly. It seemed as if the words came from his lips without conscious thought.

"If anything happens and I'm unable to claim it within a month, deliver it to the person to whom it is addressed," the girl went on, still speaking scarcely above her breath "Promise me, on your honour, not to read that address until the month is up."

"I promise," repeated Hugh; then he added swiftly: "My friend—the man who just left us—is an excellent fellow. Won't you let me confide in him? You couldn't have a better man if there's likely to be trouble brewing—"

Her red lips curved in a bitter smile as she interrupted.

"Rest assured there'll be trouble enough! But tell no one what I have given you—not even your staunchest friend. There are some secrets which, here on the moor, one must not whisper even to oneself, and—"

"But—"

"Hush!"

Her quick ears must have caught the faint sound of Ronnie's returning footsteps, for a moment later he re-entered the room with a decanter and tumbler.

"No need to trouble, old chap . . ." Hugh began, only to curse himself for a thoughtless fool. For at the moment of his friend's entry the girl had sunk back on the cushions, her eyes closed, her figure limp and apparently unconscious. Luckily Ronnie was too preoccupied to notice his words. He quickly poured out some neat spirit and held the glass to the girl's parted lips.

A feeling of amazement, not entirely untinged with uneasiness, took possession of Hugh as he noted the perfect artistry with which she simulated a gradual return to consciousness. Who, he asked himself, was this accomplished actress who had drifted in without warning from the bleak and desolate moor? That she was quite capable of fooling his friend he had just had ocular proof—what if he too were being fooled?

"That's better," Ronnie said encouragingly, as the girl sat up weakly, her half-veiled eyes looking about the room with an expression much different to her former keen regard. "You'll soon be all right again. Would you like to rest? We have a spare bedroom where you'll be quite comfortable until the morning. Sergeant Jopling is coming over first thing, and I'm sure he'll be willing to give you a lift as far as Excombe, or wherever you wish to get to."

Hugh was watching the girl closely, and he could have sworn a sudden light of fear illuminated the girl's eyes at the mention of the police officer. Strive as he would, he could not rid his mind of the impression that it was something more than mere chance that had brought her to the house.

"Oh, I shall be quite all right sitting by this nice fire," she answered, with a pretty little gesture of protest. "I should never forgive myself if my uninvited visit were to deprive either you or Dr. Trenchard of a bed."

Hugh started as though he had been stung. From the girl's words, artless and spontaneous though they seemed, two ugly facts stood out like sinister, jagged rocks rearing their heads above the surface of a smiling sea. She knew his name, in spite of the fact that he was a mere chance visitor to the district, and she was acquainted with the interior of the house sufficiently well to know that every bed would be occupied that night! Even the unobservant Ronnie was struck by the first fact.

"What, are you two already acquainted?" he cried with a laugh. "And that sly dog never let on that he knew you—actually tried to make out that he thought you were a furry banshee or something!"

The girl turned her eyes in Hugh's direction, and there was a warning gleam lurking in their blue depths.

"We met in town," she smiled. "Surely you haven't forgotten Joan Endean?"

"Of course," assented Hugh, dutifully taking up the cue which was so adroitly given him. "I knew your face was familiar, although your name eluded me. As some excuse for my lapse of memory, you must realize it is some time since last we met."

She smiled again at the dry tone in which he spoke.

"You are already forgiven—if there is anything to forgive in failing to remember an unimportant person like myself," she said, lifting her shoulders in a careless shrug. "Really it is I who ought to be pleading forgiveness for putting you to so much trouble. But I had been wandering about the moor for hours and hours, and I felt so desperately cold and fagged that I just made for the first light I saw."

"Which direction did you come from, Miss Endean?"

She waved her hand unerringly toward the north. "From the coast."

"Then you have had a longish tramp." With difficulty Hugh repressed a scornful smile; her instinctive gesture had betrayed a knowledge of direction simply marvellous in one who had wandered in the dark for hours. "I suppose you did not meet with any alarming adventures during your wanderings on the moor?"

Joan Endean laughed somewhat ruefully.

"If bogs and mire, and darkness, and pouring rain are adventures, then I had plenty!" she said, with a glance down at her bedraggled skirt. "My frock is simply ruined."

"You did not by any chance encounter the weird creature that is known as 'The Terror of the Moor'?"

Hugh was observing her closely as he put the question, but the beautiful face that was turned toward him was as devoid of expression as a graven mask. But the perfection of her self-control defeated its own purpose—the very absence of the slight surprise or alarm, which any girl would experience on having such a question put to her, told that she was controlling her features with a will of iron.

"I saw nothing of that sort." Her look of interested wonder came just too late to be convincing. "But it sounds fearfully creepy and exciting. What *is* 'The Terror of the Moor'?"

It was Ronnie Brewster who answered her.

"It's just moonshine and fiddlesticks, Miss Endean," he laughed. "My friend here is suffering from an obsession that the moor is haunted by a strange half-human monster which calls itself King of the Moor and goes about bashing people over the head with something which the newspapers delight in calling 'some blunt instrument'. Hugh is a delightful old scout, but he simply refuses to give up his belief in the Bogie Man, which I, personally, was sceptical about even when the tears were streaming down my pinafore!"

Joan Endean turned a glance of mingled wonder and amusement on the young doctor, and Ronnie immediately proceeded to enlarge on the subject of local superstitions.

"It's curious how these out-of-date beliefs survive in remote country districts; scarcely surprising, too, that such a lonely place as Exmoor should have its apparition. Curious, how the fancy of primitive civilization always turned toward monsters of a fantastically composite kind—witness the Centaur of classical times, the Sphinx of ancient Egypt, the Chimera, the Faun, the Satyr—why, the instances might be multiplied indefinitely from the early legends. And you may just as well pin your faith on one of these mythological monstrosities as on Hugh's pet delusion. Why, in these enlightened days even the kids scoff at such tall yarns! This Terror of the Moor' has arrived about a couple of hundred years too late to be convincing. He—or it— is an anachronism—"

"Silence, scoffer!" hissed a voice, low, but seeming to be uttered close at hand. *"Another gibe from you, and my magic lightning will blast you as you stand!"*

In an instant both men were on their feet. A single sweeping glance was sufficient to show that, with the exception of themselves and the now trembling girl, the room was empty. Their eyes met in a bewildered, questioning stare.

"Well, I'll be—"

The end of Ronnie's dazed ejaculation was drowned in a sudden crash of distant thunder. He stood motionless, his face hard as steel, every muscle contracted. When he spoke it was like the snapping of a cord too tightly stretched.

"Give me your pistol, Hugh!" His tone was very different to his former light-hearted bantering. "I'm off on a little tour of investigation."

"Any theory?" inquired his friend, as he relinquished the weapon.

Ronnie Brewster nodded grimly.

"I fancy the sick man upstairs is not quite so sick as we thought him to be!"

With his weapon held ready for instant use, he hurried from the room. Hugh waited until he heard his friend's cautious footsteps die into silence, then turned and looked full into the bloodless face of Endean.

"Isn't it about time you stopped trying to hoodwink me?" he asked quietly. "I've already guessed part of your secret—why not tell me all?"

"All?" she repeated. "You mean about the packet I gave you? You know I cannot tell you that—the secret is not mine to tell."

Hugh shook his head.

"I was not referring to the packet, but to yourself."

"I have already told you—"

"A pack of lies!" he interrupted, his face hardening. "You know too much about me, and this house, for a chance visitor. I've played up to you blindly before my friend—I could have torn your story to rags at any minute —and now I want the truth."

She made to turn away, but he gripped her by the shoulders, holding her so that she was forced to look into his eyes.

"Who and what are you?" he demanded.

For an instant she hesitated. Then the staggering answer came:

"I am an escaped lunatic and I came to save your life!"

CHAPTER VI

HUGH TRENCHARD POSSESSED a keen sense of humour, and at the girl's breath-taking declaration he felt an almost irresistible desire to laugh. An escaped lunatic?

That might explain all if it were true—her wanderings on the moor on such a night—her palpably false statement that she had lost her way—her mysterious injunction of secrecy regarding the sealed envelope. But *was* it true?

He made no pretensions to being an alienist, but one need not be an expert in mental diseases to know that the average person of deranged intellect is the very last person to admit that he is not normal. The lunatic may believe the whole world to be mad—but not himself. And the collected, almost offhand manner in which she said the words was in itself their own refutation. He looked again into the eyes which were still regarding him fixedly, and the last vestige of doubt was torn from his mind. Whatever else she might be, he decided, she was no lunatic. Still keeping his hand on her shoulder, he drew her toward the chair she had just vacated.

"Sit down," he said gently, "and explain yourself. You have made two very amazing statements, and I find one as hard to believe as the other."

Her colour deepened suddenly and her eyes flashed.

"You mean that I am lying?"

"I mean," Hugh said slowly and deliberately, choosing his words, "that you appear to be a young woman with an intelligence and wit far above the average."

Her full red lips curved in a bitter smile.

"And yet two of your fellow doctors have certified that I am insane!"

"Their names?" cried Hugh, a sudden suspicion flashing through his mind. "What were their names?"

"Dr. Lucien Felger and Dr. Nathaniel Mutley."

Hugh Trenchard slapped his thigh.

"Just as I thought—as pretty a pair of scoundrels as ever disgraced an honourable profession! But allow me to inform you, Miss Endean, their certificate is not worth the paper it's written on. Dr. Lucien Felger, by his own admission, has no status in this country, and if—as I suspect to be the case—you have been forcibly confined by reason of a trumpery certificate, you've a first-class case for damages."

Joan Endean nodded her head.

"Yes, it is true that I escaped from the Excombe Private Asylum—"

"Then we have a common bond between us," laughed Hugh. "I may as well admit that I was very glad to do the same thing myself no later than yesterday!"

Again she nodded her well-poised head.

"I know," she said swiftly. "I overheard you turn the tables on the doctor, and I made up my mind to fly here if I could give them a miss. I could see you were no friend of Dr. Lucien's, and so I thought you might be willing to help one of his unfortunate victims."

Victims! The word struck a jarring note, for Hugh well knew that the delusion of being persecuted is one of the most common symptoms of a disordered intellect; but at the same time he realized, from his own experience of Dr. Lucien Felger's establishment, that the girl might have good grounds for her words. He stooped and patted her hand reassuringly, and even that chance contact sent a thrill to his heart such as it had never before experienced.

"You may count on me as your friend, Miss Endean," he said with quiet earnestness. "But whatever happens rest assured that you have seen the last of the Excombe Sanatorium and its rascally proprietor."

Even as he uttered the confident words there came a loud and imperative knock on the door of the house. A look of utter consternation swept across Joan Endean's face as she started to her feet.

"They've come for me—heaven alone knows how they tracked me here!" Her eyes sought Hugh's in pleading entreaty. "I implore you, don't let them take me back to that horrible place. Please please! Tell them I'm not here—anything—but don't hand me over to that inhuman fiend!"

"Don't worry about that, Miss Endean. I'll see you don't go back there."

He spoke with an air of quiet determination although every impulse urged him to take her slender body in his arms and defy the world to part them. Until then love at first sight had meant little more to him than a stereotyped stock-phrase of novelists and playwrights, but just at that moment her beauty, her helplessness, her almost childlike trust thrilled and exhilarated him with a new and delightful sense of protection. For her he felt that he could face most desperate odds and be victorious. To win her no task would be too difficult—no peril too great.

He hastily caught up her discarded coat and hat and thrust them into her hands.

"Quick! Upstairs with you!" he said in an urgent whisper. "Hide somewhere—I'll put them off the scent."

Together they passed into the shadowy hall. At the foot of the stairs she turned, her face glimmering whitely in the dusk.

"If we do not meet again"—there was a catch in her voice—"I want you to know that I will be grateful to you as long as I live."

"Buck up!" he whispered, and immediately a louder knock sounded on the door.

There was a queer half-smile on his set lips as he pulled back the bolts. Gratitude is a cold word when one is hungering for love. Yet what else could he expect? Was he not a mere chance-met stranger—her refuge in a moment when she was ill and unstrung? What was he to her? "A blind, willing tool," was the answer given by his coldly logical brain. Yet all the while his pulses were throbbing wildly, keeping time to a new and wonderful song—without tune, without words—a song as old as the human race itself. It was with a feeling of fierce joy that he flung open the door and faced the three dim figures which stood outside. In the tallest of the three he thought he recognized the giant gate-keeper, Dawker.

"Well?" Hugh demanded crisply, unconsciously repeating Felger's greeting to him the previous day. "To what do I owe the honour of this visit?"

There was a slight pause, during which the tall man cleared his throat huskily.

"Beg pardon for disturbing you, sir," he said, and it was the unmistakable voice of Dawker. "One of the mental patients has got away from the sanatorium—rare dangerous case, sir; homicidal, in fact. If you don't mind, we'd like to have a look round."

"Well, what's stopping you?" asked a cheery voice, coming from behind Hugh. Half turning, he saw Ronnie leisurely descending the stairs, and something in his chum's manner told him that Ronnie had a very shrewd suspicion how matters stood. "It's very flattering of you to ask our permission, but you're quite mistaken in assuming that we own the surrounding countryside. Exmoor, to the best of my knowledge, is public property, and you are at liberty to search it as much as you please."

Dawker shifted his feet uneasily.

"I—we—thought the patient might have made for 'ere," he said slowly.

"Indeed?" said Hugh, with an expression of ironical surprise. "And what on earth put that idea into your head—or heads?"

"Oh, it was just an idea, gentlemen, just an idea," said Dawker airily. "I suppose you have no objection to us searching the house?"

"On the contrary, my dear Mr. Dawker, I have a very great objection to your setting your foot over the doorstep!"

Dawker glared at Hugh. It was evident that he was longing to renew the contest of the previous day.

"I'm afraid it's my duty to come in." With difficulty he managed to swallow his rage and speak civilly.

"Then it will be *our* painful duty to throw you out again! There's a man seriously ill in this house, and I can't have you tramping all over the place. You'll have to be satisfied with my assurance that we have no person of unsound mind on the premises—unless you or your friends here come under that category."

Dawker stood his ground stubbornly. But he appeared to realize that he was pursuing the wrong tactics; his voice took on a whining tone which was even more nauseating than his former bullying.

"Surely, Dr. Trenchard, you don't mean ter say that you're going to refuse us a few minutes' shelter from the storm?" he whined. "Why, it's not fit for a dog to be out on a night like this."

"In that case, old bean, I'm surprised that you didn't stay indoors!" observed the imperturbable Ronnie. "But if it's shelter you want we can soon fix you up."

"Now that's talking like a gentleman," exclaimed Dawker in a tone of satisfaction.

"Yes—there's a nice dry tool-shed at the bottom of the garden. You're quite welcome to the use of it until the weather clears."

Dawker's manner changed again.

"Funny, ain't yer?" he ground out savagely. "But you'll be laughing the wrong side of your mouth presently. You're asking for trouble—and you'll get it soon!"

"We're gluttons for trouble here," Hugh assured him cheerfully, "but we don't mind giving some away. If you doubt my word, just you start some and see!"

But Dawker seemed in no hurry to accept the invitation. He remained where he was, a leering grin on his face as he slowly shook his head.

"Oh no, my young cock-sparrow. Jem Dawker's too fly to put hisself on the wrong side of the law. I'll leave the perlice to make all the trouble that's necessary!"

"The police!" Hugh could not help exclaiming. Here was a contingency that he had not foreseen.

Dawker gave a coarse, triumphant chuckle.

"Yus—the perlice! Before I set out I telephoned to Sergeant Jopling, asking him to meet me here. How does *that* suit you, hey?"

Hugh checked the first words that came to his lips and then lifted his shoulders in a shrug of assumed carelessness.

"It suits me excellently." He turned to Ronnie with a laugh. "Our friend Dawker is quite an expert on the 'phone. It's true that he makes some intriguing mistakes in the numbers, but he always answers the calls promptly. Did I tell you about his impersonation stunt which missed fire the other day?"

Dawker cursed beneath his breath, for the home thrust had touched him on the raw. He made a quick step forward, murder gleaming in his eyes. His myrmidons each made a similar movement, but before they could come to grips Hugh withdrew his hand from his jacket pocket, and it was gripping something which gave forth a bluish gleam as it reflected the lamplight.

"Up with them, my beauties—as high as they'll go!" he ordered crisply. "The first man who makes a step forward will step into hell."

Three pairs of hands jerked upward with a smartness which would have gladdened the heart of a drill-instructor, for the hand which held the revolver was firm and unwavering, and the voice which gave the order was that of a man who meant what he said.

"I shall count ten slowly," Hugh announced steadily, "and then I shall drop any man who remains in sight. Got that? Good! *One . . . two . . . three . . . four—*"

The men had already turned and fled, when Ronnie laid his hand on his chum's shoulder.

"Too late, old chap," he said with a despondent shake of his head, at the same time pointing to a pair of distant headlights moving rapidly toward them. "The police are here!"

With a smothered groan Hugh thrust the weapon back into his pocket. "We must trust to our wits—they're the only weapons that will serve us now, Ronnie."

"You can count me in for any stunt to get the girl away," whispered the other. "Of course, you won't let those beggars take her—she's no more mad than I am! Only say the word, old bean, and I'm game for anything. Shall we bolt the door and stand a siege? Or shall I play the dashing hero at the garden gate like Horatius on the Bridge? You have only to say the word, dear boy."

Hugh could not repress a slight smile at his friend's light-hearted offer. But he shook his head.

"Thanks, Ronnie, but it would be madness to resist. We must settle this matter right now."

A moment later the burly form of Sergeant Jopling loomed through the darkness.

"Hullo! What's the trouble here?" he demanded.

Dawker, hovering cautiously in his rear, took it upon himself to give his version. The policeman looked grave.

"Be good enough to stand aside, sir," he said curtly. "I must search the house."

With a resigned shrug Hugh allowed him to ascend the stairs. In less than two minutes the police-sergeant reappeared, his ruddy face a picture of horrified amazement.

"It seems as if I'm too late," he said, looking at Hugh and the other doctor with a queer expression in his eyes.

"The girl is not there?" cried Hugh, his heart buoyed up on a sudden wave of hope.

"No," said Jopling, shaking his head. "I've not seen the mad girl, but I've seen her handiwork all right! Old Silas Marle has been murdered in his bed—stabbed to the heart with this!"

He held up his gloved hand, revealing a bloodstained dagger whose hilt was fashioned in the shape of a cloven foot.

CHAPTER VII

IT WAS DAWKER'S HOUR OF TRIUMPH, and for the fifth time he was emphasizing to Sergeant Jopling the fact that the murder would not have been committed if he had not been hindered in the execution of his duty by Hugh Trenchard and his friend.

"I told 'em she was a homicidal lunatic—told 'em again and again—and they swore black and blue that they hadn't clapped eyes on such a person. And all the while—"

"Excuse me," Hugh interrupted at this stage, addressing the police officer. "I fear that Mr. Dawker is letting his zeal outrun the inherent love of truth which I am sure he possesses in his calmer moments. If he will carry his mind back, he will remember that all I did was to deny having a person of unsound mind on the premises. And that statement was nothing more or less than the exact truth. As a medical man I can assure you that Miss Endean is as sane as you or I."

A mocking smile spread over the coarse features of the asylum attendant as he jerked his thumb toward the stained dagger which lay upon a sheet of newspaper on the table.

"Ho yus! Looks like it, don't it?" he jeered. "Why, she did it with the very dagger that she'd pinched from Dr. Felger's study at the sanatorium, and—" He stopped abruptly like a man who realizes he has said too much.

"I must ask you to make a note of that fact, Sergeant," Hugh said swiftly. "It may be an important clue to the real murderer." Then he turned to Dawker. "Go on, my man, tell us the rest of the story. You said that the dagger was in Professor Felger's possession, that he usually kept it in his study, and you were about to add something else, when, for reasons best known to yourself, you suddenly stopped. Come, now, out with it. What were you about to say?"

Dawker ceased biting his lips, and his face twisted into something which was intended to be an innocent smile.

"Lord love yer! There ain't no call to jump down a fellow's throat just because he happens to make a slip of the tongue. I meant to say that the dagger *was* in Dr. Felger's study until a few days ago. That is"—he corrected, with a malicious glance at Hugh—"we missed it soon after you called yesterday."

Hugh turned to the policeman with a laugh.

"Our friend here seems very hazy about his dates, but I suppose he means *I* am the suspected person. That rules out his former theory that Miss Endean committed the crime."

Jopling said nothing, but his face wore a confused expression. It was Dawker who answered.

"The first thing to do is to find the girl and take her back," he cried impatiently. "While we're jawing here she'll get clear away."

"Then why jaw? Find her by all means, if you can, but"— Hugh's tanned face grew set and hard, and into his eyes there crept a look which made the attendant shrink back as though to ward off a blow—"at your peril I defy you to take her back to your so-called sanatorium. Whether she be innocent or guilty of this crime, the police are her proper custodians henceforth. And I would a thousand times sooner that she occupied a prison cell than be in the power of Professor Lucien Felger."

Dawker and his fellows trooped out, followed shortly after by the two constables whom the sergeant had brought with him. But Jopling seemed to have no great faith in their chances of effecting an arrest.

"Like looking for a needle in a haystack," he grunted moodily as he returned to the living-room and seated himself in the chair which happened to be nearest the decanter. "It's a nasty night to be poking and ferreting about the moor. Rare cold, too, for the time o' year."

"Help yourself, Sergeant," said Ronnie, fetching a clean glass and placing it beside him.

Jopling shook his head, but there was no heartiness in his action.

"It's agin regulations, sir," he declared, his eyes fixed wistfully on the amber liquid. "But on such a night as this—"

"The regulations don't apply?" laughed Hugh. "I will absolve your conscience. As a medical man I hereby declare that your strength is exhausted, your nerves shaken, your circulation impaired, and I likewise declare that the only prescription that will meet the case is a stiff, man-sized bracer, to be taken immediately!"

The patient dutifully complied with the orders of his medical adviser.

"Well, there's no going agin you doctors!" he laughed. "Here's to your very good healths, gentlemen, and may you both have plenty of rich incurables on your visiting-lists!"

He drained his glass with undisguised relish, afterwards wiping his heavy moustache with a red cotton handkerchief which he took from a pocket in the rear of his tunic. Replacing it, he produced a shiny black notebook and pencil stub from another mysterious recess in his uniform and assumed a judicial air.

"With all due respect to you, sirs, this is likely to be a serious business," he declared solemnly. "Speaking for myself, and of course unofficially, I am willing to believe that you acted without malice aforethought, as the law terms it. But you must admit the fact remains that you have harboured, sheltered, and otherwise comforted—"

"My friend did all the comforting that took place," Ronnie interposed, with a sly glance at Hugh.

"Harboured, sheltered, and otherwise comforted a dangerous lunatic," pursued Jopling, ignoring the interruption. "And in the course of the aforesaid harbouring, sheltering, and otherwise comforting, the aforesaid dangerous lunatic has allegedly committed an alleged murder."

"Suppose we have a look at the alleged corpse," Ronnie suggested gravely.

"That's a good idea, sir. I was just about to make that suggestion when you took the words out of my mouth, so to speak."

He rose to his feet as he spoke, and the three men quitted the room, Jopling, by virtue of his official status, taking precedence, Hugh following, and Ronnie bringing up the rear. Ascending the cramped staircase, the police-sergeant halted for a moment on the little landing, then turned the handle and slowly opened the door.

The room might almost be termed an attic, for one half of the ceiling sloped at a steep angle, so that at the farther end of the room there were but a few inches of wall above the top of the long, low window. By daylight it might have appeared a light and cheerful apartment, for the window was composed of no less than six sections of latticed panes and occupied the greater part of one wall. But the dim light of the lamp invested it with a sombre and mysterious gloom—a fit setting to the tragedy which had so recently been enacted there. The few pieces of furniture it contained had the appearance of being genuine antiques, the bed in particular being one of those imposing but unhygienic four-posted arrangements, elaborately carved and surmounted by a canopy of faded crimson silk, with the sides shrouded by curtains of the same material. It was an interesting relic of a bygone age, but Hugh was puzzled at the manner in which Jopling remained on the threshold of the room, staring at the bed with wide-open eyes.

"Someone's been up here since I came down," the policeman whispered at last. "I left those curtains open—but they're closed now!"

"It's a wild night," suggested Ronnie. "Perhaps the draught from that open window—"

"*Open* window?" Jopling whirled round as if he had been shot. "Why, the place must be haunted! I distinctly remember that every window was shut!"

"I suppose you made quite sure that Marle was dead?" said Hugh.

In spite of his bewilderment, Sergeant Jopling smiled.

"I'm not likely to be mistaken about *that,*" he said emphatically. "I served in the R.A.M.C. during the war, and I reckon I know a corpse when I see one!" He stepped to the bed and laid his hand on the curtains. "But you're two doctors—have a look for yourselves—"

There was a low, eldritch sound as the rusty curtain-rings screeched back, followed by a gasp of amazement from Jopling.

The bed was empty!

For a full minute the sergeant remained staring at the vacant bed as if he were testing the power of his concentrated gaze to bring back its vanished occupant. Then, without a word, he dashed to the open window and sent forth three long, piercing blasts from his whistle.

"That'll bring my men back—and I feel as if I need 'em!" He took off his helmet and wiped his glistening forehead. "I have a mind that there's something or somebody fooling round this house that'll need a whole heap of catching. My men will be here in a minute; meanwhile, let's search the place."

The only fact which emerged from their rapid examination of the room was the indubitable fact that the corpse of Silas Marle was not in it. The other two constables had returned by this time, and Jopling, after ordering them to search the rest of the house, turned his attention to the open window of the bedroom. Leaning out as far as possible, he brought his hand-lamp into play, sending its beam downward through the darkness like a miniature searchlight. Presently he gave a grunt of satisfaction and withdrew his head.

"There's the sloping roof of a low outhouse immediately below, and there's a few smears of blood still remaining on the wet tiles," he informed Hugh and Ronnie. "That's the way the body was taken out, depend on it. But there was more than one person on the job—I'm sure of that! It would be quite possible for a powerful man to lift the corpse from the bed to the window, and let it slither down the sloping tiles to the ground, but it would need the strength of more than one to carry it far."

"So it would, Sergeant," Ronnie agreed, adding thoughtfully, "Unless that one man were as strong as a horse!"

"Or as swift as a deer!" said Hugh Trenchard.

The policeman made no reply, though he favoured the speaker with a long, hard stare. With a gesture which was an unspoken invitation to the two to follow him, he descended the stairs and made his way outside to the rear of the house.

"Stay where you are, gentlemen," he warned when they had got within a few yards of the outhouse. "There may be footprints in this soft earth." He switched on his lamp again and threw its light on the muddy path. Immediately an exclamation broke from him. "By George, there *are* footprints! Look there—and there!"

Hugh stepped to his side, and his eyes followed the white beam of the lamp as it jerked from one deep impression to the next. Something familiar in their outline caused him to catch his breath sharply.

"Look closer, Sergeant," he said, "and tell me if you notice anything very peculiar in those footprints."

Jopling bent his burly form almost double.

"Well, come to think of it, there *do* look something mighty odd about 'em," he admitted. Then his roving beam fell upon one more distinct than the rest, and his jaw dropped and his eyes opened wide. "Gosh!" he muttered. "If that's not the trail of a cloven foot I'll eat my helmet and swallow the badge!"

Hugh was unable to restrain a slight laugh at the man's almost comical air of mystification. It was a complete change of front from the cocksure manner in which he had ascribed the previous trail to 'an old stag'. Hugh felt tempted to indulge in a little gentle sarcasm.

"You seem rather surprised, Sergeant. Have you forgotten that there are plenty of deer roaming about the moor? Is it so surprising that one of the old stags should have paid us a visit?"

Sergeant Jopling slowly straightened himself up and played the beam of his lamp over the side of the outhouse and up the slope of the roof until it rested on the window of the room they had just quitted.

"Old stag?" he repeated, giving a twisted grin as he shook his head. "I'm thinking it's my words I have to eat instead of my helmet, Dr. Trenchard. A stag might have climbed up that wood-pile and up the roof; but it 'ud take a stag with a pair of human hands to open that window and haul out Silas Marle's body. Old stag be danged! I'm thinking that we're up agin summat 'ere that needs a parson more than a policeman!"

CHAPTER VIII

HUGH TRENCHARD CONTRIVED to snatch a few hours' sleep that night, but at the first streak of dawn he was roused by a chorus of deep-throated barks, mingled with the cracking of whips. Throwing open the window, he saw a pack of hounds on the green in front of the house. With them were four horsemen and three other mounts whose saddles were at that moment empty. The sight took him by surprise until he remembered Jopling's announced intention of sending for the Exmoor Staghounds to follow up the trail which he had discovered in the coombe immediately after the first murderous attack on Silas Marle.

"They will have a fresher trail to follow now," was the thought that flashed through his mind as he dressed and made a hasty toilet. "Unless I'm very much mistaken, there'll be queer sport afoot this morning!"

On descending to the living-room he found Sergeant Jopling in close consultation with a bluff-looking, middle-aged man in riding tweeds and top-boots.

"Come in, Doctor," cried the policeman as Hugh hesitated. "This is the man I was talking to you about—Nick Froude, the Harbourer of the Exmoor Staghounds. He's an old hand at the game, believe me, and what he doesn't know about stag-hunting isn't worth the finding out."

It was soon apparent that the Harbourer had been informed of the latest developments of the case, for a slight smile passed across his weather-beaten face at the policeman's words.

"With all my experience, I've never come across anything exactly like this," he admitted, thoughtfully stroking the strip of grey side-whisker which ornamented his otherwise clean-shaven face. "Last night will make the third time that a stag has come to this house, and it's very unusual for them to approach human beings at all, although they might possibly charge anyone who approached them during the rutting season. I'd like to have a look at those footprints before I bring the hounds to them."

"By all means do so," assented Jopling, and led the way to the rear of the house.

The Harbourer's keen eyes picked up the trail at once. Kneeling down, he examined each footmark in turn, measuring its length and breadth by the rough-and-ready expedient of comparing it with the fingers of his clenched hand.

"Yes, it's a stag, sure enough," he declared at length, "and a big 'un, or he would not have pushed his feet so far into the earth. You can always tell a stag's slot from a hind's, because a stag's hoof is rounder and wider at the heel and blunter at the toes, and his dew claws point outward, while a hind's are smaller and point inwards. And there's a difference in the gait, too, for a stag crosses his legs right and left in walking."

"You're sure it was not another kind of animal altogether?" Jopling queried.

"What else is it likely to be?" asked the Harbourer in his turn.

Sergeant Jopling shook his head.

"I dunno—I only wish I did," he returned with a shrug of his broad shoulders. "But I've never heerd of a stag what climbs roofs and opens windows!"

Nick Froude laughed.

"You'll soon see what kind of a stag it is when my hounds force it to break cover," he declared confidently. "I'll tell my men to put six couples of steady tufter on the scent at once. I suppose you'll want to ride with us. I've brought over a couple of spare mounts."

Jopling hesitated, finally shaking his head.

"I've got my report to write out, and the Superintendent is coming over from Bath and may be here any minute." He turned to Hugh. "Maybe you and the other young doctor would care for a run?"

"Nothing would suit me better, and I think I can say the same of Dr. Brewster," said Trenchard eagerly. "All that we ask is ten minutes in which to snatch a mouthful of breakfast."

As he had anticipated, Ronnie proved as eager as himself to see the outcome of the strange adventure. Long before the ten minutes were up the two were standing by their horses, ready to take the saddle the moment Nick Froude gave the word.

The sport of hunting the wild deer is, though shorn of much of its former pomp and ceremony, still carried on in much the same manner as when William of Normandy rode forth to the chase in his New Forest. Firstly the 'tufters' were separated from the rest of the pack and laid on the slot. They were old, experienced hounds and knew perfectly well what was expected of them. Each uttered a short bark as he picked up the scent, afterwards running mute. With tails in the air and noses to the ground, the dogs set off at a loping trot, making almost due east in the direction of the high ground near the old Roman camp above Ashcombe.

"Mount, gentlemen—it's a burning scent," said Froude as he sprang into his own saddle. "Ride steady and do not press the hounds. The hunt doesn't really begin until the quarry is roused."

For over two miles the trail ran straight as an arrow over the gorse and heather. Suddenly the foremost tufter swerved off almost at right angles, followed by the rest. Froude swore under his breath.

"The varment be up to his old games again. He intends to soil like he did last time."

"Soil?" Hugh repeated with a puzzled shake of his head.

"Yes, sir. That's how we call it when a stag takes to the water and swims or wades up a stream to throw the hounds off the scent. Usually they do it after they are properly roused—but this particular beast has the cunning of Satan himself. Look—what did I tell 'ee?"

Before them stretched a long rocky coombe, its sides covered with oak scrub and firs; at the bottom a silvery gleam of water showed here and there. Hugh viewed the precipitous sides with something like dismay.

"Surely you're not going down there?"

The Harbourer shook his head. "No horse could do it. But where a stag can lead a hound can follow. We'll let 'em bide for a bit and trust 'em to cast about on the farther side of the stream and pick up the scent again. Depend on it, sir, he won't travel along that stream far. There's a bog at the upper end and a bridge a matter of a quarter of a mile down. I've never known a stag yet that passed over a bog or under a bridge. And by the same token, there's a road which leads down to the bridge. We'll get across so as to be on the right side if the stag should still be harbouring there—though I suppose he's a good many miles off yet."

They were half-way across the low stone bridge when a deep, bell-like note rose from the cover.

"That's the challenge—the sign that one of the hounds has picked up the scent. I'll wager it's old Whiteboy—I'd recognize his note in a thousand. He's the oldest tufter of the lot, but he's got the finest nose for a cold scent. Look! They've broke cover—but there's no stag in front of 'em."

He pointed with his whip to where the dogs had emerged from the wooded slope on the farther side of the coombe, their bodies half hidden in the tall heather. Setting spurs to their horses, the little cavalcade breasted the steep rise and again fell into position behind the hounds. Glancing at the sun, Hugh saw that the trail was now taking a westerly direction. Their quarry was gradually circling back on its own tracks.

"Ay, he be making for water again," said Nick Froude, when Hugh commented on this change of direction. "That's an old trick of his. Other stags may put up a hind, so that its scent will confuse his own trail, or he may go to herd—mix with the others—for the same purpose. But this fellow always plays a lone hand. He's a cunning creature, and I'm minded he'll show us a trick or two before I sound his mort."

Hugh Trenchard nodded without speaking. In his own mind was an ever-increasing suspicion that the creature they were hunting would prove to be an even stranger creature than the old Harbourer imagined.

Presently they found their progress barred by a broad stream, one of the tributaries of the River Exe. Without hesitation, the hounds plunged into the water, only to be at once recalled by the whipper-in.

"He's swum downstream," declared Froude.

"How can you tell that? Surely the scent does not lie on the water?" Hugh could not help exclaiming.

"No, but the hounds entered the water with their noses pointing downstream. The only danger is that the cunning brute may take that direction, come ashore for a minute or two, then swim in the reverse direction and break soil—land, that is—higher up than the place where he first entered the water; so that while we're wasting time on a false scent downstream, he's miles off in the other direction. But we'll cast downstream first, anyway."

The pack was divided, one half being sent to the farther bank in charge of the whipper-in; then both parties made their way in the same direction as the flowing current, the dogs nosing about in that eager yet crestfallen manner which they assume when at fault. More than half an hour passed thus, and Froude was thinking seriously of casting back, when old Whiteboy—in front as usual—lifted his head in the air and gave vent to the eager 'challenge'. Nick Froude urged his horse to the spot, his keen eyes searching the muddy shingle at the river-bank.

"Hark forward!" he cried. "The slot is as plain as print, and not more than two hours old. It'll be a kill this time, gentlemen! Hark forward!"

A shrill blast from his horn brought the remainder of the dogs from the farther bank, and the chase was resumed. Another hour and Hugh Trenchard began to be aware of a vague sense of familiarity in the changing face of the countryside. He looked again at the densely wooded slope of the beacon they were approaching, asking himself when and where he had seen just such another. Just then the trail took a turn, and a second later he caught sight of a roof among the trees, and the mystery was a mystery no longer. The cloven trail was heading straight toward the gates of Professor Lucien Felger's private sanatorium—the place from which Joan Endean had made her escape!

To the wild excitement of the chase was added another, even keener, emotion. What could be the connection between the sinister, cloven-footed monster, the self-styled King of the Moor, and the equally sinister scientist from Vienna? Was it mere chance that their quarry had, after endeavouring twice to cover its tracks, made for that spot? It would not seem so, he decided, for the pack was in full cry now, running without check or swerve, straight for the closed gate. A sudden sense of exultation filled Hugh Trenchard's heart—the next few minutes would prove whether the so-called Terror of the Moor had a real existence or was nothing but the figment of a disordered imagination. The gate was less than a hundred yards off now; Hugh pressed forward until he was the foremost rider. If the hounds were refused admittance—as was more than likely—he was determined to climb the gate and admit them with his own hands. The suave professor might be an adept in throwing dust in the eyes of human beings, but it would need someone cleverer than he to deceive the natural instincts of old Whiteboy and the pack.

But even as the thought crossed his mind there came an unexpected interruption. When little more than a dozen yards from the gate, each hound came to a sudden halt, snuffled the ground for a few seconds, then set off with renewed speed in a totally different direction.

Nick Froude drew rein, his bronzed face a picture of bewilderment.

"Are the hounds bewitched?" he cried. "If this were thick cover I'd say our quarry was lying close, having turned out another stag, for I'll swear they've gone off on a fresh scent—first time I've

known old Whiteboy do such a thing. Head 'em back, Jem!" he
shouted to the whipper-in, then rode forward to the pack, endeavouring with voice and whip to make them return to the former
trail. "Ho, Whiteboy! Romper! Teazer! Back, Whiteboy, back!
Damn the hounds! They *are* bewitched!"

But for once the well-trained animals were heedless of threats
and coaxing alike. They were in full cry now, each hound giving
tongue as loudly as his exertions would permit. They seemed frenzied—maddened. They could not have dashed forward more rapidly if their quarry had just broken cover and was standing 'at
gaze' before them. Realizing that his efforts to turn them were useless, Nick Froude fell in behind the pack.

"Let 'em bide, Jem," he directed the whipper-in. "This is the
queerest run I've ever heard tell of."

Like an arrow aimed by a master-hand, the pack headed
straight across the purple moor. Gradually they left the heather
behind them and emerged on to a plateau of naked rock. Here they
suddenly stopped, barking loudly and struggling round their
leader, who was frantically snuffling and pawing something which
lay on the ground. A minute later Froude galloped up and threw
himself from the saddle, cracking his long whip and trying to sepa-
rate them. Seizing Whiteboy by the haunches—for no hound
wears a collar—he dragged him off the thing he was trying to
worry. It was a pocket-handkerchief which had once been white
but now was soiled and torn.

"A handkerchief!" cried Hugh. "Now what on earth made—"

Silencing him with a gesture, Nick stooped and sniffed the
grimy rag. When he straightened up, the expression on his face
told that he had encountered something that was beyond his experience of woodcraft.

"It seems as if our quarry has remarkable intelligence—or else
he has a human ally who is not anxious for him to be sighted," he
said slowly. "That handkerchief has been soaked in aniseed and
deliberately drawn across the trail. Aniseed has the same effect on
dogs as valerian has on cats—nothing can stop them making
straight for it. No pack on earth would run true in the face of that
drug, and if the joker who played the trick had not thrown the
drug-soaked rag away, they would have followed him to the ends
of the earth. But he was artful enough to drop his lure when he'd
carried the false trail far enough. Anyway, gentlemen, that's the
finish of to-day's sport—it would be sheer waste of time to hark
back to where the hounds were at fault, for they'd only make for

this spot again. I'll have to destroy the handkerchief before I'll be able to get them away."

He searched about until he found a small heap of dried heather. Placing the torn handkerchief on it, he drew out a matchbox.

"One moment, if you please."

Ronnie Brewster had dismounted and approached the miniature pyre. His manner was one of studied carelessness, but Hugh seemed to sense a note of suppressed excitement in his voice as he went on:

"I'm rather curious to know what aniseed smells like. Do you mind if I have a sniff before you send it up in smoke?"

"You're quite welcome, sir."

Ronnie knelt and bent over the grimy scrap of linen; then he smilingly beckoned to Hugh.

"Come and have a sniff, old bean—this stunt may come in very handy if you happen to be trailed by a man-eating bloodhound at any time."

Secretly wondering what lay beneath his chum's strange request, Trenchard knelt by his side. As he did so, Ronnie, with no perceptible movement of his lips, whispered rapidly:

"Look in the corner of the handkerchief!"

For a moment the young doctor paused uncomprehendingly. Then his eyes sought the indicated spot, and he stiffened as though at a sudden numbing blow. Worked in tiny letters of silk were the initials 'J.E.' —Joan Endean—the girl who had appeared from nowhere in that night of rain and storm, to disappear afterwards as mysteriously. Was this yet another link connecting her with the Terror of the Moor?

"Curious smell, isn't it?" Ronnie's drawling voice roused him from the stupor of amazement into which the discovery had plunged him.

"Yes." Hugh paused, struggling to control his voice. "Very curious indeed."

Nick Froude struck a match and applied it to the little heap. With a slight crackling sound the flames licked up and encircled the scrap of cambric, and in a few seconds it was nothing but a shred of glowing tinder. Like a man in a dream Hugh watched the Harbourer grind his foot on the still smouldering heap, leaving not the slightest spark that might start a heath fire.

Looking up, he caught Ronnie regarding him curiously, "Quite an impressive little ceremony, eh?" laughed his friend as they remounted. "Quite funereal—'Ashes to ashes . . .' and all the rest of it."

Ashes to ashes! In spite of the warm sunshine, Hugh felt himself shivering. Coming when they did, the symbolic words seemed like a warning—a portent of impending peril to the girl he had grown to love.

CHAPTER IX

HUGH TRENCHARD'S MIND was the prey of a host of perplexing thoughts as he jogged along in the rear of the little cavalcade on its way back to tell Sergeant Jopling of the amazing finish of the chase. The tragic and mysterious events of the past few days had followed one another so rapidly that he had not had time to grasp their full significance. From the even tenor of a quiet walking tour he had found himself plunged into a real-life drama so full of weird and seemingly supernatural happenings that it might have had its setting in the Dark Ages, instead of the prosaic twentieth century. Now, as his wiry little pony ambled along the bridle-path without needing a touch on the reins to guide it, he gave his mind up to an endeavour to consider each event in its proper order.

That old Silas Marle had made elaborate preparations to guard himself was not surprising in view of the fact that his wife had met her death on the moor just over a year previously; the massive bolts on the doors and bars across the windows, to say nothing of the numerous weapons which the house contained, proved that he had taken precautions against such a fate overtaking himself. He had indeed admitted as much on recovering consciousness after Hugh had carried him to the house, and the old man's horror-stricken utterance had caused his words to be imprinted on Trenchard's brain with an exactitude which approached that with which the recording needle of a gramophone engraves its message on the waxen disc. "The Terror of the Moor! The Terror that walks by night—the foul, cloven-hoofed shape that glides through the darkness, seeking but to destroy! . . . I swore that I would destroy it, but it has destroyed me instead." Wild and frenzied words, and words which the young doctor might have attributed to the ravings of delirium had it not been for his own experience that night—the demoniacal voice issuing from the mist and the unmistakable imprint of the cloven feet in the soft ground.

A supernatural monster? Hugh dismissed the thought the instant it came to him, but close behind it came the recollection of the passage in the ancient black-letter volume in the library of Silas Marle:

> . . . ye Foule and Namelesse Thynge whyche, fearsome beyonde measure, haunteth ye Desolate Moore of ye Aunctient Kyngdome of Wessex . . . It slayeth wythe Arte and Cunnynge beyonde very belief, nathless it leaveth ye Cloven Trayle of its Devyl's Foot wheresobeit it walketh.

With a start he called to mind the uncanny fact that it was just as he was reading of this weird monster's power of assuming the shape of

> a Maiden, rauvishynge to the eye and fair withal, who knocketh on ye Casement, beseechynge entry,

that he had heard the light tap which heralded the arrival of Joan Endean.

Hugh could not repress a smile as his thoughts reached this stage. The quaintly spelt adjectives of the long-dead necromantic author of the old book might not be a bad description of the personal charms of the girl who had emerged so opportunely from the sometimes desolate Exmoor; but he could not reconcile the expression of her frank blue eyes with the attributes of a bloodthirsty monster of diabolic origin. Indeed, he was surprised at himself for allowing his mind to dwell on the subject with any degree of seriousness.

'This legend-infested moor must have inoculated me with some of its supernatural virus!' he thought, his lip curling in a smile of self-contempt. 'I'd better be getting back to the saner atmosphere of London before I make a public confession of faith in vampires, hobgoblins, and Black Magic generally!'

But even as the thought of return presented itself to his mind, he knew he had no intention of putting it into effect. Truth to tell, he knew that he would never leave the neighbourhood of the great sweeping moors until he, or somebody else, had solved the problem which at present baffled yet enthralled him with its eerie mystery. In his character was a streak of dogged pugnacity which had often served him in good stead in his encounters in the amateur boxing-ring, and now it asserted itself in no uncertain fashion. Come what might, he would see the matter through, and if the trail of the cloven foot led him to Joan Endean, so much the better.

True, he recognized the possibility of his quest ending in something much more sinister and less desirable than the renewal of his acquaintance with the beautiful girl who had crossed his path under such exciting circumstances; but he accepted that possibility with a confident shrug. He would take lodgings somewhere in the immediate neighbourhood and play a lone hand against the dreaded Terror of the Moor.

Sergeant Jopling met them on their return to Moor Lodge, and there seemed to be an undercurrent of excitement beneath the worthy officer's stolid exterior. He listened in silence while the Harbourer gave an account of the unexpected check which had brought the run to a premature end. A gleam of increased interest came into the sergeant's eyes when he heard the means that had been employed.

"Aniseed?" he repeated, busy with his ever-ready notebook. "Well, there doesn't seem to be anything supernatural about a thing you can buy at any chemist's shop. Now if it had been a whiff of brimstone . . ."

Hugh felt secretly amused at the eloquent manner in which the sergeant left the rest of the sentence unspoken.

"I should imagine that one could just as easily procure brimstone as aniseed," he remarked. "But at least the employment of such means seems to indicate that whatever you're after is substantial enough to wear a pair of regulation handcuffs—when you catch him."

Sergeant Jopling slowly closed one eye in an elaborate wink.

"Maybe when that time comes we may find it isn't a 'him' at all," he said in a whisper that was intended for Hugh's ears alone. "It might possibly be a 'her'!"

Hugh Trenchard regarded the man with quickened interest. Plainer than words his manner indicated that he had got a clue.

"Any fresh developments, Sergeant?" he asked in the same low tone.

"Maybe—maybe not," was the non-committal rejoinder. "Will you please step into the next room for a moment?"

When they were alone the sergeant slowly and impressively drew a letter from his pocket and laid it on the table.

"This was delivered while you were away, sir. It's addressed to Hugh Trenchard, M.D., and the writing betrays feminine characteristics, as the saying is. Would it be indelicate to ask if there is any lady of your acquaintance that is likely to be writing to you here?"

Hugh could only shake his head. His circle of friends was a small one, and none of them, he felt positive, knew of his present whereabouts, unless—he started, and his heart gave a quick throb as the thought flashed to his mind—it was the mysterious Joan Endean. He felt the flush rise to his cheeks, and cursed as he saw a look of suspicious comprehension light up Jopling's dull features.

"Why, anyone would think you were about to charge me with stealing somebody's affections!" he said, forcing a light laugh. "If you intend to arrest every young man who gets written to in feminine handwriting, you'll have to sell your village lock-up and buy a county gaol! Odd, but it's not stamped," he added, struck by a sudden thought.

Sergeant Jopling slowly shook his head. "If it 'ud been posted I shouldn't be questioning you now, sir."

"Was it delivered by a messenger?"

"Not so far as I knows," said the policeman, with another shake of his head.

"Then how on earth did it get here?" cried the now thoroughly bewildered Trenchard.

"Ah, that's the very question that I'd like to be able to answer." With exasperating deliberation, Jopling insinuated his bulky form into an inadequate-looking armchair and crossed one leg over the other. Again his eyes roamed toward the ceiling as though he were seeking inspiration from the age-blackened beams; when at length he spoke, he seemed to go off at a tangent.

"I happened to go up to Lunnon once, on a matter of identification, and having a few hours to spare before my train left, I strolled into one of the theatres. I forget the name of the piece that was being played, but one of the scenes were an old, lonely house—just such another as this 'ere house we're in at this moment. I don't remember much of the plot—if there was a plot— but I *do* mind that every time the villain came on—he wasn't the villain at all, as it turned out at the end, but someone who was trying to catch the real villain, who was a detective—I hope you catch my meaning, sir?"

"Oh, quite. I've seen plays something like that myself," said Hugh wearily. "Please go on."

"Well, as I were a-saying, this villain-who-wasn't-the-villain-at-all seemed never to dream of entering the room like an ordinary Christian—through the door. He'd pop in through the window at most unexpected, unlooked-for moments, or through the ceiling, or the floor, or a secret panel in the wainscot—once he comes through an old grandfather clock, though how he managed it without being mixed up with the works is a thing I've never rumbled from that day to this! I remember thinking at the time how puzzling it would be to us policemen if things like that happened in real life, which same I was quite sure at that time they did not. And I was quite sure, sir, up to no later than yesterday. But now—well, *now* I ain't quite so sure!"

"I'm afraid I don't quite follow you." There was no pretence about Hugh's puzzled air. "What do you mean?"

Sergeant Jopling jerked his head toward the letter which still lay unopened on the table.

"I mean the way that letter came to be delivered 'ere. It were something like half an hour arter you had all rode away with the hounds. I was sitting on this window-seat, trying to straighten matters out in my mind and making a few entries in my notebook. One o' my men, P.C. Wimple—a good lad, though he *is* too fond of reading those detective stories—was out by the front-garden gate, looking for cigarette-ends and whatnot among the grass. Another, Hardy, an experienced officer (between you and me, he's next for promotion when I retire), was at the back taking plaster-of-paris casts of the cloven footprints. My third man was on the roof lowering a bag of sand down the chimney to see if it was wide enough for a body to pass through. Please to bear in mind those positions—me in here, Wimple at the gate, Hardy at the back door, the other man on the roof. You'd say it was impossible for anyone to enter the house without one of us spotting him, wouldn't you? Well, someone *did* enter it, for when I finished my notes and came out to tell Wimple not to waste his time scratching about like an old hen, the first thing that caught my eye was this letter lying on the hallstand!"

"It's certainly very curious," Hugh admitted.

Apparently the worthy sergeant appeared to consider the adjective inadequate.

"Curious?" he repeated with a grunt of contempt. "To my mind it's a jolly sight more curiouser than merely 'curious'! I've heard of messages being sent through the air by wireless, but it's the first time I've heard of 'em being delivered all written out, sealed, and addressed! Why, a dog couldn't have entered the house without one of us seeing it—much less a man! I'm thinking there be a secret passage or two about this old place, and that's the way old Marle's body were spirited away."

"And where do you imagine this wonderful secret passage leads to?" Hugh inquired with a slight smile.

Jopling waved his hand vaguely.

"Out on the moor—anywhere—maybe only a few hundred feet outside the walls," he replied, eyeing the ancient panelling with a resentful scowl. "I've been tapping the woodwork down here and in the bedroom all the afternoon, but it all seems hollow alike to me."

"You ought to confine your investigations to looking for the hidden spring—all the best fiction insists on a hidden spring being present on these occasions," said Hugh gravely. "While you are searching for it, I'll read my letter, if you have no objection."

"Certainly, sir—by all means." The policeman gave a tentative cough. "Maybe the contents will be interesting."

His meaning was unmistakable; but Hugh had no intention of taking the somewhat obtuse hint.

"I have no doubt that they will be—to me."

Hugh took up the letter as he uttered the dry rejoinder. In spite of his assumed nonchalance he found his fingers trembling with eagerness as he slit the envelope and extracted a dainty sheet of notepaper. Long before his eyes had scanned the signature, his instinct told him that the missive was from his mysterious visitor of the previous night.

Dear Dr. Trenchard [it ran],

When I gave the sealed packet into your keeping I little thought that I should want to claim it so soon, but unforeseen circumstances have made it necessary for me to have it without delay. Meet me at the Devil's Cheesepress, in the Valley of Rocks, near Lynton, bringing the packet with you. I shall be waiting there between eleven o'clock and midnight. Please do not fail me.

Joan Endean.

Jopling was searching his face with curious eyes.

"Anything of interest?" he asked after a long, expectant pause.

"Yes—but only of interest to myself."

"It has no bearing on the disappearance of Marle's body?" the other persisted.

"Not the slightest bearing."

Hugh Trenchard made the statement quite believing it to be true; it seemed little short of sacrilege to regard that frank-eyed girl as being a prime mover of the dark mystery which hung over the lonely house on the moor. He was like a man who walks beneath a magnificent star-sown sky, admiring the splendour of the heavens, his upturned eyes unheeding the chasm which yawns beneath his feet.

He thrust the letter into his pocket, nodded to the sergeant, and hurried from the room. The little town of Lynton was some fifteen miles distant, and the Valley of Rocks beyond that again. A glance at his map told him that there was no railway that would serve his purpose; he would have to trust to luck to get some kind of conveyance from one of the villages; failing that, he would have to tramp the whole distance. In the end he did tramp it, and it was a very weary Hugh Trenchard who breasted the summit of Shilstone Hill and saw the lights of Lynton shine forth one by one against the dusk-dimmed waters of the Severn Sea.

CHAPTER X

THE TWIN TOWNS of Lynton and Lynmouth, no larger than villages, doze like sentinels over the rocky mouth of the River Lyn. It is quite possible to throw a stone from one village to the other, though the experiment is not one to be recommended, as the missile hurled from Lynton might gain a dangerous momentum in dropping the several hundreds of feet which represent the difference of altitude between the two villages; for Lynton crowns the brow of a lofty hill while Lynmouth nestles in the valley beneath.

A church clock was announcing the hour of ten as Hugh Trenchard made his way along the Lynbridge Road; and, confident that he had plenty of time in which to cover the remaining couple of miles, he turned his steps seaward, emerging on the cliff overlooking the spot where the united waters of the East and West Lyns form a tiny tidal harbour, sheltered on the west by a breakwater with a lighthouse in the form of a mediaeval-looking tower, machicolated and weather-scarred, and bearing a curious resemblance to the structures which crown the heights on the banks of the Rhine. Stretching his weary limbs on the grass, Hugh lit his pipe and prepared for a quiet hour, for he had no wish to attract attention by arriving at his destination before the appointed time.

Although it was still the tail-end of the holiday season, the place seemed almost deserted. Beyond the lighted windows of the single row of houses fronting the harbour, the waters of the Severn Sea stretched dark and mysterious to where the faint flash of the Mumbles Light marked the coast of Wales. Nearer at hand were the white and green lights of a tramp steamer hugging the coast on its way to Bristol or Cardiff. Hugh had slowly smoked one pipe and was in the act of lighting a second, when he was conscious of a burly figure coming along the edge of the cliff.

"Voine night, zur."

The greeting was uttered in the broadest Devon dialect, and Hugh, straining his eyes to pierce the gloom, saw that the speaker was attired in a peaked cap and rough pilot jacket. Although his appearance was distinctly nautical, he looked slightly different from the usual fisherman or longshoreman.

"It is indeed a fine night," Hugh agreed, "though it blows a trifle chilly up here."

The man nodded his head sagely as he cocked a weatherwise eye toward the clouds.

"Thacky wind's blawin vrom the zea. It'll bring rain afore morn, I wadge."

"I hope not," laugh Hugh. "We've had enough wet these last few days to last us quite a long time. These Exmoor showers are no joke—they wet you through in five minutes."

"Ay, vor sure, it do rain cats and dogs zumtoimes," the old man assented. "I mind my varther a-telling me that volks used to wear stag-skin suits afore they mackintoshes were invented."

Hugh Trenchard was conscious of a suddenly awakened interest.

"Stag-skin suits?" he repeated.

"Ay, zur, suits made out of the hides of stags, tanned o' course, and worn wi' the hair outstanding. It were Dr. Wade, of Dulverton, who first thought of the idee. He had a suit made like a pair of overalls, with a large overhanging cape and a hood for his head—just like one o' the old monks—with holes left for the eyes and to breathe through. On the day that Sir Thomas Acland were nominated as the Conservative candidate, the doctor wore it when he rode down to Exeter to support him. Eh, but what laughin' and jokin' he caused! All the gentlevolk were a-calling him 'Robinson Crusoe' and 'The Wild Man o' the Woods' and zuchloike, but Doctor, he didn't moind a scrap. It were raining cats and dogs that day, zur, an' every one o' 'em were drenched to the skin, bar him. Comin' home he were riding through Raddlecombe just as the 'Royal Oak' were a-turning out their customers at closing-time. No sooner did the lads zee what were riding at 'em afore they lets out a screech that could be heard t'other end o' Zummerset a'most, and then every man-jack of 'em skedaddled for their lives. They thought the Phantom Hunter had coom for 'em, I wadger!"

Hugh removed his pipe from his mouth and glanced sharply up.

"The Phantom Hunter?" he repeated, striving to conceal the eager note that would creep into his voice. "What on earth is that?"

The ancient mariner regarded him with a kind of pitying amazement during the pause which followed.

"Lord sakes! Do 'ee mean to say 'ee never heerd o' the ghostly horseman that rides with his ghostly pack over Exmoor?"

Trenchard shook his head, repressing the smile which at first threatened to betray his incredulity. Like a flash his mind had recalled the staggering events of the past few days—events which so far had defied a rational explanation. Though still far from willing to credit the moor with possessing a supernatural habitant, he was nevertheless surprised to learn of the existence of a definite local legend to that effect. It at least seemed to indicate that Silas Marle was not alone in his belief that the moor was haunted.

"I have heard a rumour to that effect," he admitted warily. "But tell me more about this Phantom Hunter. What does he look like?"

Apparently delighted at finding such an interested listener, the old man seated himself on the turf beside Hugh, and, having filled his clay pipe from the proffered pouch, plunged into his tale with relish.

"What do 'e look like, sez you? Well, mister, that theer be a hard question to answer, surely—some volks zay one thing, some volks say contrariwise. According to some 'e be dressed like the huntsmen of the days gone by, with a plumed hat and high buff boots, mounted on a gurt black horse, bewhiles a-blowing of his hunting-horn and halloing to his hounds as he follows the Phantom Herd."

"Herd of what?" questioned Hugh. "Deer?"

The old man nodded as he sucked reflectively at his pipe.

"Deer, to be sure," he assented. "Many a varmer on Exmoor— ay, and on Dartmoor, too—will tell 'ee how he has laid awake at night a-listening to the baying of the Wild Huntsman's hounds as the chase swept past his cottage. They do zay it all began over a witch's curse, years and years agone, mister, and I've often heerd my old varther repeat the rhyme that some poet vellow made up about it."

"Do you think you could remember it?" Hugh asked the question with an interest that was not wholly due to the possible bearing which the old legend might have on the recent puzzling events. He knew that the oldest traditions of folk-lore were often cast into verse, so as to be more easily remembered and passed on orally from father to son through the ages, when the bulk of the common people were illiterate.

"Aw, iss, for sure I remember it," the old man answered, and in a quavering sing-song treble he repeated a doggerel legend which, judging by its archaic phraseology and barbaric metre, must have originated somewhere about the time of Chaucer.

"Lord Tybault, of Haddon, a huntsman he,
Deep-skilled in the Art of Venerie,
Handsome and proud as a hart in the glen,
Beloved by maidens and envied by men.
He laughed at Love's shackles—his love it was free,
And freest of all that for Sweet Marjorie,
Dame Elspeth's daughter—she who, 'twas said,
Was learned in witchcraft, art deep and dread.
But Marjorie spurned him, laughed long and loud
At the tenderest vows of Lord Tybault the proud:
'Go, seek other hunting—you're riding at fault!
This heart will elude you, my proud Lord Tybault!'
But he carried her off in the dead of the night,
And she in the greenwood bewailed her sad plight.
About her white throat a kerchief she tied,
And Lord Tybault had a corpse for his bride.
The aged witch-mother, she wept and she swore
By the Powers of Darkness she'd plague him full sore.
As the bell tolled out midnight she cast a dread spell,
Written in blood and recorded in Hell.
When forth next morn rode proud Lord Tybault,
His palfrey was lame, his hounds were at fault;
The bolts from his cross-bow flew wide of the mark;
The stags in the glen, the hinds in the park
Went alike scathless, and never a mort
Sounded that day to enliven his sport.
The hottest of scents, the plainest of slot,
His fiend-ridden hounds e'er overshot.
Anon, rousing himself, he cried, 'Hark away!
I'll kill if I ride till the Judgment Day!'
The hounds quested back in the depths of the wood,
With snuffle and traverse, thirsting for blood;
A hart bounded out, they hot on his spoor'—
Lord Tybault in chase dashed over the moor.
Away went the quarry, away went the hounds,
'Hark away! Forward!' the hunting-horn sounds.
He rose in his stirrups and swore, 'By the Rood!
Ne'er will I dismount till I have drawn blood!
Up hill and down dale, o'er forest and combe
I'll harry that stag till the last crack of Doom!"
Up hill and down dale, through heather and brake,
The hart took its way, with him in its wake.

The sun sank down in a sea of red flame,
But hunted and hunter sped on just the same.
His vow had been heard by the God he defied—
Condemned was Lord Tybault for ever to ride.
And through summer's fair days and the dull winter gloom,
Lord Tybault must ride till the last Day of Doom."

"H'm—very interesting," Hugh commented when the old fellow came to the end. "Allow me to congratulate you on your excellent memory."

"I knaws heaps more, zur. I'll tell 'ee the one about the ghost that used to haunt the trading-ketch that plied atween Minehead and Waterford—"

"I'm afraid it will have to be some other time," said Hugh as he rose to his feet. "It's getting late, and I shall have to be going."

"Right you are, zur. Any time ye be passing this ways, just ask anyone for Zacary Durdon's cottage. I'll allers be glad to have another crack wi' 'ee. Good night, zur, good night."

The old man touched his forehead and hobbled off in the direction of the village. Hugh Trenchard swung off in the opposite direction, entering the North Walk, a mile-long terrace hewn midway down the face of the cliff, a mere ledge five feet wide and four hundred feet above the surface of the sea.

It seemed as if Zacary Durdon's prediction were correct, for, as Hugh walked onward, the ragged rain-clouds began to drive in from the Atlantic, and, scudding across the face of the rising moon, sent their crawling shadows over the heaving sea and the jagged wilderness of peaks which presently opened out before him. By the fleeting moonbeams he was able to take his bearings. That stupendous mass of stone, its summit reared some eight hundred feet above the waves which frothed against its foot, was the Castle Rock; the more regularly outlined pyramid of cyclopean dimensions could be none other than the hill called Ragged Jack. Almost opposite, on the inland side, where the Valley of Rocks took a sudden turn, was a fantastic, isolated mass of granite jutting from the slope of the hill. It was the Devil's Cheesepress—the spot where he was to meet Joan Endean,

Trenchard slackened pace as he sighted his destination. A glance at the illuminated dial of his watch told him that he had a good twenty minutes to spare before the appointed hour. He knocked the ashes from his pipe, felt to make sure that the precious letter reposed in his pocket, then began to pick his way across the floor of the Valley to the lonely, upstanding rock.

He fell into a curious train of thought as he slowly advanced. The scene around him, with the exception of the narrow metalled road threading the Valley, had probably remained unchanged since the eyes of the first man had beheld it. What a story that solitary crag could tell were it endowed with speech! In its shadow, low-browed savages had patiently chipped their rude flint axes and smiting-stones; if antiquaries were right in their interpretation of the rough circle of surrounding stones, white-robed Druids had enacted their solemn mysteries there. It had watched with the same inscrutable face the Celts retreating westward before the coloniz-ing Saxons, and the same breezes that rippled through the heather at its feet had swelled the painted sails of the ships which brought the Danish rovers, and the mail-clad Norman knights. Elsewhere, the face of England had changed with the passing centuries—here the very heart of Time seemed frozen and dead. That stark, Na-ture-hewn monolith was like an everlasting link connecting the present with the past.

Five minutes' leisurely walking brought him to the irregular path which sloped up to the rock. His heart was beating a little faster than usual as he started to mount. Try as he might, he could not repress a creepy feeling as, alone amid the prehistoric stony wilderness, he awaited the hour that would herald the birth of an-other day to add to the vast toll of days that were past and dead.

Suddenly he halted and stood stock-still, listening. In that world of silence he had caught the sound of a footstep—not such a sound as a shod human foot would make, but light, soft, almost inaudi-ble, like the padding of some prowling beast. Surely, he thought, the girl would have recognized him as he had crossed the open; it could not be she who was approaching with such sinister stealth!

He shifted his gaze to the patch of shadow cast by the Devil's Cheesepress, examining a portion which seemed to have changed its position without apparent cause. But before he could make sure that his fancy had not deceived him, a cloud drifted before the moon, and all was dark. Moving forward quickly, his outstretched hand came in contact with the rough surface of the rock. Guiding himself by touch, he began to creep round the shoulder which separated him from the suspicious object.

The moonlight flickered, waned, then shone through a rift in the moving clouds—the dim, wavering beams not bright enough to illuminate the recesses of the rock-girt gloom, yet sufficiently so to reveal something which made him catch his breath sharply and feel for the butt of his revolver.

Two greenly luminous eyes were looking into his own!

It was not the cold malignity of that fixed, unwinking stare that made Hugh Trenchard's heart feel as if it were being squeezed by a hand of ice, neither was it the half-bestial, half-human character of the eyes themselves. It was the remembrance that the last time he had seen them was when they watched his approach through the window of Professor Felger's so-called sanatorium. In a flash he remembered, too, that Joan Endean's handwriting was unknown to him—the letter which had been delivered in such a mysterious fashion might well be a forgery designed to lure him, with the precious sealed packet, to that lonely spot. Like a fool he had walked into a trap!

He turned to fly—a fraction of a second too late. Even as he whirled round, he was conscious of the whistle of a slung-shot through the air—a crashing blow which made the scene dissolve into a thousand dancing stars—an ocean of blackness rushing up to engulf him, and, as he sank into what seemed death, the purring laugh of triumph of Professor Lucien Felger.

CHAPTER XI

WHEN THE FIRST GLIMMER of returning consciousness trickled into Hugh Trenchard's brain he was at first uncertain whether a minute, an hour, or many hours had elapsed. All that his bewildered brain could grasp was that he had a splitting headache; the rest was chaos.

It was a long time before he began slowly, almost subconsciously, to piece together the events of the night. He had gone somewhere to meet somebody, but where and whom he had but the foggiest notion. Yet all the while his disjointed thoughts kept circling round two words, like dancing moths round a candle. Those words, were "the Devil". At one time he caught himself gravely reviewing the possibility of his having received a weekend invitation from His Sulphureous Majesty, and only rejecting the theory on account of the inconsistency of the atmospheric conditions. For a pleasantly cool wind was fanning his throbbing forehead as he was being borne swiftly and smoothly through the night air. But his ideas were jumbled and confused, as if—the simile came without conscious effort—his brain had been squeezed in a gigantic cheesepress.

Cheesepress! The absurd word was like a magic key. The Devil's Cheesepress—the forged assignation—the sealed letter . . .

The memory of Joan Endcan's trust was like a douche of cold water. What of the sealed letter? His hand fumbled in his inner pocket, and he knew the answer and groaned. The letter was gone!

Without altering his position, he opened his eyes to discover that he was huddled on the cushioned seat of a large car. Darkness hemmed him in on every side, save where the headlights revealed a section of the rough moorland track ahead. Was he a prisoner? Hugh slewed his eyes to his right and saw the dim profile of a man seated by his side. He seemed to be a youngish fellow, clean-shaven; but little more could be discerned by reason of his upturned coat collar and downturned hat brim. Another, burlier figure sat on Hugh's left hand, and this one seemed to be dressed in some sort of uniform adorned with metal buttons.

"That will be the amiable Dawker!" Hugh thought grimly. "Wonder if the other fellow is Professor Felger minus his highly convenient antiseptic mask!"

Hugh closed his eyes and did some rapid thinking. Out of the queer jumble of the events of the past few hours three facts appeared to stand out clearly. The sealed packet had been stolen—he was a prisoner in the hands of those who had stolen it—and, he felt sure, he was being carried to the Excombe Private Sanatorium. He did not allow his mind to dwell on the probable motive of such a proceeding; nor did he speculate on what would be his fate when once incarcerated in that lonely and forbidding house. He had no intention of allowing himself to be shut up there—not without a fight, anyway. But a fight, unarmed and single-handed, against such odds could only have one end. Yet, if he could get his hands on the throat of Professor Felger before he was overpowered, he'd teach that treacherous devil . . .

A great wave of hope rushed through his heart as he caught sight of the scattered glimmer of lights ahead. The car was about to pass through a village—perhaps a small town. Help would be within call. It was a chance such as he had scarcely dared to hope for. He did not pause to ask himself why his captors should not have chosen another route, or at least secured his silence by an effective gag. His eyes were fixed on the lighted cottage windows which loomed nearer every second as the car sped on; his heart was oppressed by the dread that they should suddenly swerve into a road which would avoid the village.

He felt his heart beating almost to suffocation as they ran past the first house. Then another, and another—on both sides of the road. It was a small country town that they were passing through —surely the crucial moment had come!

On the left was a row of old-fashioned shops; on the right was a slightly larger building having over the door a blue lamp inscribed with the welcome word POLICE. Hugh clenched his fists and braced himself for a fight for life. Twenty yards—ten . . .

The man on Hugh's right made a movement and spoke:

"Here we are, Sergeant," he said in the cheerful voice of Ronnie Brewster.

Sergeant Jopling rose from his seat on Hugh's left, put on his helmet, and alighted.

"Thanks for the lift, sir," he said to Ronnie, shaking him warmly by the hand. "I'll be across to your surgery to-morrow morning. Good night, sir."

In the grip of an amazement too deep for words, Hugh watched Sergeant Jopling enter the police station; nor did he trust himself to speak before the car was moving off.

"Say, Ronnie, what in the name of thunder does all this mean? How did I come here? How did you—and Sergeant Jopling? Have I been wandering around in my sleep or something?"

Ronnie Brewster turned and surveyed his companion with a smile.

"Oh, you've been asleep all right. When we found you we thought you were sleeping the sleep that knows no awakening, as the poet says."

"Found me?" Hugh passed his hand across his forehead. "Where?"

"Lying beneath the Devil's Cheesepress, where you'd been lured like an innocent little lamb." Ronnie laid his hand on Hugh's shoulder as he went on: "Why, you poor old chump, couldn't you guess that note was a trap? Why, even Jopling—who has about as much intelligence as an automatic cigarette-delivery machine—suspected *that!* When he saw that you had taken the road to Lynton he got me to give him a lift in my car. We went a roundabout way, parked the car at Lynton, and waited and shadowed you from the moment you entered the town. At first we thought you had met the man you came to meet on the cliffs, until we crept nearer and heard the old boy spouting poetry to you. We were close behind you when you started off again, but when you got into the open we had to fall behind, and we lost you altogether when you entered the Valley of the Rocks. Jopling was inclined to give up the chase as a bad job; but I offered to scout round on my own for a bit. I made my way up to the high ground and saw you making for the Cheesepress arrangement down in the Valley. I had to lose sight of you as I hurried down among the rocks, and when I reached you it was to find you lying senseless."

"Did you see anybody near?"

"Not a soul."

"Or any animal?"

Ronnie glanced sharply at him before answering.

"I saw two or three goats scampering up the hillside. Why do you ask?"

Hugh parried the question with a careless shrug. He knew well enough that the eyes he had seen did not belong to a goat, but he was in no mood to invite his chum's banter by voicing his suspicions. He turned the conversation into a different channel by asking a question.

"Where are you going now?"

"Home, sweet home," was the laughing reply. "And that's the best place for you for a day or so. I've got a spare bedroom at my shanty just round the corner, and I absolutely insist that you shall stay with me—at least until I can engage a nursemaid to look after you!" he added with cheerful insult. "What with seeing hobgoblins, and cloven hoofs, and getting sloshed over the nut—well, I'm beginning to think it's not safe to let you go wandering about alone. Were you robbed, by the way?"

Hugh Trenchard nodded.

"But don't ask me any more questions, old chap," he said wearily. "I'll take you into my confidence as soon as I've got things straightened out a bit. Just now everything seems like a crazy jigsaw puzzle."

Ronnie laughed good-naturedly.

"I understand all right, Hugh. In other words, 'Your lips are sealed! Ha! Ha!'—as they used to say in the dear old melodramas which we used to delight in during our salad days. This is my shack," he went on, bringing the car to a standstill before a neat little house on the outskirts of the town. "Up to bed you go, like a naughty little boy! I'll bring you a sedative and a pyjama-suit. Then not another word until the morning."

Hugh Trenchard slept heavily that night. When he awoke it was broad daylight, and the first thing his gaze lighted on was the figure of his friend, now clad in a dark professional suit.

"Hullo!" cried Hugh. "What's up now? Are you about to attend the funeral of one of your unsuccessful cases?"

"I don't have any unsuccessful cases," Ronnie declared calmly, settling his tie in front of the mirror. "The fact is that I am about to make my usual round of patients, and my grave attire is merely a concession to their prejudices. When you go into practice for yourself you'll soon discover that the average middle-class country tradesman would sooner expire than be attended by a doctor wearing a tweed suit or grey flannel bags, and it pays a new man to deal tenderly with the local superstitions. I'm afraid you'll have to breakfast on your lonesome, for I must be off. Make yourself thoroughly at home, old man, and if you want anything in the way of kit, don't hesitate to borrow mine. How's your poor old nut?"

Hugh put up his hand and tenderly fingered a lump the size of a pigeon's egg.

"I'd just like to have five clean, straight, two-minute rounds with the blighter who gave me that!" he said wistfully. "He'd know how to fight like a white man by the time I'd finished with him!"

Ronnie showed his white, even teeth in an appreciative grin.

"May I be there to see the fun when that happens! But I must rush now. So long!"

Left to himself, Hugh made a leisurely toilet and a still more leisurely breakfast. He was in the act of glancing through the pages of a local paper, when there came a ring on the surgery bell. At first he took no notice, naturally assuming that the maid would answer; but when the ring had been repeated several times he came to the conclusion that he must be alone in the house. As it was not the usual surgery hour, it must be an urgent case. He rose to his feet and made his way to the door.

"Good morning. I must see Dr. Brewster at once."

The caller was a tall, elderly lady, grey-haired and aristocratic-looking. Her carefully modulated voice held a tremor which showed that she was labouring under deep emotion.

"I'm sorry to say that he's out at present—on his rounds, you know."

"When will he return?"

For a moment Hugh was at a loss for an answer. It had not occurred to him to question Ronnie about the size of his practice.

"Oh, in an hour or two," he said vaguely. "Would you care to leave a message?"

She made a gesture eloquent of despair.

"An hour will be too late. It is an urgent case—an—an accident—a matter of life and death!" She turned and gave him a long, searching look. "Are you a medical man?"

Hugh could not do otherwise than admit the fact.

"But I am here only as a guest. This practice belongs to my friend, and professional etiquette—"

"Etiquette!" she repeated with fierce scorn. "My child is dying—and you talk of etiquette!" She covered her face with her hands and burst into a fit of passionate weeping. "Have you a heart of stone that you stand here wasting moments that may be precious?"

"Of course, since it's really urgent . . ." Hugh turned and hurried into the dispensary, thrust into his pockets a few articles that he would be likely to need in dealing with such an emergency, caught up his cap, and closed the front door behind him.

"Is it far?" he asked.

"Just across the road."

Almost immediately the tall woman pushed open a gate in a high, close-set hedge. The house was large, but somewhat dilapidated, and, although the windows were furnished with lace curtains, it bore a curious, undefinable air of being unoccupied, and the long front garden which separated it from the road was weed-grown and neglected. But Hugh was too much intent on his mission to take note of such details. The moment she opened the door with a key, he stepped inside, only to stop dead at something that could not be overlooked.

The hall and staircase were not even carpeted; the dust lay thick on the banisters; the open door of the one room visible revealed bare walls. He had been brought to an empty house. He wheeled, his mind alight with suspicion.

"What jest are you trying to play on me?" he demanded.

The woman closed the door and set her back against it.

"It's played," she said, and her voice was deeper, fuller, with not the slightest trace of its former tremulousness.

For a moment Hugh could only glower at her in silence.

"You have tricked me—" he began sternly; but she cut him short with a soft, rippling laugh.

"Neat, was it not?" she asked coolly. "Not quite sporting of me to take advantage of your better feelings, but it was the only ruse I could think of at short notice. You see, I only rented this house yesterday, and there has been no time—"

"This foolery has gone far enough!" Hugh cried, furious at being duped a second time. "Why have you brought me to this place?"

"To ask you for the sealed packet that was given you by Miss Endean," said the woman slowly. As she spoke, still keeping in the shadow cast by the closed door, she stealthily raised her right hand behind her head.

"Packet?" Hugh stammered, for the cool demand had caught him unprepared. "I know of no such packet."

"Think again, Dr. Trenchard."

Hugh laughed.

"Even if I had such a thing in my possession, I certainly would not hand it over to a stranger!"

The strange woman made a swift but incomprehensible movement.

"Indeed? Then will you be good enough to hand it over to *me?*"

She stepped forward as she spoke, so that the ray from the fanlight fell full upon her. Hugh started backward with a shock of surprise. Standing before him, her blue eyes dancing with merriment, her soft red lips rippling back in a mischievous smile, was Joan Endean!

CHAPTER XII

JOAN—MISS ENDEAN! Is it really you?" The words came from Hugh impulsively as he caught her hand in his. "Thank God you are safe!"

The girl smiled a little bitterly as she gently released her hand.

"It may be rather premature to say that either of us is safe if you go shouting my name like that," she returned dryly.

"Then you are in danger?"

Joan shrugged as she held up the grey wig and bonnet, a wry smile playing on her lips.

"You may be sure that a girl does not add forty years to her age just for the fun of the thing," she said grimly. "Just at this moment there are quite a lot of people who would like to know where to find me."

"The police?" he queried; but she shook her head.

"Oh, I'm not worrying about the police." Her tone was careless and indifferent. "Though I suppose Sergeant Jopling has already sworn a warrant against me for the murder of Silas Marle."

"He could not do that," said Hugh quickly. "The body has disappeared."

"Disappeared? How?" The words came in startled jerks, though it was plain that she was striving to control her voice. "How did the body disappear?"

"Stolen, apparently"; and he went on to give a succinct account of the affair. "It all seems so mad, so fantastic—"

"Maybe it is fantastic, but you'll find there is a very cool and calculating sanity behind its apparent madness."

"You mean that you have guessed the motive?" Hugh cried.

Joan Endean nodded her head.

"The motives, for there were two," she corrected. "Surely you must be aware that it is a principle of English law that no one can be condemned for a murder without the production of the *corpus delicti,* or some identifiable part of it? Then again—and this gives the key to the second motive—on the death of a person who possesses property, the will cannot be proved until the actual fact of the death is made clear, and it is a fair assumption that with no body forthcoming there would be no death certificate. Of course it might be possible to get the Probate Court to presume death, but in this instance it would be a long and costly business, and the mere delay which would have occurred before Silas Marle's effects were handed over to the heir would have served the purpose of whoever removed the body."

"I think I'm beginning to understand. Marle had in his possession something—probably a document—containing a secret, and his body was stolen to prevent that document falling into other hands. Now I come to think of it, I remember that the old man *did* say something about making his will, and even went to the length of engaging a couple of doctors to certify that he was in a fit state of mind. But that does not clear up the mystery of his death."

A slow, enigmatical smile came over Joan Endean's features.

"That is no mystery—to me."

"You know who did it?" he cried, staring. "Why, of course—you were upstairs at the time. You saw the murder committed? That's great! You have only to go to the police—"

"And be arrested myself! I think you have forgotten the indefatigable Sergeant Jopling. No, no, I think I will retain my liberty for the present, for I have much to do." There was a perceptible pause; then she held out her hand with the question which Hugh had been dreading ever since she had revealed her identity: "Please may I have the sealed packet?"

He felt himself flush under her expectant gaze. How was he to tell her that he had failed in the trust she had reposed in him?

"I—the packet . . ." he stammered, then stopped.

"You mean that you have allowed it to be stolen from you?"

Hugh nodded mutely, devoutly wishing that the ground might open and swallow him. He seemed to live an age during the pause which followed. With dogged determination he choked back the excuses which rose to his lips. He felt a self-confessed, over-confident fool who had proved himself incapable of a simple task. Why didn't she speak? He could have borne her anger, scorn, recriminations—but not that long, reproachful silence. He dared not raise his eyes to hers, but in imagination he could visualize a look of despair in those eyes of blue—perhaps now brimming with tears. . . .

A faint, unexpected sound made him glance up. Heavens, the girl was actually laughing! Was it hysteria?

"I'm sorry I bungled"—his words came in a rush. "I received a note that was signed with your name, and I went alone to keep an appointment at a deserted spot in the Valley of Rocks. There I was suddenly attacked from behind and robbed of the packet. But I'll recover it!" he went on eagerly. "I'll move heaven and earth—"

"I hope you will not dream of attempting any such herculean task." She smiled. "I should never forgive myself if I allowed you to undertake such exertions over a few sheets of blank paper."

"Blank paper?"

"Yes, it is I who ought to be begging your forgiveness for using you as an unconscious decoy. I was certain that an attempt would be made to steal the packet, and the only means of saving it was to draw a red herring across the trail."

"I see," Hugh said stiffly. "And I was the red herring. I hope you will at least admit that I was an effective one." He told her what had happened at the Devil's Cheesepress, and the breathless interest with which she listened, no less than the look of gratitude on her face as he finished, was some balm to his ruffled feelings at having been given a dummy packet to guard.

"And now," he said, when his story was at an end, "I have no wish to appear inquisitive, but I really think I'm entitled to a little explanation on your part. What does it all mean?"

Her eyes avoided his.

"I'm afraid I must ask you to be patient a little longer," she said, and there was a note of almost wistful entreaty in her voice. "I will gladly tell you everything, for God knows I need someone I can trust. But not now."

"You mean that you will give no explanation?" His gaze was like a sword piercing her through.

The girl gave a little hopeless gesture.

"I mean that I cannot," she said simply. "Were I to do so, I would be compelled to reveal matters on which I have been sworn to secrecy. Oh, I know that everything about me must look suspicious," she went on quickly, "the way I came to you—the lies I told—my sudden flight when Marle was killed. I cannot blame you for doubting me—indeed, I should have a very poor opinion of your reasoning powers if you had obeyed me blindly without debating in your own mind whether you were being made the tool of an adventuress, or at least a woman who was not responsible for her actions. Even if you wash your hands of the whole matter now, I shall always be grateful for the service you have already rendered me—and, through me, to the whole civilized world. That surprises you, no doubt," she went on, as she noted his change of expression. "But you have stepped into something much bigger than you imagine. It is not merely a question of the murder of Silas Marle, or of the unknown thing which haunts the Moor. You may regard those incidents as being merely the first moves in a game of chess—the pawns that are sacrificed to secure the desired opening before the *real* struggle has commenced."

She made the explanation, such as it was, rapidly and unfalteringly, and every word rang true. Her very reticence was in her favour, for he realized it would have been easy to concoct a plausible tale instead of courting suspicion by silence. He moved closer to her, looking down at the beautiful upturned face.

"And are you, too, one of the pawns that may be sacrificed?"

She parried his question with a shrug of seeming indifference.

"A pawn may become a queen—when she penetrates the enemy's lines," she returned lightly. "But enough of metaphor—the time has come for plain speaking. Will you throw in your lot with me in an endeavour to overthrow the most far-reaching, subtle, and diabolical peril that ever threatened the human race?"

"It sounds rather an ambitious undertaking for two people, Miss Endean, but you may count me in on your side. Just tell me where to begin."

She smiled at the light-hearted way in which he assumed his duties. "I'm afraid the initiative does not rest with us; we must wait for Professor Lucien Felger to make his next move. Rest assured it will not be long in coming when he finds that the sealed packet contains blank papers. In the meantime, do not breathe a word to anyone about my presence here."

"Not even to Ronnie Brewster?" he said in surprise.

"Not to anyone," she repeated firmly. "A chance word might ruin everything. Be wary, be silent, and, above all, be prepared to defend your life."

Trenchard took his departure with these ominous words still ringing in his ears. Slipping through the garden at the rear of the house, he followed a narrow lane and reached the street a few hundred yards down. Brewster had already returned from his round of visits, and he looked up with some surprise as Hugh entered.

"You're out early," he remarked in a tone which seemed to invite explanation.

"Yes, I thought a little fresh air would do me good," Hugh replied evasively.

Apparently satisfied with this vague answer, Ronnie applied himself to reading the letter which he held in his hand. Presently he looked up with a question which sent his friend's pulses tingling.

"I've just received a communication from a man who is very anxious to know your present whereabouts. Do you happen to be acquainted with a solicitor named Andrew Shale?"

Hugh recognized the name as being that of the solicitor whom he had brought to Moor Lodge at Silas Marle's request. "He was the man who came in the car with you that night," he explained.

"What, the old boy with the grey side-whiskers? Oh, so his name was Shale, was it? Apparently he must know *me* all right, for he has written asking me if I can furnish him with your present address. It might save time if you were to trot down to his office. It's in the High Street—about ten minutes' walk from here."

Hugh agreed and at once set out. He had no difficulty in finding the solicitor's office—it was the only one in the town—and soon he was seated opposite a keen-eyed man of about fifty.

"I scarcely hoped that I should get on your track so soon, Dr. Trenchard," the lawyer remarked. "Last time we met I was given to understand that you were on a walking tour and that your address would be uncertain for some time to come."

"I fear the tour is abandoned for the time being," Hugh informed him.

The old lawyer beamed through his gold-rimmed glasses.

"So much the better, since that will leave you free to fall in with the plans of my client."

"Who is your client?"

"Mr. Silas Marle."

"You mean *the late* Mr. Silas Marle."

The lawyer shrugged.

"I am obliged to you for the correction, Doctor, although I am not quite prepared to admit that my original statement needs amending."

Hugh Trenchard gave him a quick look. "You mean that you think your client is still alive?"

"I do not recollect having said so."

Hugh gave a slight exclamation of impatience.

"I make no claim to be an adept in splitting legal hairs, Mr. Shale. I try to speak plainly myself, and I like plain speech in others. If words mean anything, yours must mean that you have a doubt about the fact of Silas Marle's death. Have I interpreted your meaning correctly?"

There was a pause during which Andrew Shale carefully adjusted his glasses, pushed aside some documents, and leant his elbows on the desk.

"I have been in the legal profession long enough to have a profound reverence for facts—legal facts," he explained in dry, precise tones. "In the eyes of the law, Silas Marle is still alive, inasmuch as he is not legally dead. On several occasions in the past, men commonly supposed to be dead have turned up safe and sound, and in two historic cases innocent men had in the meantime suffered the extreme penalty for their murder. I may add that it was in consequence of the last terrible miscarriage of justice that the law was altered to its present form."

The lawyer selected a document from the pile at his side, opened it, and appeared to run his eye through its contents.

"Curiously enough," he went on, "my client seemed to have a premonition that his death would be disputed, for in addition to making his will in the usual manner, he instructed me to prepare a document, usually termed a Letter of Attorney, which was to become effective in the event of his disappearance. You will observe that his death was provided for by the usual will—which, however, does not interest us at the present juncture because that same death cannot be legally proven. But there is not the slightest doubt as to his complete disappearance, so the deed conferring Power of Attorney automatically becomes operative."

"I follow you. But what has all this got to do with me?"

"Because you are the sole person who benefits," was the astounding answer. "This deed, executed under the hand and seal of the said Silas Marle, Scientist, of Moor Lodge, near Worplecombe, in the County of Somerset, confers on you, Hugh Trenchard, Doctor of Medicine, the legal and unrestricted possession of the whole of real and personal estate of the said Silas Marle—"

"Good lord!" ejaculated Hugh, springing up as though a bomb had exploded beneath his chair. "Why, I was a complete stranger to him—"

"Always provided," the lawyer went on, oblivious to the outburst of astonishment, "that the beforementioned Hugh Trenchard agrees to undertake and to carry out to the best of his skill and ability a certain task, the undertaking of which shall be a necessary condition."

"Task?" interrupted Hugh, more bewildered than ever. "What task does he want me to undertake?"

The lawyer laid down the document, and for the first time the ghost of a smile hovered about his shaven lips.

"The necessary condition is somewhat unusual—indeed, I may go so far as to say that it is so extraordinary that my client was well advised to get two medical men to certify his complete sanity before he executed the deed. For in order to become possessed of the not inconsiderable fortune of Silas Marle, you must solemnly covenant to use your utmost endeavour to destroy the supernatural monster which he refers to as 'The Terror of the Moor'."

CHAPTER XIII

THERE WAS A LONG PAUSE after the lawyer had made his startling announcement. He carefully folded the document, laid it on the pile by his side, then once more leant forward on his desk, his chin resting on his interlocked fingers, his shrewd eyes fixed on the young man's face.

Hugh Trenchard, on his part, found himself utterly at a loss for words. The news of the unexpected legacy—for legacy it was, in spite of the lawyer's respect for legal nicety of expression—followed so swiftly by the fantastic, knight-errant task on which it was conditional, filled him with an amazement too deep for words. His mind groped in vain for a rational explanation. Was it the mere desire for revenge that had induced Silas Marle to offer his fortune as a reward for the destruction of the mysterious thing that had caused his death? Or was there another, a deeper motive?

"Well, Dr. Trenchard," the voice of the lawyer snapped his train of thought, "I suppose you would like a little time in which to think over things, before coming to a decision."

"It certainly seems to call for a little serious thought," Hugh answered with a smile.

The smile was reflected on Shale's features as he shrugged his shoulders.

"I should imagine that the answer to that depends on your own belief in matters supernatural. If you are convinced that this so-called 'Terror of the Moor' existed only in the imagination of my client, you may be inclined to settle the matter by accepting at this moment. It would not be a very dangerous or difficult task to rid the earth of a thing which is non-existent!"

"That's very true, Mr. Shale. But I fear the matter is not so easily to be disposed of. In my own mind I am quite certain that the moor is haunted by a—well, for the want of a more definite name, let us call it a monster, which, though not necessarily supernatural in the general meaning of the word, is certainly unknown to science. I had already made up my mind to get to the bottom of the mystery, and intended to take lodgings in the nearest village so as to be as near the scene as possible. But that will not be necessary now, as you inform me that Moor Lodge is my property. Would there be any objection to my taking up my residence there immediately?"

Andrew Shale shook his head.

"Your claim to the estate is incontestable, the more so in view of the fact that Mr. Marle has no living relatives. The legal formalities may take a day or two, but I will hand you the keys of the house now, if you wish to take possession immediately. I think you may rest assured that no one will dispute your presence there"—Mr. Shale paused, and a slow smile twisted his parchment-like features—"unless it be the fabled 'Terror of the Moor'!"

A few minutes later the interview terminated, and Hugh hurried back to tell his friend of the new and unexpected development that had taken place. Ronnie was profuse in his congratulations.

"Well, if you're not the luckiest lad ever!" he exclaimed. "You can't even get lost in a fog without barging up against a millionaire with a fortune to give away!"

"What makes you think that Silas Marle was a millionaire?"

Ronnie laughed gaily.

"I know because I've been using the highly specialized grey matter which I carry beneath my hat. My mode of deduction would do credit to the superest super-sleuth that ever sleuthed. Listen, and I will expound; I have sufficient knowledge of the habits of my fellow bipeds to know that when a man wears a suit as old and as shabby as that of Silas Marle's he's either very rich or very poor. Silas Marle could not have been poor, or he could not have bequeathed you anything. Therefore he was a very rich man. A millionaire is a very rich man; therefore Silas Marle was a millionaire. Q.E.D., as my friend Euclid used to say."

"I only hope you're right," said Hugh, laughing at the other's specious reasoning. "But you seem to forget that I shall have to do something for the money."

"Slay one full-sized dragon," nodded Ronnie. "Saint George up-to-date! What a pity Miss Endean has disappeared—she could have fitted in with the general scheme of things by taking the role of the Enchanting Princess! But you are surely not taking that Terror stuff seriously, are you?"

Hugh drew meditatively at his pipe.

"Upon my word, old chap, I hardly know whether I do or not," he said presently, a look of indecision on his tanned face. "Sometimes the whole affair seems so fantastic that it would be a positive relief if I could think it was all a nightmare. But I can't, and that's the trouble."

"But, hang it all, this is the twentieth century—not the Dark Ages!" expostulated his friend. "What data have you got? A few footprints made by a cloven hoof—footprints which the Harbourer of the Staghounds, a man who has grown grey on these moors, declares to have been the slot of an old stag."

Hugh Trenchard shook his head.

"I would be only too glad to accept that explanation if I could, Ronnie. But I know well enough that it was no stag that I encountered the night Marle was attacked."

"Then what on earth was it?"

"That's what I'm going to find out—and before long, too." Hugh started to his feet and began to pace the room restlessly; his lean jaws were tightly clenched and there was a light of battle in his eyes. "There *must* be some explanation—a natural and logical explanation that will fit the facts as we know them. The trouble is that I've grasped the tangled skein haphazard, and every attempt to straighten out the snarl only makes the confusion worse confused. Once the end of the thread was in my hands the whole tangle might straighten out with one pull—"

"You remind me of my old granny soliloquizing over her knitting!" Ronnie interrupted flippantly. "What do you say to getting the car out and having a look at your new house? You may pick up a few clues, you know," he added with a grin.

Hugh needed no second invitation. Ten minutes later he was seated in Ronnie's small but powerful car, being piloted through the winding lanes which led to the uplands of the moor. Each was busy with his own thoughts, and it was not until half the distance had been covered that Ronnie broke the silence.

"So you have really decided to take up your residence at Moor Lodge?"

Hugh glanced round in some surprise. "Of course. What better centre could I have for my investigations?"

"Ho, ho! Investigations?" His friend chuckled as he repeated the word with exaggerated dramatic emphasis. "That seems as if you're going into the detective business in real earnest. But surely you can't be thinking of living at that all-forsaken place like Robinson Crusoe on his island?"

"Well, I had thought of asking you to act as my Man Friday for a bit, but it's not fair to make you neglect your practice."

Ronnie Brewster gave a somewhat rueful laugh.

"Up to the present my practice is still in the nebulous stage of development," he confessed. "If Moor Lodge were connected with the town by 'phone I could almost as easily make my calls from there. But it wouldn't be worth while to run a line out here—"

"Why not install a couple of wireless sets?" Hugh made the suggestion half in jest, but to his surprise Ronnie jumped at the idea.

"The very thing!" he exclaimed. "It ought not to be difficult to get a transmitting licence, and then we could be in touch with each other even when I was not stopping at your place. And it would be very handy to be able to send out an S O S if you happened to wake up in the night and find a gentleman with a cloven foot leaning over the bedrail, asking you if it is to be roast or boiled!''

Ronnie was on his favourite subject now, and he kept on in the same vein of half-cynical banter until they came in sight of the red-tiled gables and quaint, twisted chimneys of Moor Lodge softly outlined against the greyish-purple sweep of the distant hills.

"Creepy-looking shack, isn't it?" was his final comment as they alighted. "If there isn't a genuine, blown-in-the-glass, dyed-in-the-wool family spook on the premises—well, all I can say is that the builder ought to be prosecuted for obtaining shudders under false pretences!"

"Obtaining shutters?" Hugh repeated, in a tone which showed his thoughts had been wandering from the other's light-hearted chatter.

"Wake up!" cried the indignant Ronnie, "Who said anything about shutters? I was talking about *shudders*—s-h-u-d-d-e-r-s— two 'd's', and the 'h' is silent, as in 'pudding'."

"I understand you," laughed his friend, "What a lad you are for a joke, Ronnie! You really must take up your quarters here—the murmur of your baby prattle will be like a ray of sunshine in this gloomy old house."

"Anything to oblige, old bean," Ronnie smirked with the air of one acknowledging a well-deserved compliment; but the next moment his grin vanished as he laid his hand on the other man's shoulder. "But, seriously, Hugh, I hope you don't mind my silly nonsense," he went on in an altered voice. "You see, I have to be so preternaturally wise and solemn when I've got my bedside manner on that it's quite a relief to blow the cork out now and again."

"Come and stay with me," invited Hugh Trenchard, "and you never need put the cork in at all."

Ronnie gave a laugh and smacked his lips with mock gusto.

"That sounds alluringly festive. I'll think it over."

Hugh had not been jesting when he had described the house as a 'gloomy old place', for it looked almost as eerie in the bright sunshine as it had looked in the mist-dimmed moonlight when he had first seen it. It was a structure of tolerable antiquity, and had probably been built as a lodge for one of the Yeomen Rangers when Exmoor was one of the Royal preserves. One had not to look very closely to detect the patina imprinted by the passing years. The tiles of the high-pitched roof were toned to a deep, mellow red; the oaken beams of the half-timbered walls were weathered to a greyish drab; the intersecting plaster was in places stained a sickly green by the drippings from the eaves, and its whole surface starred and cracked until it resembled the face of a wrinkled hag. There are some houses upon which the hand of Time seems to have been laid with a benign touch—grey havens of peace and quietude, or stout old manor-houses whose wide hearths seem to remind one of the crackling of Yule logs; whose cheerful, paneled walls still seem to retain a kindly echo of the songs and laughter of top-booted, red-faced squires; oak-roofed halls which still seem to ring with the merry strains of Sir Roger de Coverley; painted and gilded salons where one seems to catch the measured rhythm of viols and harpsichord, and the light tapping of red-heeled shoes in the stately minuet.

But there are others whose dusty chambers are shadowy, aloof, and mysterious—fit settings for whispered plots, cloaked and masked figures flitting like sinister shadows, or stealthy deeds which shunned the light of day. And of such was the house of which Hugh Trenchard had come to take possession.

The footsteps of Hugh and his companion echoed eerily as they passed along the passage on the ground floor, entering each room in turn and throwing back the curtains which shrouded the windows. Passing through the darkest part of the passage, Hugh's left-hand sleeve caught in something which projected from the wall. He drew his hand over the surface of the panelling and uttered an exclamation as he felt an unmistakable doorknob.

"Hullo! I never noticed a door here before. I wonder where it leads to!"

"If it leads to the wine-cellar I'll give an unsolicited testimonial to your detective abilities right now!" laughed Ronnie. "Come on, let's see what sort of a tap the old boy kept."

"It's locked," said Hugh, tugging in vain at the handle.

"Try some of the keys that Shale gave you," suggested his friend. "If they fail we'll have to try a little gentle persuasion with the kitchen poker."

But there was no need for the proposal to be put into operation, for the lock clicked smoothly back when Hugh inserted the third key on the bunch.

"Ah-ha! The mystery deepens!" Ronnie exclaimed dramatically, as he peered through the open doorway.

"Who would expect to find an up-to-date chemical laboratory in the wilds of Exmoor?"

Hugh nodded in silent agreement; for the room in which they found themselves could have been used for no other purpose. The whole of one wall was covered with glass-fronted cupboards, and inside could be seen row upon row of jars, bottles, and phials. Standing against another wall was a long, breast-high bench bearing an orderly array of retorts, test-tubes, scales, and recording instruments; a powerful electric battery stood in one corner, flanked, in the opposite angle of the room, by a large and very modern-looking safe. A roll-top desk and a filing-cabinet occupied the centre of the room, and toward these Ronnie gave an expressive nod.

"There ought to be plenty of data for your investigations here," he observed with a smile. "There are enough papers and memoranda to clear up a thousand mysteries. And the desk is not even locked—or the cabinet, either. Look here!"

He thrust back the cover of the desk and began to rummage among the papers, only to give vent to a grunt of disappointment.

"Nothing that is likely to help us here," he declared. "Bills, invoices for chemicals and apparatus supplied—the old boy seems to have been a whale for experimental chemistry. Stop a moment, though!" he added suddenly as he opened the lowest drawer. "Here's something that may shed a little light on our darkness. Just run your eagle eye over these . . ."

Glancing at the official-looking documents which Ronnie spread on the desk, Hugh saw that one was a printed form bearing the Royal Arms at its head. It was an official certificate of discharge, and the words which had been filled in by hand intimated that: MARLE, *Silas James, has been employed in the* INVESTIGA-

TION BRANCH *of* THE RESEARCH LABORATORIES *of the* ROYAL AR-
SENAL, WOOLWICH, *from April the 23rd,* 1915, *to October the
11th,* 1918, *being discharged therefrom at his own request.* Another was a well-worn pass, enclosed in a leather case, authorizing
the same MARLE, *Silas James,* to enter the area of the Danger
Buildings at the Royal Arsenal.

Evidently our friend was a retired expert in explosives," Ronnie
remarked. "I don't think there's much to be gathered from these
papers beyond that not very interesting fact."

Trenchard did not answer immediately. He was staring at the
blue-grey papers, his mind working rapidly. At length he turned to
Brewster with an unexpected question.

"Does the date, April the 23rd, 1915, suggest anything to you?"

The other man thought for a few moments, then shook his head.

"Of course the war was on at that time—that accounts for
Marle being employed in manufacturing, or inventing, explosives—

"But he need not have had anything to do with explosives at
all," Hugh broke in excitedly. "It was on April the 23rd that the
first German attack was made in which they used asphyxiating
gas! Silas Marle may have been employed in evolving counter-
measures."

Ronnie Brewster received his friend's suggestion with a careless shrug.

"Interesting, but scarcely informative," was his comment. "I
flatter myself I'm not particularly slow in the uptake, but I'm
hanged if I can see any connection between a retired Government
chemist and that precious cloven-hoofed Terror of yours. Why not
see what is in the safe?"

Hugh nodded and, selecting the likeliest-looking key on the
ring, inserted it in the brass-rimmed keyhole. It fitted—it turned—
the ponderous bolts slid back. Grasping the handle, Hugh gave it a
half-turn and the heavy door swung open, and as it did so a loud
gasp of amazement escaped his lips.

Until that moment he had scarcely paused to consider what a
safe of those dimensions might contain—for all he knew he might
be confronted with the dead body of Marle in a repulsive state of
decomposition. But the object which met his gaze was less grue-
some, though not less surprising.

The sole content of the safe was a long, bulky, sealed packet—
in every respect the counterpart of the one given to him by Joan
Endean!

CHAPTER XIV

A LOOK OF THE BLANKEST MYSTIFICATION spread over Hugh's features as his eyes fell on the duplicate sealed packet. For it was an exact duplicate, not only in its general size and bulk, but down to such details as the peculiar texture of the paper and the heraldic device which adorned the large red seal. Such a likeness could not possibly be accidental; either the packet lying before him was the same one that had been stolen from him in the Valley of Rocks, or else this was the genuine packet which the decoy one—containing nothing but blank papers—had been intended to safeguard. In any case, the presence of the letter m Marle's safe formed a strange and unexpected link between him and the mysterious Joan Endean.

"What's wrong, old man?" Ronnie's voice, tinged with a note of amused surprise, brought Hugh's speculations to an abrupt end. "You've been staring at that letter as though you were expecting to see it vanish in a whiff of brimstone. I believe the greedy beggar is disappointed because the safe wasn't packed tight with wads of banknotes!"

"Scarcely that." Hugh forced a smile as he shook his head. "But that letter happens to be a perfect facsimile of . . ." He paused, suddenly calling to mind Joan's stipulation of secrecy; adding, a trifle lamely, "Of—of another letter that I have seen."

"Nothing wonderful in that," was the other's careless rejoinder. "Most letters have a family likeness on the outside—it's what is inside them that makes all the difference between a tender missive of love and a curt intimation that a cheque by return will oblige."

Trenchard picked up the letter and balanced it thoughtfully in his hand as he read the inscription:

To Hugh Trenchard, M.D.

Beneath, apparently written by the same hand, though in weak and shaky characters, was the injunction:

> *Only to be opened in the event of the Death or Disappearance of Mr. Silas Marle.*

"Pardon my idle curiosity," said Ronnie, trying to speak indifferently in spite of his impatience at his friend's tardiness. "Aren't you going to open the thing?"

Hugh again weighed the letter in his hand; then he shook his head.

"Not here, old chap. Judging by its weight, this is a somewhat lengthy communication. I think it would be more cheerful and comfortable to read it before a nice bright fire. Besides"—Hugh pointed to the single window of the laboratory, already dimming in the early dusk—"probably it will be dark in here before I've finished, and—unless I'm very much mistaken—the contents of this packet will not sound any the better for being read in the gloaming."

Returning to the library, they lighted the lamp, drew the curtains, and set a match to the fire which was ready laid in the grate. Then and then only did Hugh break the seal, draw forth several closely written sheets of foolscap, and commence to read:

"Dear Doctor,—When you read these lines I shall be dead (or I shall have disappeared, which practically amounts to the same thing), and you may regard what I have to state as a revelation coming from the grave.

"Considering the very short time I have known you, it will undoubtedly come as a surprise to you that I should single you out as my confidant. But you may believe me when I say that I have not reposed this trust in you because my time is short and I have little choice in the matter. I flatter myself that I am a keen and accurate judge of character, and I know that your acceptance of the strange task which I have imposed on you will not be actuated by the mere sordid desire to possess my money. Moreover, I have travelled in the East long enough to have my mentality tinged, and more than tinged, with the fatalism of the Orient. I do not believe that it was mere blind chance that led your footsteps through the mist, guiding you to me in my hour of need, sending in you a champion, young, clear-thinking, with sound nerves and a healthy body. Surely it was Fate—maybe a Power even higher—that ordained the appearance, at the very moment I was stricken down, of the very man whom I should have chosen out of all the world as the one best fitted to carry on the work I had begun.

"That the work is not free from danger, my own fate will be sufficient proof; whether the end justifies the risk; you must judge for yourself. But this much I will say here—no mail-clad Crusader knight ever rode forth on a holier or more righteous cause than the one you will follow in ridding the earth of the Terror of the Moor.

"It would be both tedious and unnecessary to give even a brief account of my eventful life; suffice to say that the outbreak of war in 1914 found me a lecturer on chemistry at a university in the North of England. I soon found my post a sinecure, however, for the whole of the students joined up in a body one afternoon, and I was left facing rows of empty benches. I myself was too old for military service, so I transferred my activities to a munition factory that had been newly opened in the neighbourhood, and for the next six months or so I was employed in the simple routine work of checking the purity of the various chemicals used in the manufacture of explosives. The work, though of course responsible and fairly dangerous, was not hard in itself, and I frequently found myself compelled to wait for hours in the great, well-equipped laboratory with nothing whatever to do.

"It was during these periods that I began to make a few experiments on my own account, and as a result I was able to suggest some minor improvements both in the mode of handling and the actual proportions of the ingredients used. But beyond a mere formal acknowledgment of my communications, the War Office took no notice, and I quite thought that my letters were reposing in some dusty pigeon-hole, when, on April the 23rd, 1915, I received an urgent and imperative order to proceed to London.

"Upon my arrival at King's Cross Station I was met by an eminent statesman, a man whose features the cartoonist and cameraman have made familiar to every inhabitant of the kingdom.

" 'Professor Marle, I presume?' he said, coming forward with outstretched hand.

"In the shock of surprise I blurted out his name, but he immediately shook his head in smiling remonstrance.

" 'I fear I cannot lay claim to such a famous name'—even at the time I noted the ambiguous nature of his disclaimer; 'a moment's reflection should convince you that you have been misled by a chance resemblance.' He spoke coolly, but the twinkle in his eye told me that I was not intended to take his words too literally. 'As a matter of fact, you must consider me as belonging to the good old Welsh family of Jones.'

" 'An extensive clan,' I said, falling in with his humour. 'And what might your business be with me, Mr. Jones?'

" 'Important, but in no way official. I hope you understand that perfectly'; he repeated the words slowly and emphatically, *'In no way official.* You must make up your mind to regard me as being merely a certain Mr. Jones, a private and undistinguished Englishman who has the welfare of his country at heart. Is that quite clear?'

" 'Quite.'

" 'Then please follow me.'

"A big limousine was waiting a few yards away, the door held open by a liveried footman whose stature quite dwarfed my companion. As we emerged into the station courtyard, two other cars started into motion, taking up their position one ahead and one behind the car we were in, and my wonder grew as I noted the burly forms and watchful eyes of their occupants. Mr. Jones might modestly proclaim himself an ordinary private citizen, but it was evident that he had the resources of Scotland Yard at his beck and call. The three cars turned west, zigzagging through the mean streets which lie between King's Cross and New Oxford Street, and as we headed south I made sure that we were bound for Downing Street. But we skirted the north side of Trafalgar Square, swinging down the darkened Mall, leaving Buckingham Palace on our right. There was a traffic block opposite Victoria Station, but a brief, silent signal from the leading car cleared a way as if by magic, and a few minutes later we were heading down the King's Road at racing speed. I caught a glimpse of the river as we passed over Putney Bridge, but lost my bearings completely in the dimly lighted suburban roads beyond. When at last we pulled up before a large country mansion, I knew that I must be somewhere in the neighbourhood of Richmond, but that was all.

"The door swung open as we ascended the front steps, and I was ushered into a cheerful dining-room where a meal lay already spread. Mr. Jones was a brilliant talker, and throughout the meal he kept up a flow of interesting conversation, without, however, once hinting at the nature of the business which he had brought me there to discuss. It was only when we had adjourned to the smoking-room, with one detective patrolling the gravel walk in front of the windows and another keeping watch in the passage outside the door, that he placed his hand in his pocket and produced a small sheet of paper.

" 'Did you write that?' he asked in a conversational tone.

"I nodded, wondering what was coming next. For the thing was merely one of the letters that I had sent to the Ministry of Munitions, suggesting a quite minor and unimportant modification of the formula of one of the stock explosives. But before I could frame the question that was in my mind, he turned the sheet over and pointed to some chemical symbols scribbled in pencil on the back.

" 'And this too, I presume?' he went on, watching me keenly the while.

"I took the paper in my hand and read $C_4H_7N_3O_2$, $C_6H_{12}O_6$, $C_{216}H_{338}N_{51}S_5O_{68}$, $C_{12}H_{14}O_4(NO_3)_6$, $C_3H_5(NO_3)_3$. There was a sixth combination of symbols, but this I must not divulge—even to you—so, for the purpose of this narrative, I will refer to it simply as the 'X Formula'.

"In a flash I realized what had happened. I must have been jotting down some notes respecting my experiments, and I had inadvertently used the same sheet of paper on which to write my letter to the Ministry.

" 'Yes,' I was forced to admit, 'that is my handwriting. But I certainly had no idea that there was anything on the back of that sheet when I sent that letter to you.'

" 'I can well believe that!' Mr. Jones smiled somewhat grimly. 'It's extremely fortunate that the communication did not fall into other hands. However, I have not brought you here to call you over the coals for being so careless. It is rather to ask you for a friendly explanation of what was in your mind when you made those notes.'

" 'You know the meaning of the formulae?'

"Mr. Jones nodded his grey head. 'Naturally, in these days, when every newspaper is full of the spy peril, we should not allow a set of mysterious-looking letters and figures to pass through our hands without wanting to know the meaning of it. Within an hour of its receipt that letter was in the hands of a Government analyst. But his report only seemed to deepen the mystery. He states that the first three formulae respectively represent Creatine, Inosite, and Albumen—three organic substances which are to be found in every human body; while the last three combinations of symbols represent Gun-cotton, Nitro-glycerin, and the newly invented Devastite—three of the most powerful explosives known to science.'

" *Yet the same chemical elements occur in each!* ' I said slowly. 'Carbon, Hydrogen, Nitrogen, and Oxygen—combined in certain proportions they form substances, not only innocuous in themselves, but substances that are absolutely vital to the human organism. Combine the same elements in different proportions, *and you have the deadliest explosives!'*

" 'My God! You mean to say—'

" *'That every human being is a potential living bomb!'*

"The effect of my words was electrical. The man who would have faced a hostile House without a tremor now sank into his chair, deathly white and unnerved. It did not need more explanation to enable his keen, far-seeing brain to visualize the awful possibilities of my discovery. Yet I could see that he was struggling to disbelieve me.

" 'It—it's incredible!' he gasped at last. 'Why, if what you say is true—'

" 'Why waste words? Words may sway the thoughts and actions of men, but the most transcendent eloquence is powerless to affect the elements of Nature. Compare those sets of symbols, and tell me honestly if you—without the assistance of a chemical expert—could say offhand which represents, say, Creatine, the crystalline substance which is contained in your own muscles at this present moment, and the high explosive which goes by the name of Devastite. Consider again that the very air we breathe consists of four-fifths of Nitrogen— and it is scarcely necessary to remind a man occupying your post that Nitrogen forms the basic principle of almost every explosive known—and then ask yourself whether it is beyond the power of modern science to make practical use of those facts.

" 'I know that you will probably remind me, in your turn, that the use of that particular explosive, Devastite, has been discontinued because it has been found liable to detonate spontaneously through decomposition. But my answer is that such a defect is a defect only so long as the explosive is within our lines—the moment it is within the *enemy* lines, the more easily it explodes the better! Each soldier in the vast armies arrayed against us contains within himself the means of his own destruction. It needs but one single element, harmless in itself, to be incorporated in a gas and sent over the enemy trenches, and the next few hours would see a holocaust such as the world has never known.'

"For a long time my companion looked at me without speaking. 'So *that* was your idea?'

"I felt myself flush at his tone. 'It certainly *was* my idea, but I abandoned it.'

" 'Why?' he asked quickly.

" 'It was too horrible, too fiendish, too frightful—'

" 'Frightful?' He pounced on the word like a swooping hawk. 'Do you know who has taught us that word? Who has advocated the doctrine of ruthless frightfulness, backing it up with specious arguments; that the most terrible weapons are the most merciful because they make the struggle of opposing nations shorter? Our foes have taught us that—and now they shall be confounded by their own text—"hoist with their own petard" in real earnest! Put whatever price you please on your own services—we must have that gas! I hope, I pray that we may never need to employ it, but we must have it—or the knowledge of its preparation—to use as a last resort.'

"I will not weary you with a recapitulation of the arguments he employed before I consented to renew my researches. But I made one stipulation. The secret of the gas must remain in my own possession, contained in a sealed envelope that would only be handed to him when I was convinced that no other alternative remained than the complete destruction of the British Empire. But fortunately I was not called upon to make that momentous decision, for when the United States of America became our Allies there was very little doubt as to the ultimate result of the war. The peril has passed—but has it passed for all time? If I could have answered that question with an unhesitant affirmative, I would have committed the secret to the flames. But ever at the back of my mind there lurked a fear that the world might be confronted with another, even graver crisis, when the possession of my secret would be the deciding factor between victory and defeat. For you may rest assured that whoever holds the sealed packet, which I hereby give into your hands, holds in his hands the destiny of mankind. Guard it, I entreat you, as a sacred trust; as something even dearer than life. For, once it falls into the hands of the emissaries of a nation whose ambition is the domination of the world, carnage and hideous chaos will follow as surely as the night follows day, and—"

A harsh command cut through Trenchard's voice like the stroke of an axe:

"Up with your hands—both of you!"

Three shadowy figures, each holding a levelled revolver, stood in the doorway.

CHAPTER XV

THE GRIM COMMAND, backed as it was by muzzles of three weapons trained with such deadly accuracy as to make them appear like so many circles of steel, left no alternative but to obey. Hugh and Ronnie raised their hands above their heads.

"Keep 'em there, and don't move until I tell you," said the man who had spoken before to his companions he added, but without turning his head: "Keep the red-headed chap covered, Dawson; I'll see that the other one behaves himself. Regan, kindly remove the suspicious bulges."

One of the men stepped forward and ran his hands lightly over Hugh's clothing. In a very few seconds he had found and removed the revolver which Hugh had carried in his hip pocket ever since the death of Silas Marle.

"Well armed, eh?" The spokesman of the party took up the weapon with his disengaged hand and glanced at the conical bullets which nestled in the chambers of the cylinder. "See what sort of artillery the red-headed chap's got."

"Look here, old sport," remonstrated Ronnie, "not so much of the 'red-headed chap'. I know I'm not exactly coal black, but—"

"Don't speak out of your turn! You'll have plenty of time to—" The rest of his remark was drowned in Ronnie's sudden cackle of laughter as the searcher inserted his fingers beneath his armpits. "What's the game now? Getting hysterical?"

"No—ticklish. I never could bear anyone to touch me there. If you do not desist, I shall give one long scream and bite your face. I will—if it poisons me!"

"Completely ga-ga." The searcher gave a shrug.

Ronnie looked pained.

"Ga-ga? What vulgarity of expression! Well, if you're going to probe my anatomy until you find a gun, you'll wear your fingers into fists before you find what I haven't got. If you manage in fact to find anything on me more deadly than a fountain-pen I'll present you with a fiver for your trouble."

The searcher paused and glanced round at the man who appeared to be the leader of the party.

"You heard that, sir?" he asked, and on his lean features there played a flickering smile. "I call on you to witness he offered me a bribe."

"Your duty?" gasped Hugh, a light beginning to dawn on him. "You don't mean to tell me you're the police?"

"Certainly," was the answer, given somewhat stiffly. "We are detectives belonging to the Special Investigation Branch of Scotland Yard. I am Detective-Inspector Renshaw, and it is my duty to take you into custody for being on enclosed premises at night for an alleged unlawful purpose."

"Oh, my sacred aunt!" wailed Ronnie, suddenly collapsing in the nearest chair and hiding his face in his hands.

Hugh straightened his tie with complete indifference.

"Ever heard of the Habeas Corpus Act, Inspector?"

But the inspector did not appear to have heard.

"I'll trouble you for your names and the last addresses at which you slept."

Ronnie's shoulders ceased shaking as he rose to his feet.

"Put down the red-headed chap as Auburn Harry of Wapping," he said gravely. "You know—the man who strangled five policemen with his bare hands. My accomplice in crime—'pal' is the correct term, I believe—is Cross-eyed Dick of Shadwell—"

"Shut up, you ass!" Hugh interrupted; then he turned to the detectives. "I'm afraid there have been mistakes on both sides, Inspector. You apparently took us for a couple of crooks, and your dramatic entry certainly made us think you were three gentlemen of the same kidney. As a matter of fact, I am Dr. Trenchard, the present owner of this house, and this is my friend Dr. Brewster."

Inspector Renshaw looked at him half incredulously. "I suppose you have some proof of what you say?" he asked at length.

"Not here, I'm afraid. But Mr. Andrew Shale, Marle's solicitor, will vouch for me, as will also Sergeant Jopling of the local police."

The inspector's action was eloquent. He handed the revolver back to Hugh.

"Hope we didn't scare you with our gun-play, sir."

Hugh laughed.

"Oh, I'm getting used to scares since coming down here for a quiet holiday."

"The rest cure hasn't been a success, eh?" Inspector Renshaw nodded in a manner that was intended to convey sympathy. "We've heard all about the funny business that has been going on here, and for the past few days the place has been under observation. When my man reported that he'd seen two men enter, I rushed over at once and thought I'd got a capture."

"You must have hustled," Ronnie put in, speaking in a tone of admiring respect. "Unless you were camping somewhere on the moor, you must have started soon after we entered this house. I am rather curious to know how your man managed to tip you off so promptly."

The inspector shrugged and permitted himself a cryptic smile.

"Oh, we have our methods, sir," he said with an air of mystery. "Some people are very fond of sneering at us and hinting that the mental development of the C.I.D. got atrophied somewhere in the mid-Victorian era. They are apt to remember our failures and forget the fact that Scotland Yard delivers the goods—in the shape of the wanted man—nine times out of ten. We don't advertise every new invention we adopt, but I can tell you this—at one hour's notice I could get enough men here to search every square yard of this moor, big as it is."

"That's the stuff to give 'em!" cried Ronnie approvingly. "I bet you've got a wireless set, and a few aeroplanes, and half a dozen tanks up your sleeve somewhere! I thought I and my friend were going to enjoy a nice little spook-hunt all on our own, but now you've come in all we'll have to do is sit tight and read all about it in the papers. Of course you have a theory?"

Inspector Renshaw gave a non-committal shrug.

"I don't set much store on theories when I can get hold of solid facts. You seem to have got hold of a few"—he made a gesture toward the sheets of manuscript on the table. "I suppose you have been going through the dead man's papers?"

"As he had a perfect right to do," Ronnie interposed briskly. "Seeing that the whole of Silas Marle's property devolves on him—"

"Of course, of course," Inspector Renshaw hastened to say. "My remark was not intended as a criticism of your action, Dr. Trenchard; I was merely anxious to know if you have found anything that will shed light on the mysterious happenings here."

"Well, not directly," Hugh answered, after a pause during which he did some hard thinking. "The only salient facts contained in the papers I have already read are that Marle was a chemist who had made a special study of the chemical warfare which the late war brought into being, and had invented a novel and—at any rate theoretically—effective method of wholesale slaughter. You are quite welcome to hear the remainder of his narrative, but I warn you I shall skip any passage which appears to be of a private or personal nature."

"That's fair enough," assented Renshaw; to his subordinates he added: "You two keep watch outside and see that we are not disturbed."

When they had the room to themselves, Hugh took up the thread of Silas Marle's story:

"My conditions were accepted without the slightest demur. I was to be given an absolutely free hand in making my researches, but, merely as a matter of form, I was entered on the pay-roll of the laboratory staff of the Royal Arsenal, Woolwich. But it was very seldom that I entered the gates of that establishment, for I quickly realized that my work was too hazardous to be carried on in the same vicinity where large quantities of explosives were being manufactured and stored. I looked out for a spot, lonely and remote from human habitations, and at last I decided to buy a dilapidated and reputedly ghost-haunted house known as Moor Lodge, situated on the most desolate part of Exmoor.

"Needless to say, I did not go out of my way to refute the grisly legends respecting the old house, for I counted on them ensuring me the seclusion I so much desired. One of the rooms I fitted up as a laboratory, and there I laboured to convert my dream into a tangible, practicable reality. No galley-slave ever toiled harder at his oar than I toiled at my bench during the first three months. We lived here alone, my dear wife and I, and sometimes whole weeks would go by without either of us seeing a strange face. She knew that I was engaged in confidential work for the Government, but little did she guess the nature of that work!

"But gradually the strain began to tell on me. I was far from being a young man, and in addition to my experiments I was obliged to perform the rough work of the house, for my wife was not strong physically, though nothing could have exceeded her love and devotion to me.

"It was almost impossible to hire a domestic servant at that time, when the prospect of earning high wages was tempting every able-bodied girl to the munition factories; even in normal times I doubt whether any local girl would have consented to spend a single night in a house with such a ghostly reputation as Moor Lodge. I even journeyed to Plymouth and interviewed several discharged soldiers and sailors who had been disabled in the war. But they all seemed too intelligent for my purpose—I simply dared not risk having a man on the premises who might so much as guess at the nature of the work on which I was employed. Things were at a deadlock when Fate brought to my door the very man I needed.

"No doubt you will call to mind how severe the weather was in the winter of '16-17. It was by far the worst winter in the war; the ponds and wells were frozen solid, and the very earth seemed blighted with the intense cold. Toward evening, on one of the bitterest days, I was working in the laboratory when there came a light, timid tap on the front door. The sound was so unusual in that desolate region that for a moment I attributed it to a fall of half-melted snow from the roof; but presently there came another tap, this time accompanied by a low, half-articulate moan. I caught up the nearest weapon handy—which happened to be a short iron bar which I had been using as a poker for my furnace—and made my way to the door. Outside was a man dressed in a ragged and mud-plastered khaki uniform. The badges and buttons had been roughly torn off, so that the tunic was open, showing the grey shirt beneath. He wore no cap, and his hands and face were blue with the cold.

" 'Hullo!' I said, staring at him.

"He was leaning against the door-post, as though for support, and at the sound of my voice he raised two deeply sunken, lack-lustre eyes to mine.

" 'Hullo, matey," he responded weakly.

" 'What are you doing here?' I demanded. 'You'll catch your death of cold if you go about half-dressed in this weather!'

" 'I'm half dead already, matey . . .' And as though to prove his words, he staggered forward and would have fallen if I had not caught him in time.

"When I put my arms round him I got a shock. The man was nothing but skin and bone, and when I lifted him he weighed no heavier than a large child. He was starved—not 'starved with the cold', as they say hereabouts, but literally starved with hunger. I got him into the living-room, pulled him round with a stiff glass of brandy, then ransacked the larder and watched him eat. Eat! I thought he would never stop eating, and as he wolfed the platefuls I took a good look at him.

"His age could not have been more than eighteen or twenty, but he was tall and big-made, and when in his usual health he must have been unusually strong. His hair was fair and inclined to be curly, and I judged by its length that some considerable time had

elapsed since it had last received the attentions of a military bar-
ber. His features were prominent, but not unpleasing —indeed,
had it not been for the curious expression in his eyes he might
have been considered handsome. I find it difficult to convey that
expression in words; it was at once wary, alert, shifting, and rest-
less. But the only way in which I can make my meaning clear is to
describe it as an *animal* look—not that which one sees in the eyes
of an intelligent dog, or even a cat, or any domesticated animal;
rather was it the look of instinctive hostility and distrust which one
may see in the eyes of a wild beast, untamed and untamable, as it
roams its native wilds. I took but little heed of this strange trait at
the time, naturally attributing it to the hardships which he had obviously undergone. Later on I had good reason to recall it to mind.

"When he had cleared his plate for the third time, I began to put
a few questions:

" 'What's your name?'

" 'Jake.'

" 'Jake what?' The length of the pause which followed my
question warned me that the answer was likely to be a he.

" 'Jake Thomas Smith.'

" 'Have you any more names?' I queried sarcastically, and to
my surprise he nodded.

" 'The blokes in my platoon call me "Crazy Jake",' he informed me solemnly.

"I looked hard at him, suspecting that I was being paid back in
my own coin. But he went on unconcernedly finishing up the remaining scraps of food, cracking the bones with his strong teeth,
the canines of which were unusually long and pointed. When he
licked up every scrap of gravy off his plate, just like a dog, I began
to glimpse something of the truth. He was one of those rare exam-
ples of extreme atavism, a throw-back to primitive type, an
unlucky being who had been cursed with more than his fair share
of the thin streak of animalism which is the compulsory legacy of
the human race.

"Later on, when I had the opportunity of examining him more
closely, I found that he was able to exercise those muscles (represented in the normal man as mere rudimentary survivals) which
move the ears; his sense of smell was unusually keen; his eyes
possessed the power of reflecting the light in exactly the same
manner as the eyes of certain species of carnivores. It came as
something of a shock to think that such a man had been accepted
for military service, but, after all, then was nothing wrong with

him in a physical sense; on the contrary, as is so often the case with these reversions, the man was exceptionally strong and active, and his peculiar mental traits might well have passed unnoticed in the perfunctory examination to which recruits were subjected in the latter days of the war.

"By degrees I got his story from him. Of course he was a deserter, though to do him bare justice he seemed quite unconscious of the gravity of his offence—or, indeed, that he had committed any offence at all. He had simply got tired of his surroundings and the irksome restraints on his liberty, and had wandered off, his instinct drawing him to the great open moors, living on herbs and roots and scraps that he could find or steal, until the intense cold had beaten him.

" 'And what do you intend to do?' I asked him where he had finished his vague and rambling tale.

"He gave a vacant stare. 'I dunno,' was the extend of his future plans.

" 'Do you know what they'll do to you if they catch you, Jake?'

" 'Make me slope arms by numbers?' His accompanying grimace was eloquent of his distaste for that form of exercise.

"They'll do more than that, my poor lad. They will shoot you.'

" 'Me?' he cried with a sort of simple wonder. 'Shoot me dead?'

" 'Dead as mutton,' I had to tell him.

" 'Why?' he demanded in an aggrieved tone. "I never hurt 'em—I never hurt a fly.'

" That's just the trouble, Jake. You became a soldier in order to hurt people. That's what a soldier is for in time of war—to hurt soldiers wearing another sort of uniform—or to get hurt by them.' I tried to explain the matter as best I could, but after I had finished I very much doubted whether the enormity of his offence had penetrated his intelligence. Not that he was an idiot in the ordinary sense of the word; I classed him as a 'mattoid', a man whose brain could not be gauged by comparison with ordinary standards. He might be trained and taught to perform certain tasks, much in the same manner as an intelligent dog goes through certain tricks. More than that, he might be capable of having certain fixed and elementary ideas instilled into him by simple repetition, for later on I had good reason to know that he possessed an unusually retentive memory. But beyond that, and as far as original and self-conscious thought and reasoning were concerned, his mind was an absolute blank. And as I realized the fact I knew that here was the very servant I had been praying for—strong, willing, docile, and no more capable of understanding the work on which I was engaged than was a horse or a dog.

"I sat up late that night, watching Jake sleeping curled up on the floor in front of the fire, debating with myself whether I should turn him over to the military authorities or keep him myself. In the end I decided that he would be serving his country more effectively by doing the menial work of Moor Lodge than by endangering his own life and the lives of all around him by handling a loaded rifle and experimenting with Mills bombs. In the morning I put the matter to him, and he was only too glad to stay with me. He soon picked up the routine of his simple duties and for a time all went well.

"My experiments proceeded apace; I succeeded in isolating the missing element and gasifying it in a form that could not be detected when mingled with the ordinary atmosphere; complete success was within my very grasp, when I was brought up short by an unexpected and disquieting discovery.

"You must understand that I had never attempted to keep Jake confined to the house—indeed, I doubt whether he would have obeyed me had I forbidden him to leave it. I had provided him with a suit of clothes such as might be worn by a lad working on a farm, and he was accustomed to spend his hours off duty roaming freely about the moor. One evening he came home at dusk, after having been absent most of the day, took off his coat, and began to sweep out the laboratory where I was still working. At first I took no notice of him, but presently I began to see that he was not giving much attention to what he was doing. Every now and then he would stop sweeping and furtively take something from his trousers pocket, glance at it, polish it on his sleeve, examine it again, and then transfer it to his pocket and go on sweeping.

"Secretly amused, I watched his antics for a while out of the corner of my eye, and when he was admiring the thing for the umpteenth time I purposely made a sudden movement. Jake tried to conceal his treasure, but in his hurry to replace it in his pocket the thing slipped out of his hand, falling on the stone floor with a jingle that was unmistakable. It was a brightly polished halfcrown.

" 'Hullo, Jake,' I laughed. 'I didn't know you were a moneyed man! Where did you get that from? Have you been robbing a bank or something?' For I knew well enough that he had not had any money when he arrived.

"Instead of saying that he'd found it—which I quite thought he had—he jibbed at my question and stood silent, his hands fumbling with the broom-handle while he shifted his feet uneasily, the very picture of conscious guilt.

" 'Where did you get that money from?' I repeated more sternly. 'Did you steal it?'

"He bridled at that. 'Jake is not a thief!' he declared, looking me full in the face.

" 'Then where did you get it from?'

" 'Someone give it me,' he said at length.

" 'Who's the someone?'

" 'A man.'

" 'What man?'

" 'The man that lives in the big house.'

"His evident reluctance to answer only increased my suspicions that something was wrong. I kept questioning him until I learnt that the 'big house' was the place which is now known as the Excombe Private Sanatorium. Turning this piece of information over in my mind, I handed him back his coin, and as he dropped it into his pocket I heard it jingle against other money.

" 'Ah, have you got many of those pretty bits of silver, Jake?' I asked carelessly, pretending to resume my work as though the matter were of no importance.

"He fell into the trap at once. He was unable to count, but he proudly held up the outstretched fingers of one hand.

" 'Five, eh?' I commented with forced geniality. 'He must be a nice, kind man to give away all that money. Do you think he might give *me* some?'

" 'Not all at once,' Jake explained innocently; 'he only gives me one at the time.'

" 'Oh-ho!' thought I. 'So he has been at the "big house" four times before to-day.' The mystery was deepening! 'I think I'll have to pay a visit to this kind gentleman who gives money away,' I smiled. 'I've been wanting to meet someone like that all my life.'

" 'You'll have to sing first,' said Jake, eyeing me as though doubtful as to my vocal abilities.

" '*What?*' I cried.

" 'I always have to sing before he gives me anything.'

" 'And what on earth do you sing?' I asked, utterly bewildered.

" 'Songs,' grunted Jake.

" 'Sing one to me,' I said, struck by a sudden idea, 'and I'll give you another half crown.'

"He needed no further inducement, but immediately put down the broom and struck up one of the very unofficial marching tunes that he'd learnt in camp. But it wasn't the tune that caused the colour to drain away from my face and my heart to be filled with a sickening horror—it was the doggerel words which he had adopted in place of the quasi-French of the original. *They were a crude but recognizable parody of the chemical equation which represented the composition of my secret explosive!*

"In a flash I realized what had happened. Underrating the creature's intelligence and forgetting his marvellously retentive memory, I had not troubled to keep my notes out of sight. Somebody had got hold of him and bribed him to learn them off by heart—and who was likely to do such a thing except a secret enemy agent?

"Cold sweat broke out on my forehead as I saw how narrowly irretrievable disaster had been averted; for, once the secret of the gas was in the hands of the enemy, it would be a mere matter of days—perhaps only hours—before their immense and well-equipped system of gas-producing factories would enable them to wipe out the Allied Armies *en masse*. At that time it was known in official circles that the German guns were firing more than fifty per cent of gas and war-chemical shells, besides using their apparatus for cloud attacks and batteries of short-range Liven's projectors. Was it likely that they would refuse to use this new and terrible weapon when once it lay ready to their hands?

"Steadying myself with an effort, I turned to the innocent cause of all the trouble:

" 'So that was the song you sang to the nice gentleman at the big house, eh? Did he seem to think that it was worth the money?'

"Jake shook his head. 'No, he was angry and said I must have learnt it wrong. He said he wanted to hear the *last* song that was in that book'—and he pointed to the large notebook in which I entered the results of my experiments. A great wave of relief swept over me as I realized that the fool had not yet betrayed the secret—yet he must now know the final and ultimate formula, for he had just repeated it to me. But the explanation was not far to seek—he had taken another look at the book and memorized the last formula since he had returned that evening. So far, my secret was safe; but how long would it remain so after Jake had paid another visit to the 'big house'?

"That visit must be prevented at all costs. But how? If he chose to quit the house that minute, I had no power to stop him. How could I ensure the silence of a creature of such mentality unless I silenced him for ever? *For ever!* I felt myself trembling as a thought flashed through my mind like a blinding electric flash traverses a vacuum tube. Within the reach of my arm was a phial containing a liquid preparation of the deadly formula. So far it had never been tried on a living organism, but here—forced on me by circumstances over which I had had no control—was the opportunity to test its efficiency in a practical manner and at the same time ensure the silence of the only man likely to betray it to the enemy!

"Averting my head lest my very expression should betray the sinister project I had in mind, I addressed Jake: 'When have you arranged to see the kind gentleman again?' I asked as carelessly as I could.

" 'To-night—after supper,' he answered; and with those words he sealed his own fate.

"There could be no turning back now; one man must be sacrificed in order that humanity might be spared a scourge such as had never fallen on it since the world was evolved. What was one single life—and such a life!—compared with the millions of clear-minded, sentient beings who would dissolve in smoke and flame if he were allowed to reach the big house that night?

"During the hour which elapsed before supper-time I probed my soul as I had never probed it before, weighing the matter, sifting each argument for or against, as meticulously as did any judge before assuming the black cap. I shrank from my task with horror, but I went through with it to the bitter end.

"Its actual accomplishment was simplicity itself. A few drops of the colourless liquid poured into the mug of cider that he always drank at supper, and the thing was done. It only remained to get him well away from the house without delay.

" 'Your friend will be waiting for you, Jake,' I reminded him.

" 'Ay, so he will.' He rose and took up his cap. 'Good night, sir.'

" 'Good-bye, Jake,' I answered, adding under my breath, 'And God help you!'

"I allowed him five minutes' start, then hurried on my overcoat and followed. Outside, the night was dark and forbidding, with the sky overcast by a murky veil of cloud which shrouded the face of the moon. Before me stretched the moor, a waste of empty blackness, devoid of even a film of low-lying mist to denote the winding coombes which ran between the heather-clad beacons. As I made my way along the well-defined track I seemed to be walking through an infinity of shadows; the only sounds which broke the eerie stillness were the slight crunching of the gravel beneath my hurrying footsteps and the far-off mournful cries of curlews.

"When the slope of the ground told me that I had passed the brow of the ridge, I glanced at the illuminated dial of my watch and saw that twenty minutes had elapsed since I had administered the drug to Jake. This told me little, for I had not the slightest idea how long the stuff would take to work; still, I walked more slowly down the slope, and only quickened my pace in order to mount the farther side of the coombe in order to get a view of the path ahead. Not that I could see anything in that pall of darkness as yet, but I wanted to have an uninterrupted view of what was about to happen.

"Of course, I had not caught sight of Jake since quitting the house, but I knew that the path I had followed was the only means of his reaching the 'big house'. Somewhere in the darkness ahead he must be hurrying along, his poor brain filled with childish delight at the prospect of soon possessing another big, shining coin; as blissfully unconscious of his impending fate as are the microscopic infusoria before the drop of sterilizing solution wipes them out of existence.

"At last I reached the summit of the soaring beacon from which I knew I could command a view almost to the gates of the house for which Jake was making. I paused and glanced at my watch again. I started when I saw that a full hour had elapsed without anything happening. Had the experiment failed? Was the whole thing nothing but an empty, impracticable dream? Had my days and nights of labour been wasted in a quest as useless and futile as those of the madmen who strove to square the circle or evolve a system of perpetual motion? Throwing aside all caution in my desire to know what had happened, I pressed onward almost at a run. Nor did I pause or slacken speed when my onward progress brought into sight a single pin-point of light, telling me that the inmates of the sanatorium were awake and stirring.

"Then, slowly but inexorably, the conviction was forced on me that my experiment had failed—that, though theoretically flawless, it had proved useless when subjected to the acid test of practice— and I can truthfully say that my first emotion was a feeling of profound relief.

" 'Thank God the formula is harmless!' I cried, and laughed aloud in the darkness. 'Let him tell the spy the secret—and much good may it do him! I have failed—but again I thank God and am content. At least humanity has been spared the menace of—'

"Coming from a spot barely a hundred yards ahead, a flash of blood-red fire stabbed the night, and a fraction of a second later a dull, muffled concussion smote my ears. It was the death-knell of Crazy Jake! That was my one conscious thought as I stood, stunned by the awful manner in which my theory had been proved. It was some minutes before I could pull myself together.

"Prudence warned me to leave the spot as soon as possible, for it was but a short distance to the spy's house and he could not have failed to hear the explosion. Yet a horrible fascination—an irresistible desire to look upon my fell handiwork—drew me onwards like a magnet draws a needle. Almost before I was aware of what I was doing—the danger I was courting in risking being seen near the spot—I found myself running forward, my eyes following the dancing beam of my flashlight as it searched the ground.

"I will not harrow your feelings by describing the sight which finally met my eyes. Sufficient to say that the explosion had expended its force in a downward direction, in precisely the same manner as dynamite does. The whole of the lower portion of his body had been blown to atoms, but the upper part of his chest, his arms and head, were comparatively uninjured. One look was enough—more than enough! I snapped off my flashlight and fled . . .

"You can well imagine the eagerness with which I scanned the first newspapers I could get hold of. But there was no account in the morning paper of a mutilated body being found, nor in the next morning's, nor the next; and as the days lengthened into weeks without a single hint of the tragedy, my relief gave place to wonder, and finally to a vague, nameless fear. Had I not seen the uninjured half of Jake's body lying in the roadway, I should have dismissed the matter with the assumption that it had been completely destroyed by the explosion. But the moor is not so utterly deserted that such an object could remain unnoticed in the public highway for any length of time. It must have been removed on the same night as the tragedy occurred. But by whom? And for what purpose? But as the months went by without a single hint or rumour of the affair being brought to light I could only come to the conclusion—a fantastic one, maybe, but the only theory that would explain the facts—that the remains had been carried off and devoured by some prowling animal.

"Gradually my fears became lulled into a sense of security; whether his remains were above ground or below, Crazy Jake was dead and unrecognizable by this time, I argued with myself, and his secret had perished with him. My fears slept so soundly that the rude shock of their awakening almost unsettled my reason.

"It happened like this. It was a night in winter, six months, almost to the very day, after the affair that I have just described. It was intensely cold, and the snow, which had fallen heavily throughout the day, lay thick upon the ground. But I was cosy enough, sitting in my easy chair in front of a roaring fire in the library of Moor Lodge, with my pipe alight and a recently published scientific volume on my lap. My wife had retired early in consequence of a slight chill, and I was alone.

"A faint, fumbling sound at the window made me glance up, though there was nothing more in my mind than a mere idle curiosity as to the origin of the sound. But the moment I rested my eyes on the casement I felt my limbs grow stiff with stark, paralysing terror.

"*Gazing fixedly at me through the glass, his face, and figure clear and unmistakable in the bright rays of the moon, was Crazy Jake—the man whom I had last seen a hideously maimed corpse, blown literally in halves by the terrible fulminator whose secret he had been about to betray!*"

CHAPTER XVI

UGH TRENCHARD PAUSED to turn over another sheet of the closely written manuscript. The tense, almost breathless silence in which his two companions had listened so far proved that their interest had been gripped by the simple yet grimly dramatic narrative that had been penned by Silas Marle before he disappeared. When Hugh resumed reading, they could not help feeling an even greater sense of eeriness at the thought that the events he was describing took place in the very room in which they were sitting.

"It is useless for me to attempt to describe my feelings at that moment [the narrative continued]. I should judge you to be a man of some imagination; put yourself in my place, and ask yourself what your own emotions would be on finding yourself suddenly confronted with a man whom you had last seen injured—*shattered* would be a better term—beyond all possibility of recovery. Knowing as I did that one half of his body had been totally destroyed, I was more ready to believe that the figure before my eyes was an accusing phantom, than to admit the bare possibility of his having recovered from such—I can call it nothing else—semi-annihilation.

"At a moment such as that, time seems to stand still. I have not the faintest idea how long I remained twisted in my chair, gazing at the apparition with distended eyes. And Jake, or the *Thing that had been Jake,* remained equally immobile, with its arms raised above its head and resting on the transom that crossed the diamond-paned window. As we glared at each other, without speech or movement on either side, I began to take note of the strangeness of his attire—or rather the lack of it. In spite of the bitter cold, the whole of the upper portion of his body, indeed all that I could see of him, was devoid of clothing, though I thought I could detect part of a coarse, shaggy something which I assumed to be a pair of trousers. His hair was long and unkempt, falling in matted ringlets to his shoulders. On his head was what appeared to be a low-crowned, fantastic helmet decorated with a pair of huge stag's antlers, and in my swooning fear I half hoped that the apparition might even be one of the unceasing voyagers of Wagnerian legend. The other alternative was too horrible to contemplate . . .

"Until that moment I had never regarded myself as a superstitious man, and it was with a subconscious feeling of something very much like self-contempt that I found myself wanting to face up to whatever stood between me and a rightful, happy existence. My very fears spurred me to action. I gained my feet with a jerk and advanced toward the window—advanced, as it seemed, through timeless aeons, until I was gazing into the luminous, beast-like eyes of the nameless Thing, with but the thickness of the leaded panes between us—until I could see the slow and regular heaving of the massive chest and note the glistening of the melted snowflakes as they trickled down the knotted muscles.

"It seemed unbelievable that such a fearsome shape should draw the breath of life and radiate animal heat like a normal living thing, yet I felt some measure of confidence as I noted these natural signs. I did not stop to ask myself what devilish arts must have been employed to bring that erstwhile shattered and disembowelled body back to life—it was enough to know that it was no pale, bloodless phantom come from the grave in that dreadful guise to tax me with my crime. It lived! It breathed! It might even be endowed with speech . . .

" 'Who are you?' I cried in a voice I scarcely recognized as my own. 'What do you want here?'

" 'I am the man who in life was known as Crazy Jake—the man you slew by foul and damnable treachery!' came the answer, muffled by the intervening glass, yet every word falling on my heart like drips of ice-cold water. 'Look upon me and tremble, Silas Marle! For I, being dead, live again! In tumult and rending fire I was hurled to my doom—I come again in the silent watches of the night, creeping like a shadow drifting by the moon, slaying swift and sure as the shrouded Angel of Death whom I have gazed on face to face! *Look to yourself, murderer!* The poor puzzle-brained Jake has passed through the sable halls of death and has returned, strong, virile, cunning, and thirsting for revenge!'

"I listened like a man in a dream as the creature threw back his elf-locks and sent a laugh that echoed through the limitless galleries of the frozen night.

" 'Ho! Ho! Ho! You've had your hour of triumph, Silas Marle —mine is still to come! These eyes, once glazed and lifeless, shall seek you out. These hands, once cold and stiff, shall send a dagger-thrust into your false heart—ay, and tear it smoking from your body and glut my vengeance with a feast of blood! The poor and friendless wanderer has been transformed into a being such as the eye of man has not looked upon before. I am a king—a god—a monster! The Demon Monarch of the Moor! Fleet as the hunted hare—wary as the prowling fox—fierce as the bayed stag, I sweep like the wind over the broad bosom of my desolate domain, hunting by the glimpses of the moon, slaking my thirst at the mossy pools which mirror the rosy dawn; the eternal granite crags my rough-hewn throne, the starlit vault of heaven my justice-hall. And woe to him that falls under my displeasure. Woe to *you*, who have made me what I am! Look well upon your handiwork, Silas Marle, and tremble! When next you look upon me you will know that your last hour of life is speeding to its close!'

"With a swift, threatening gesture of his naked arm, he turned and slipped from my sight, leaving me like a man who suddenly awakens from a nightmare and asks himself if it be nothing but a vision of the night. I turned and looked at the familiar room—my book lying where it had fallen from my hand, my pipe smouldering unheeded on the carpet.

"Moved by a sudden thought, I snatched up the lamp and hastened to the door. Heedless of what might be lurking in the shadows, I threw back the bolts and passed outside, lowering the lamp until its rays fell on the spot where the apparition had seemed to stand. Then indeed did I know that it was no figment of my fancy. *In the deep snow was a trail of footprints made by cloven hoofs!*

"Well, I have nearly come to the end of my long story, and you who read this must form your own conclusions as to the real meaning of the events which I have here set down as fully and as exactly as my memory serves me. I myself was completely at a loss to decide whether the thing I had seen and conversed with was Jake's corporeal body, restored to life by some unprecedented feat of surgical science, or a supernatural form that had taken his shape. One thing at least was certain: the Thing—be it what it might—possessed memory and the power of speech. Its denunciation of me proved that it remembered the events which preceded the explosion. What if it remembered the secret of the composition of the human detonator which had been the cause of its assuming its present awful form?

"Even in my perplexity I remember being struck by the quaint and novel problem: whether it was likely that a person insane during life would appear after death as an insane ghost. Previously he had been but feeble-minded; now he was a hopeless maniac. His egoism, his grandiloquent utterances, his vainglorious assumption of an imaginary kingship, even the sonorous phrases of the sustained rhetoric in which he proclaimed himself Monarch of the Moor, were nothing but so many symptoms of the most pronounced form of megalomania. Here was a predicament such as I had not anticipated in my utmost thoughts. Instead of being safe, my secret—the formula that could devastate a world and rend humanity to smoking fragments—was in the possession of a raving madman!

"Prudence bade me flee from the moor and hide myself in some populous, well-policed city where I could laugh at the threats of the fantastic monster; but, although I toyed with the project, it was a foregone conclusion that I could not leave Exmoor until I had safeguarded my secret by destroying the Terror of the Moor. It was to be a duel to the death between us, and I hope you will not accuse me of empty bravado when I say that I was fighting for something far more precious than my own life.

"It would be superfluous for me to detail the precautions with which I surrounded myself, for you have already seen them. I converted Moor Lodge into a veritable fortress and always kept a loaded weapon within arm's reach. I wished to face my ordeal alone, but my dear wife resolutely refused to leave me, and in the end (as you already know) she paid the price of her devotion with her life. She was returning to the house at dusk when the Terror pounced upon her, no doubt mistaking her for me. She received no wound beyond a slight bruise, but she must have had full sight of the thing, and what she saw killed her as surely as a bullet in her heart. One shriek—I shall carry the echo of it in my brain to my dying day—and she never spoke again.

"After I had seen her laid to rest in the shadow of the little grey church on the hill, I returned to my empty, desolate house, nursing a hatred in my heart such as I pray that you, my friend, will never experience. Till then I had fought the Terror with much the same feelings as a soldier might seek to outwit and slay a soldier of the opposing army; now I resumed my quest with a fierce and unholy joy. Before, I had been content to remain on the defensive behind barred windows and bolted doors, awaiting the attack; now, I flung caution to the winds and boldly sought the attacker instead. Day and night I roamed the great moors, armed and watchful, asking—praying—for nothing more than to meet the cloven-footed man-monster face to face.

"But well has it been said that the Devil protects his own! For a whole year I pursued my self-imposed task in vain. Vague and wild stories of a Demon Stag came to my ears now and then. Once it was an old crone, gathering dry sticks for her cottage fire, who fled screaming at the horned apparition she glimpsed amid the trees. Now it would be a benighted shepherd who had cowered in a ditch while a herd of wild deer thundered by, led by a four-footed creature that was neither beast nor man. A gamekeeper who openly boasted that he would get to the bottom of the mystery was found next morning with the life choked out of him. 'A poacher's revenge', the papers hinted—but I knew better! Time and again I found the devil footprints beside some stream, or crossing some marshy hollow, but the Thing itself I never saw—until the night you came.

"With the memory of your own experience still fresh in your mind, you can imagine what happened to me. I heard the sound of hoofs on the gravel path, threw wide the door, and charged the shape that loomed dimly through the mist, firing as I ran. Three shots—misses—then it got me. The rest you know.

"And now, my friend, you understand something of the nature of the quest on which you have embarked. You will know that there is more in your strange legacy than a mere desire for revenge on the part of an old man whose race is almost run. If, knowing all, you decide to take up the task which I shall have laid down ere you read these lines, the whole of my wealth and property is yours. Accept it without scruple, for I have neither kith nor kin to dispute your claim; and, large as it is, it is no more than an adequate reward for the extermination of the monster I have unwittingly brought into being.

"The rest is on the knees of the gods. Farewell!"

There was a long silence after Hugh had come to the end of the strange epistle. Hugh looked at each of his companions in turn, endeavouring to gauge their thoughts. The expression of unwonted gravity on Ronnie's usually humorous features showed that his interest had been aroused, though the somewhat mocking glint in his half-closed eyes seemed to hint that he was not wholly convinced by the truth of the narrative. The face of Detective-Inspector Renshaw betrayed nothing; it was the stolid professional mask of a man accustomed to conceal his thoughts.

"Well, what is your opinion, gentlemen?" he asked at length.

"I hardly know what to think, sir." It was the detective who answered. "If I was not in possession of Sergeant Jopling's report, confirming the presence on the moor of just such another weird creature as Marle describes, I should be inclined to the opinion that Crazy Jake was not the only lunatic in the story. As it is"—he shrugged and shook his head—"well, I prefer to keep an open mind."

"An unprejudiced sceptic, eh?" smiled Hugh; then he added as he turned to Ronnie: "And you?"

"Oh, I'm prepared to go farther than our official friend here," declared the young doctor. "If he's a tentative sceptic, I'm prepared to declare myself an out-and-out unbeliever! Of course the poor old boy who wrote all that tosh was suffering from a lesion that is popularly known as 'bats in the belfry'."

Hugh Trenchard shook his head decisively.

"In that case you must admit that the same diagnosis applies to me," he reminded his friend. "Have you forgotten my own encounter with the cloven-footed monster?"

"By no means, old bean," drawled Ronnie. "I'm not likely to forget your extremely vivid account of that encounter. But if you'll pardon my saying so, dear boy, your description was more dramatic than convincing. If you were in the witness-box and I were the opposing K.C., I could simply tear your story to shreds. After all, what does it amount to? On a dark and misty night, while in a highly excited condition of mind, you see a series of footprints which might or might not have been made by a large deer. While examining them you are startled by a madman or practical joker declaring that he is Old King Cole, or some monarch equally mythical. Startled by his voice, the deer stampedes, bowls you over, and smashes your electric torch. How's that for a sane and commonplace explanation of *your* little yarn?"

Again Hugh shook his head.

"Your ingenious theory does not explain the voice which we heard in this very room—the low, sibilant voice which interrupted your declaration of disbelief in the Terror of the Moor. 'Silence, scoffer!' it said. 'Another gibe from you and my magic lightning shall blast you as you stand!'."

"Oh, *that!*" Ronnie Brewster grinned contemptuously. "That was friend Silas's way of amusing himself at our expense. Probably he had got out of bed, crept to the head of the stairs, and was listening to me declaiming against the spook that obsessed his poor brain. Perhaps his 'magic lightning' was a reference to the wonderful detonator that he thought he had invented."

"How do you account for the roll of thunder which sounded

immediately afterwards?"

"Pure coincidence," shrugged Ronnie.

At this point Inspector Renshaw, who had been listening to the conversation with a puzzled frown, stepped forward.

"Pardon me, gentlemen, but you have been alluding to an incident which is news to me. Will you be good enough to describe exactly what took place?"

Briefly, but omitting no important detail, Hugh narrated the events which had taken place on the night of Joan Endean's dramatic arrival at Moor Lodge. In his desire to make everything clear, he took up the same position where he had stood when the mysterious and uncanny voice had been heard, and, after some persuasion, induced the highly amused Ronnie to do the same. With Inspector Renshaw representing the absent girl, Hugh made a very creditable reconstruction of the scene. At the conclusion the detective made a few brief entries in his notebook.

"Thank you, gentlemen. I'm much obliged for the trouble you have taken to make the position clear." He snapped the clip on his notebook and thrust it into his pocket with an air at once elated and surprised. "That's the first real clue I've had handed me since I took up the case."

He spoke with such assurance that Hugh Trenchard was conscious of a sudden feeling of apprehension. "Do you imagine that Miss Endean is involved in this matter?" he demanded sharply.

A grim smile twisted the detective's features.

"Very much involved, I'm afraid," he answered, shooting a quick glance at the tense, drawn face of his questioner. "If I might be permitted to offer you a little friendly advice, Dr. Trenchard, I would warn you to keep as far away as possible from that young lady during the next few weeks."

Hugh took a quick pace forward and gripped him by the arm.

"What—you know her?" he gasped in a voice that betrayed the pent-up emotion he was endeavouring to repress.

At the question there came a flicker of amusement in Renshaw's keen eyes. The expression was but fleeting, and was gone in an instant; but it had not passed unnoticed either by Hugh or Ronnie.

"Know her?" the detective repeated, and there was an unmistakable innuendo in his tone. "I should say we do! The girl who calls herself Miss Joan Endean has been known to the police for years!"

CHAPTER XVII

THERE ARE MOMENTS in a man's life when his normal consciousness is overwhelmed and submerged beneath the
surge of emotion brought about by a sudden and unexpected
shock. Such a moment came to Hugh Trenchard when the detective's revelation regarding Joan Endean shattered the idol which
he had enshrined within his heart. He sat listening with unheeding
ears while Inspector Renshaw outlined his plan for the capture of
the Terror of the Moor; to his surprise, he even found himself occasionally contributing to the discussion of ways and means; but,
for all the impression which subsequently remained on his clouded
and preoccupied mind, the conversation might have been conducted in a language quite unknown to him.

The thought that the beautiful girl, whose eyes had looked so
frankly and so fearlessly into his own, was a clever crook—
'known to the police'—was like acid dropped into an open wound.
In spite of his first suspicions caused by her conflicting stories
when she had arrived at Moor Lodge on that night of storm and
rain; in spite of the ingenious manner in which she had made him
the decoy with a packet of blank papers; in spite, too, of the clever
masquerade by which she had lured him to the empty house opposite Ronnie's surgery—in spite of all, he had believed and trusted
her. Nay, more—he had loved this mystery girl who had come so
strangely into his life. He knew it now—now that the blunt, mat-
ter-of-fact words of the police-inspector had shown that his idol
was not even composed of good honest clay.

Masquerading under a false name, feigning to be engaged in a
mission which must remain an inviolable secret, throwing dust in
his eyes and making him the innocent accomplice in her
schemes—he had been fooled by tricks so cheap and threadbare
that he felt a flush of anger rise to his cheeks as he pictured himself as a shallow-witted modern Don Quixote, tilting at windmills
at the behest of a wily adventuress.

By heaven, she had not seen the last of him yet! He would let
her see that double-crossing was a pastime that two could play at.
"Keep as far away as possible from that young lady" had been In-

spector Renshaw's advice, and there seemed to be no doubt that it had been tendered with all good faith. But if the police officer had deliberately planned to bring Hugh Trenchard and Joan Endean together he could scarcely have hit on a better plan, for the young doctor was now all eagerness to confront her, to tax her openly with her duplicity and show that he had repudiated the promise of blind allegiance which she had exacted from him. Of course, he argued, her escape from Excombe Sanatorium and the subsequent attempt of Dawker to recapture her was a carefully staged farce intended to lull his suspicions and enable her to play the part of the persecuted heroine. He felt himself shiver as the thought crossed his mind that the seemingly obtuse Sergeant Jopling might not have been so far from the truth after all, when he had suspected that it was her hand that had guided the fatal dagger on the night Silas Marle was slain.

"Well, I suppose you two gentlemen are quite capable of looking after yourselves for to-night, so I and my men will be off." With a start Hugh realized that the inspector had risen to take his departure. "But I should not advise you to leave the front door on the latch—as it was when we entered." Renshaw laughed as he added: "The next hold-up gang that makes free of the house might not let you off as lightly as we did."

The two friends joined in the laugh at their expense.

"Oh, we shan't be caught napping the second time!" Ronnie said confidently. "I intend to lock my bedroom door and go through the early-Victorian ceremony of looking under the bed before I blow out the candle!"

Inspector Renshaw shook his head dubiously.

"Locks don't seem to be of much account in *this* house," he mused aloud. "The local sergeant was telling me that he suspected the walls were honeycombed with secret passages and I don't know what else."

"Don't take any notice of him," grinned Ronnie. "His mind is still vibrating with the thrill of the one and only crook drama he saw in London. If we had given him a free hand, I believe he'd have ripped down every square foot of oak panelling and turned the carved chimneypieces into so much firewood. He does not seem to be a man very prolific in ideas, but when one *does* happen to penetrate his brain, well, I reckon it would require a surgical operation to get it out again! I suppose he has told you all about the mysterious letter that dropped from nowhere on to the hall-stand?"

There was a faint smile on the inspector's lips as he nodded his head.

"The only thing he hasn't told me is how the thing managed to get there," he said quietly. "There was one of his men at the front door, one at the back, and one on the roof. The sergeant himself was sitting in the front room, and anyone coming downstairs would have had to pass the open door of the room. Yet the letter was found lying on the hallstand. You must agree that it is a bit of a mystery."

Ronnie Brewster laughed.

"I bet it wouldn't be a mystery if *I* had been in the house at the time. Unfortunately I had just ridden off, accompanied by Dr. Trenchard here, and Nick Froude, the Harbourer of the Stag-hounds, in an attempt to track the so-called Terror by means of the dogs."

"But," objected the detective, "you all left the house by the back entrance."

"No, by the front." It was Hugh who made the correction. "I distinctly remember taking my hat from the hallstand, and I am certain that the only thing on it at the time was the hat belonging to my friend Dr. Brewster."

"That's correct," confirmed Ronnie. "There certainly was no letter there when we quitted the house."

"Thank you, gentlemen. Your testimony on that point has been most helpful." Renshaw paused and stroked his chin thoughtfully, his brows drawn down so that they half veiled his keen, penetrating eyes. "What you have told me has relieved my mind pretty considerably—though I'll admit that, on the face of it, it doesn't seem to give one the slightest hint how the thing was managed. It seems rather to confirm Jopling's secret-panel theory, eh? Well, good night, gentlemen, and once more let me advise you to be careful. Remember that you are for the time being the guardians of a secret that would give an ambitious Power the domination of the world, and two human lives would be but a grain of dust in the balance to anyone who desired to possess it."

On this not very reassuring note Inspector Renshaw took his departure. Hugh Trenchard bolted the door behind him, and on re-entering the library stood motionless for nearly a minute, thinking deeply. The inspector's parting words had brought home to him the extremely perilous nature of the secret entrusted to him by Silas Marle. When at last he glanced up, it was to catch Ronnie's eyes fixed on him with an expression of sardonic amusement.

"Getting scared?"

To the questioner's surprise Hugh nodded.

"Frankly, old chap—yes. I am scared of what might happen if the wrong people got hold of that sealed envelope. When I came out here to spend the night I little thought that I should have in my keeping a secret that has already cost the lives of two men—"

"One and a half, to be exact," Ronnie corrected flippantly, "for the village idiot was only half annihilated, according to Marle's account. Not that it seems worth while going into fractions and decimals in a case like that. Anyway, what are you worrying about? Put the envelope in the safe and forget all about it till the morning."

"That safe makes me smile," Hugh declared, shaking his head. "Didn't you notice the rough way in which it has been put together? It appears to have been constructed by an amateur boiler-maker, and a live crook could simply rip it open like cutting through a sardine tin."

"He wouldn't be a 'live' crook very long after he'd started his job," Ronnie declared so confidently that his friend stared at him in amazement.

"Why not?"

"Come with me and I'll show you."

He led the way from the room and, crossing the dark passage with an unerring sense of direction, found and turned the handle of the door leading to the laboratory. Inside was a mere cave of velvety blackness, marked at the further end by an oblong of slightly lighter indigo which showed the position of the single window. Ronnie struck a match and lit the reading-lamp which stood on the desk, tilting the green shade so that the light fell full on the safe; then, drawing a coin from his pocket, he tapped lightly on the metal door. To Hugh's surprise the sound which came forth was not the dead vibration of solid steel but the musical ring of a substance unmistakably hollow, "*Why,* it's even flimsier than I thought!" he exclaimed.

Ronnie indulged in a superior smile.

"Appearances are deceptive, dear old top," he drawled. "In all probability this safe is one of the gadgets invented by the ingenious Mr. Marle for the safeguarding of his precious secret, and the fact that no attempt has been made to open it during the time the house was empty seems to indicate that it's no common specimen of the so-called burglar-proof variety. I say 'so-called' because it's a well-known fact that the up-to-date crook can open any safe in the world provided that he is left long enough undisturbed. But here, I repeat, we have something different. The oxy-acetylene blowpipe will cut through chilled and toughened steel like a warm knife cuts through butter, but that flimsy-looking safe would beat the best outfit in the world. The door and walls of that safe are nothing but so many shallow boxes made of ordinary iron boiler-plating. Heaven alone knows what diabolical chemical or gas is sealed up inside those hollow walls, but you may be sure that it is something quite capable of giving the *coup de grace* to the enterprising cracksman who releases it. The late Mr. Silas Marle had a very wide acquaintance of highly scientific methods of wafting his enemies into the inky black nowheres, and I bet he has provided something extra special in that line for the man who tries to steal his secret by busting that safe."

Hugh could not but agree as he examined the strange contrivance, and when he discovered a small screw-valve set in one of the inner walls and another inside the door of the safe, he felt positive that Ronnie had guessed the truth. The safe was nothing but a huge hollow tank, and the extreme care with which the outer and inner iron skins had been hermetically sealed was a silent but significant warning of the deadly possibilities which lay within. Reassured, he replaced the sealed envelope in the safe and locked the door.

There was some desultory conversation after they had returned to the library, but it was not long before Ronnie yawned and glanced at the clock.

"I think it's time that all good little boys were in bed," he declared. "I think I'll turn in now, especially as I shall have to be up pretty early in order to get to the surgery. Heigh-ho"—he yawned again—"I wish to goodness somebody would take it into their heads to leave me a country house and a nice fat income. But it is always the undeserving that get all the luck. Which room do you intend to sleep in?" he asked suddenly. "Of course you'll give a wide berth to the one from which old Marle was spirited away?"

He gave a whistle of surprise as Hugh shook his head.

"Surely you're not going to sleep *there*—and in the same bed?"

"Why not?" There was a gleam of quiet amusement in Hugh's eyes as he asked the question. "I consider it is the most comfortable room in the house."

Ronnie shrugged and made a grimace.

"Oh, well—there's no accounting for taste. Personally, I prefer to sleep in the front—with the door locked! Bye-bye, old bean. Pleasant dreams, and all the rest of it."

With a genial nod, he quitted the room, and presently the creaking of the ancient woodwork of the staircase told that he had retired upstairs. Left to himself, Hugh Trenchard made a tour of the
ground floor, closely examining the fastenings of every door and
window. Satisfied on this score, he mounted the stairs and entered
the room of tragic memories.

Setting the lighted candle on the small spindle-legged table,
Hugh took a quick glance round the apartment. It appeared exactly
the same as he had last seen it, on that night of grim excitement
when Silas Marle had been spirited away so completely and mysteriously. There stood the great four-poster bed, its fringed canopy
looking like a funeral catafalque amid the looming shadows which
stretched themselves like dusky tongues across the floor and hung
in dark masses in the corners and clustered against the oak-beamed
walls. The aged room seemed to have assumed a frown, menacing
and malignant, as though its worm-burrowed heart were register-
ing silent disapproval at this evasion of its drowsy sanctuary.

A faint and elusive odour hung in the stagnant air. It was not
exactly the stale smell exhaled by damp and decay; neither was it
the lingering trace of some old-world perfume clinging to the
faded tapestries. It seemed to be a curious combination of both,
and gave rise to thoughts unpleasantly morbid and suggestive.
Hugh lost no time in crossing to the window and throwing open
the leaded casements to their fullest extent.

For a while he stood there, inhaling the gusts of clean, sweet air
which still retained the salt tang of the sea in spite of its twenty-
mile sweep across the rolling moors. The sky was almost cloud-
less, and the slender sickle of the moon gave just sufficient light to
make the scene a world of vague shapes, sensed rather than actually seen, with here and there a glint of dull silver that marked the
course of some meandering streamlet. Once the deep stillness was
broken by the shrill hoot of some questing owl, and once again
Hugh thought he could detect the passage of a slinking animal
shape amid the tall bracken which lay beyond the confines of the
house-garden—reminders that, though the great moor seemed to
sleep tranquilly, the inexorable conflict of tooth and claw knew no
truce.

So absorbed was he in the quiet beauty of the night that when
he heard a faint creak of the swinging door he idly set it down as
being caused by a chance current of wind. Not until he caught the
sound of a faint padding footfall in the room behind him did he
realize that he was not alone.

"Hullo, Ronnie!" he said, without turning his head.

"So you don't find yourself so inclined for sleep as you imagined—"

He broke off with a quick, gasping intake of breath as he felt something cold and hard pressed into the nape of his neck.

"Do not presume to utter a sound, Dr. Trenchard! Your friend Ronnie is sleeping as he has never slept before, and you will sleep even sounder if you do not obey me instantly. I have come here for two things—the key of the safe downstairs and the information of where I can find Miss Joan Endean. If you do not give me both within the space of the next ten seconds, I shall be under the painful necessity of cutting short a most promising career by pressing this trigger!"

Hugh stiffened like a man suddenly turned to stone. There was no mistaking those sibilant, coldly enunciated accents. It was the voice of the enemy, Professor Lucien Felger!

CHAPTER XVIII

TEN SECONDS!

Twenty fleeting ticks of a watch—a dozen or so normal pulse-beats—the space during which two ordinary breaths might be drawn and exhaled. It was a short enough time in which to make the decision of the most trivial and unimportant matter, to say nothing of one which concerned his own existence—maybe the existence of thousands of others.

Yet Hugh Trenchard knew that he must act, and act at once. The menace with which Professor Felger had uttered his threat was in itself a proof that this was no empty bluff. Hugh felt quite certain that, unless he agreed within the allotted ten seconds, the eleventh would see him lying with his spine shattered by the weapon whose muzzle he could feel pressing into his flesh.

Almost before the professor had ceased speaking, Hugh had taken his desperate resolve, and in his heart he thanked God for the impulse which had led him to open the windows to their fullest extent. Without daring to flex his muscles lest the movement should betray his intention, he nerved himself for what was coming.

Meanwhile Professor Felger's watchful eyes were wavering between Hugh's head and his hands, which still gripped the window-sill. The only forms of resistance he anticipated were a sudden attempt to draw a weapon or a lightning-like swing round in an effort to grab his own. For both of these he was fully prepared, but what actually happened in the next few seconds was the very reverse to his expectations.

Without shifting his grip of the window-sill, or his eyes from their contemplation of the distant landscape, Hugh hurled himself sideways and downwards through the open window.

Felger fired—the fraction of a second too late. The flash of the discharge scorched Hugh's left ear, and the crash almost deafened him, but the bullet itself whined harmlessly away in the darkness. Breathless, but unhurt, he alighted on the great heap of peat-fuel that was stacked beneath the window, and even as he rolled into the shelter of a projecting angle of brickwork his hand groped and gripped the butt of his revolver. He felt the satisfied thrill of an armed man as he disengaged the safety-catch and crooked his finger over the trigger. If Felger was alone, the odds were something like even now!

But *was* he alone? Hugh doubted that he would have undertaken his task single-handed—and did not his boast of having overpowered Ronnie imply the presence of one or more of his satellites? The thought that his friend was lying helpless in the power of these ruffians almost goaded Hugh to madness; but he knew it would be worse than madness to attempt to force his way back into the house in the face of the hail of bullets which would greet his reappearance at the window. He must get help quickly. But how?

A sound in the bushes behind him made him whirl with cat-like agility. As he raised his revolver in the direction of the faint rustling, the branches parted and Joan Endean stepped forth.

There was a bitter smile on Hugh Trenchard's lips as he thrust his weapon back into his pocket.

"So you're in this game, too?"

If the girl perceived the implied accusation in his words she made no sign. Walking proudly and erect, she advanced until she could have touched him with her outstretched hand; until he could see the enigmatical half-smile that curved her lips as she stood regarding him.

"I was passing and I heard a shot," she said. "What has happened?"

"Passing?" he repeated with ill-concealed derision. "Passing across the moor at this hour of the night?"

Her shoulders lifted slightly beneath the dark cloak which she wore.

"Watching, then—if you like that word better. It is not the first time I have been alone on the moor."

Her tone of almost contemptuous defiance stung him like the lash of a whip.

"I can well believe that!" he flung back grimly. "This time, however, your help has come too late."

"Too late?"

"Yes. Your friend the professor has failed in his hold-up, and Marle's sealed envelope is still in the safe."

"Thank God for that!" she said quickly. "But what right have you to describe Professor Felger as my friend?"

"Is he not your friend?" he demanded bluntly.

"Not so much as he is yours," she flashed back in what seemed to be a clumsy verbal parry. "You would make me out a very dreadful person, Dr. Trenchard, but do not let your prejudice blind your eyes to the identity of your real enemy. But this is not the time for asking riddles, or answering them. Once again I must ask you to tell me what has happened."

Such was the imperviousness of her tone that, almost before he was aware of the fact, Hugh found himself giving a brief account of his late encounter.

"So you did not see Professor Felger's face?"

Hugh shook his head.

"I have never seen it. On the occasion of my former interview with him he wore a gauze antiseptic mask. But we are wasting precious time. Ronnie is inside that house, helpless, probably drugged—Felger hinted as much. I must get help—"

"Have you the key of the house?" she asked suddenly.

"Yes, but—"

"Give it to me."

He drew it from his pocket and held it out. She took it without a word, and at once stepped swiftly up the short path which led to the front door. Hugh held his breath as her slight figure rounded the angle of the house and came within the arc of fire from the windows, half expecting to see a vicious spit of flame leap from the dark casement and hear the report of Felger's pistol. But everything within the house remained quiet as the grave. Was it a trap, with Joan Endean as the tempting bait?

By this time Joan had the door open and was beckoning to him. "Come on—there is no danger," she called.

Hugh Trenchard's jaws set in a straight, firm line. There had seemed a subtle mockery in her assurance that roused his fighting spirit. In a dozen quick strides he reached her side.

"This is likely to be a man's work," he said, placing himself in front of her in order to lead the way into the house.

She resigned her position with a shrug, and laughed softly as her eyes fell on the revolver in his hand.

"I do not think there will be occasion to use *that*," she said coolly. "I shall be very much surprised if we find anyone in the house answering to the description of Professor Lucien Felger."

"Indeed?" Hugh stared at her from beneath raised brows. "You seem tolerably well informed about the movements of this gang!"

Still smiling, she shrugged again. "Search the place and see if I am not right."

"Are you armed?" he asked suddenly.

"Knowing where the danger lies, I am doubly armed," was her oracular reply.

Without further parley Hugh made his way into the house, searching each room in turn and locking the doors behind him. On the lower floor the rooms were silent and untenanted, so, holding his weapon ready for instant use, Hugh warily mounted the stairs, A single glance was sufficient to show that there was no one lurking in the bedroom he had occupied. Satisfied on this point, he turned to the one which Ronnie had chosen.

The moment he opened the door his nostrils were assailed by a familiar, sweetly pungent odour.

"Chloroform!" he gasped as he dashed forward to the still figure that lay upon the bed. "Whew! The place reeks of it. Open the windows while I see if he is still alive."

Apparently they had not arrived a moment too soon. Ronnie Brewster lay flat on his back, his ghastly white face upturned to the ceiling, his arms and legs sprawled in grotesque angles. At first there seemed no sign of breathing; but as Hugh took up his limp hand and laid his finger on the pulse, a faint, long-drawn sigh fluttered from the lips of the unconscious man.

There was no need to seek far for the cause of his condition. On the pillow was a pad heavily soaked in chloroform, and the traces of the blistering effect of the powerful drug, apparent on Ronnie's lips and nostrils, showed that the pad had been forcibly pressed over his face. Luckily for him, however, the natural spasmodic movements which always precede complete coma had caused the cotton wool to fall off. But for this he would have already been past all aid.

Hugh's first care was to snatch away the drugged pad and hurl it out of the open window; then he opened the door wide to allow a current of air to pass through the room. But it was not until he had soaked the towel in the water-jug and freely dabbed it over Ronnie's face that the first real signs of returning consciousness became apparent.

It was at least a quarter of an hour later before he opened his eyes and looked about him vaguely.

"What's happened?" he gasped. "Where am I?"

"You are safe, old chap. That's all you need worry about at present."

"Safe?" Ronnie repeated, looking more puzzled than ever. "What d'ye mean by 'safe'? Did we go on the binge last night?

My poor head feels just like the morning after the night before, and my tummy is beginning to show the first symptoms of a choppy cross-Channel trip. Sorry to trouble you, old top, but—"

Hugh lost no time in rending the needful first aid.

"You'll feel better presently," he assured him.

"That's a safe prediction on your part . . . I don't think I could feel much worse!" Ronnie grunted between his spasms. "Pah, this place smells like an operating-theatre without the carbolic. I say, what's the giddy old idea?"

"Attempted murder—with you and me as the prospective corpses!"

"Eh? Just say that over again, will you?"

Hugh's tersely worded account of what had happened acted like a tonic on the stupefied man. His blank, bewildered look gave place to an angry frown; a flush mounted to his pallid cheeks; his limply sagging body grew taut and finally jerked up into a sitting posture on the bed.

"The low hounds! Let me get my hands on that old professor and I'll teach him a lesson in dissection that'll surprise him! Here, hand me over my trousers—"

Hugh shook his head.

"My dear chap, it's quite impossible for you to get up—"

"I'll show you whether it's impossible or not!" cried Ronnie fiercely. "Give me those confounded trousers, you? If you don't, I shall go on the war-path like one of the heroes of Ancient Greece!"

"For heaven's sake don't do that!" laughed Hugh, relinquishing his hold on the desired garments. "The Professor would think you were qualifying as an inmate of his institution."

Ronnie paused in his hasty dressing and gazed at his friend in boundless admiration.

"By Jove, that's a brain-wave if you like!" he exclaimed. "If one of us could only manage to get locked up in the Excombe Sanatorium, we'd be able to pick up no end of clues and things. Suppose you pretend to be potty—"

"No, thanks!" Hugh declined, modestly adding, "You could act the part much more naturally than I—in fact, it might not be necessary for you to act at all! Just be your own sweet self, Ronnie, and you will next find the slightest difficulty in getting the necessary certificate."

But the young doctor treated this suggestion with lofty disdain, and the remainder of his toilet was performed for the most part in a majestic silence. Only once he paused and sniffed the air.

"I don't know whether it's that damned chloroform still in my head, but I seem to smell something like frying bacon—and coffee," he added, with another sniff.

"I suppose Miss Endean is exercising her culinary abilities," Hugh hazarded with a smile.

"That girl?" The other was plainly startled. "Is she still here?"

"It would seem so."

Ronnie favoured his chum with a long, puzzled stare.

"Taking into consideration the information that Inspector Renshaw gave you concerning her," he inquired slowly, "what is your candid opinion of that young lady?"

Hugh parried the direct question with a shrug. "I haven't made up my mind yet."

"And are you exercising the same commendable restraint from forming rash judgments in the case of the sinister professor?" persisted Ronnie.

"Oh, I've weighed *him* up all right," came the reply without an instant's hesitation. "He's an out-and-out crook."

"Indeed? In what particular direction does his crookedness lie?"

For a moment the bland question left Hugh nonplussed. Truth to tell, he had been so convinced of Professor Felger's guilty participation in the whole series of mysterious happenings that he had never so much as dreamt of tabulating his suspicions in a cool and orderly manner.

"Why, in every direction possible," he said at length. "Haven't I just been telling you how he attempted to hold me up in the next room a few hours since?"

"Could you swear to his identity in a court of law?" Ronnie asked calmly. "Did you recognize him?"

"You know very well that I've never seen the fellow's face," Hugh cried impatiently. "But I recognized his voice all right!"

"That's a slender thread on which to hang a grave charge, old chap," shrugged Ronnie. "I very much doubt if they'd issue a warrant unless you could offer something more convincing than the sound of a man's voice. Voices can be imitated, you know— especially voices which speak with a slight foreign accent. Please don't go running away with the idea that I hold a brief for Felger—I only want to show you the weakness of your case before you fall into the error of making a false step. Legally speaking, you haven't got a shred of evidence against him."

"What about Silas Marle's letter? Doesn't that prove that he's an enemy agent trying to get hold of the secret self-exploding formula?"

"On the contrary, it did not so much as mention his name." Ronnie smiled as he shook his head slowly. "I fear that statement is neither definite nor conclusive. Looked at coldly and logically, what does it amount to? Simply that an eccentric recluse named Marle said that a half-witted lout named Jake said that an unnamed man living at the 'big house' liked to hear him sing! Hearsay evidence to the third degree, and vague at that. No, no; we'll have to get hold of some more convincing evidence before we call in the police. By the way," he added, as if struck by a sudden thought, "our friend Sergeant Jopling was not such a fool as we thought."

"Why?"

"He was right about the secret passage leading into this house, for by what other means could Professor Felger have entered last night?"

Hugh Trenchard stood transfixed as the full meaning of this possibility rushed upon him.

"If that is so, he might have overheard every word of our discussions—to say nothing of the contents of Marle's letter!" he exclaimed. "We *are* a first-class pair of dithering bone-heads!"

"Speak for yourself, dear boy," drawled Ronnie. "Personally, I don't think we've handed the professor anything that he wasn't aware of before. For heaven's sake don't look so tragic. I've got a few stunts up my sleeve that'll rather surprise everybody—yourself included."

"Oh? And what are they?"

Ronnie grinned and shook his head, laying his finger on his lips in the manner of a stage conspirator.

"Not here, dear boy—walls have ears, you know. I'll let you into my secret when the time is ripe. In the meantime, I think I might manage to peck at a slice of dry toast and a cup of coffee."

The cold grey light of the early dawn had crept unnoticed through the windows as they had talked, and its wan illumination did not invest the gloomy oak-panelled interior of Moor Lodge with any additional cheerfulness. Hugh Trenchard felt a slight shiver pass down his spine as he descended the cramped staircase. He found himself eyeing the age-darkened walls with a new and disquieting interest, speculating which of the squares of carved wood might be concealing a lurking enemy. Secret doors might sound very romantic when regarded in the abstract, but when one has made up one's mind to live alone in a house with such a sinister reputation as Moor Lodge, they are an interesting link with the 'good old days' with which one would willingly dispense. He felt a twinge of compunction as he remembered how unmercifully he had chaffed Sergeant Jopling about his 'crook-drama theory' (as he had honestly thought it to be then), and he determined that he would take the first opportunity of offering something more solid than a mere verbal apology as a balm for that worthy officer's ruffled feelings.

As the two men entered the living-room, they seemed to step into a new and cheerier world. The lamp had been trimmed and lit, the fire replenished; its ruddy glow reflected in the coffee-pot and covered dishes which stood in the old-fashioned hearth. The place looked tidier and more homely already, and the neatly laid table, with its bunch of freshly plucked late roses in the centre, showed subtle yet unmistakable touches which indicated a feminine hand. But there was no sign of the girl herself, and Hugh stepped back to the door and called: "Miss Endean!" Hearing no reply, he made his way to the brick-floored kitchen. "It's awfully good of you to have taken pity on two helpless bachelors, and I wish to thank . . ."

The words died on his lips as he realized that he was speaking to the empty air. Switching on his torch, he hurried from room to room, yet in his heart he knew his search was useless.

"She's gone!" he announced blankly as he re-entered the living-room.

Ronnie paused in the act of demolishing a generous helping of fried eggs and bacon.

"What, again?" he queried satirically. "My word, what a girl she is for performing the vanishing-trick! She seems to be a veritable will-o'-the-wisp of the female species, but—" he gave a warning grimace before turning to refill his coffee-cup—"but don't follow her pretty little lodestar too closely, or you may find yourself up to your neck in a whole heap of trouble."

"Your metaphor is rotten, Ronnie."

"Perhaps—but my advice is sound." There was a note of unwonted gravity in the usually bantering voice. "Think it over, old chap, *and keep clear of Joan Endean!*"

CHAPTER XIX

THOUGH HUGH TRENCHARD felt half dead for want of sleep, he managed to put in a fairly busy morning. No sooner had Ronnie taken his departure in the car than he put on his cap and proceeded to make a thorough inspection of the ground in the immediate vicinity of the house.

He argued that if there really was a secret passage leading inside the house, its outlet could not be very far beyond its walls. The lodge had been built in a bygone age when such devices were not uncommon, and he was determined not to spend another night there until he had done his best to settle the question one way or the other.

The possibilities of the small garden at the rear of the house were soon exhausted. No such outlet could exist among the clipped box hedges and symmetrical flower-beds; nor did the most careful scrutiny of the paved paths reveal a single slab large enough to admit the passage of a man.

In the front of the house, and about twenty yards distant, lay the steeply sloping escarpment of the coombe up which he had raced on the night of his first arrival at Moor Lodge. Here the ground looked more promising, for the face nearest the house was for the most part a sloping wilderness of dense oak scrub, with here and there an outcropping granite ridge. At one place a narrow path, provided with roughly hewn steps at the steepest parts, zigzagged its way downwards, and at first sight this seemed the sole means of traversing the cliff.

It was not until Hugh had pushed aside the bushes which bordered the path that he discovered more than one rocky ledge by which an active man might make his way along the face of the coombe in an horizontal direction. There was one, slightly broader than the rest, that particularly attracted his attention; as far as he could trace its course amid the confusing overgrowth, it appeared to lead directly to an immense buttress of granite, a fantastic weather-scarred mass that must have weighed scores of tons, which jutted precariously far over the abyss of the gorge-like river course. Comparing its position with the brow of the cliff, Hugh came to the conclusion that its base must be less than a dozen

yards below the foundations of Moor Lodge. From the safe van-
tage-ground of the path he examined it long and carefully, and at
length his straining eyes seemed to detect a darker patch of
shadow which might possibly be a crevice large enough to admit
the passage of a man. At this he hesitated no longer. Thrusting
aside the bushes, he began to make his way cautiously along the
shelf of rock, steadying his progress by grasping an occasional
gnarled root which thrust itself from a soil-filled cranny, though he
was well aware that such would have been but a poor support
should a false step compel him to rest his whole weight upon it. It
was with a feeling of intense relief that he found the narrow ledge
resolving itself into a fairly safe path, such as might be traversed at
night by one familiar with its devious windings. The half-hearted
interest with which he had begun the adventure now gave place to
a feeling of elated excitement. Here, if anywhere, would he find
the answer to the riddle that had so puzzled him.

Suddenly he stopped, every nerve a-quiver. He was passing a
spot where earth had been washed down on to the rocky path, and
in the still moist soil was a distinct imprint of a human foot. Although it was not the mysterious cloven sign that he had learned to
dread, the sight was significant enough, for it proved that someone
was in the habit of using this secret path along the cliff.

He bent down and examined it closely. It had been made by a
fairly large-size boot, though the absence of hobnails seemed to
rule out the possibility of its being due to the chance passage of
some shepherd or gamekeeper. Straightening up, Hugh Trenchard
slipped his revolver from his pocket and silently crept toward the
fissure in the cliff face, which he had rightly conjectured to be the
entrance to a cave.

Every muscle held reads for instant action, he rounded the last
boulder; then:

"Good morning, Dr. Trencherd," said a bluff, hearty voice.
"I've been waiting for you."

For a moment Hugh stared at the smiling face before recogni-
tion came.

"Inspector Renshaw!" he gasped. "I little thought of meeting
you!"

"Evidently not," said the police officer dryly, glancing at the
revolver which Hugh still trained on him. "I'd feel more at ease if
you would put that thing back in your pocket."

Hugh complied with a muttered apology, but the other cut him
short.

"Oh, I'm not blaming you for being careful," he said smilingly, as he led the way into the cave. "I've been watching you from the first moment you appeared on the cliff, and when I saw you start along that ledge I knew you shouldn't be prepared to find a friend at the other end. So I thought it policy to speak first—in case of accidents," he added grimly.

Hugh was looking about with lively interest. Though of irregular shape, the cave was far roomier and loftier than he had expected, and there were many evidences that the inspecter had prepared for a long stay. There was a heap of tinned pensions in one corner, a couch of dry bracken covered with a brown blanket in another; a kettle, a saucepan, and an oil-cooker completed the domestic arrangements. But what attracted Hugh's attention most was the passage-like aperture which opened from the innermost corner of the rocky chamber.

"Where does that lead to?" he asked quickly.

Inspector Renshaw looked at him for an instant without speaking, apparently undecided how far to take him into his confidence.

"I will show you something that will surprise you," he said at length. "Follow me."

Unhooking a portable electric lamp from a peg driven into a crevice in the rock wall, he switched it on and led the way through the narrow aperture. With growing excitement Hugh saw that this tunnel, unlike the cavern they had just quitted, had walls comparatively smooth, and in places he could even distinguish the marks of the tools with which they had been hewn.

"This passage has been made for a definite purpose," he exclaimed, his voice sending weird echoes booming hollowly out of the wall of blackness ahead.

"Speak lower," warned his guide. "This place carries sound like a huge speaking-tube, and it would spoil my plans if its existence became known. Yes," he went on, in answer to Hugh's question, "this is nothing more or less than an abandoned mine, so ancient that its very existence has been forgotten."

"Mine?" repeated Hugh dubiously. "What sort of mineral could have been dug out of here?"

Renshaw shrugged.

"I'm afraid I'm not sufficiently expert in mineralogy, sir, to answer that question. But there are plenty of old workings in the Mendip Hills—some thirty miles away in a north-easterly direction—where they used to get lead ore and calamine, and some of them are being operated at the present time. I should say that this has been a mine of that description. You'll notice that the galleries do not run in a straight line, but wind about as they followed the veins of ore. There are about a couple of dozen side passages. There is one of them."

He swung the beam of his lamp to the left, and Hugh caught a glimpse of the mouth of a tunnel that was even narrower and lower than the one they were traversing.

"Where does it lead to?" he asked.

"I haven't explored that particular one," Renshaw answered carelessly. "I took a look down a few of them, but they all ended suddenly, some in clayey earth, others in a kind of black rock. I suppose they were abandoned when the veins petered out."

"Where does this particular tunnel lead?" Hugh was conscious of a vague feeling of uneasiness as he put the question. "We must have travelled a fairly good distance—though the air is fresh enough. Where are we?"

"You'll see in a few minutes," the detective parried, at the same time half turning and throwing a smiling glance at Hugh.

Ever since they had entered the tunnel Hugh had noticed that the ground had been sloping gently upwards. Now, however, the tunnel took a steeper incline. Presently Renshaw paused and pointed to a roughly drawn arrow, chalked on the rock at the entrance to another side passage.

"I put that there so that I shouldn't miss my way," he explained. "We turn off here."

A dozen paces in this new direction, and Hugh was conscious of a strong current of air blowing in his face. The dank smell of moist earth assailed his nostrils. Involuntarily he slackened his pace.

"Where are you taking me?" he asked again.

The man with the lamp walked on without replying. Hugh raised his voice slightly.

"I will not go another step until I have an answer. For the last time—where am I?"

"At the end of your journey, Dr. Trenchard."

Abruptly the light was extinguished, leaving him in a darkness complete and impenetrable as that of a sealed tomb.

CHAPTER XX

HERE," SAID RENSHAW'S VOICE from the darkness, and Hugh felt himself grasped by the arm and urged gently forward. "Mind your head—the roof is very low. Round to your left, and here's what I've brought you to see."

Turning an angle formed by a buttress of smooth rock, Hugh became aware of a thin shaft of golden sunlight slanting through the blackness and falling in an irregular circle on the opposite wall of rock. By its light he perceived that he was in a tiny natural chamber. The welcome daylight, as well as the twisted roots of some large tree which partly formed, partly supported, the roof, showed that he was not far beneath the surface of the ground. The hole which admitted the ray of light was about a man's height from the floor of the cave; its outer rim was fringed with grass, and it had every appearance of being a natural rabbit-burrow.

"My observation-post," Renshaw explained, indicating the hole with a wave of his hand. "Care to have a look?"

Hugh Trenchard stepped up to the hole and peered through, and it was as much as he could do to stifle a cry of amazement at what he saw. Separated from him only by the width of the grass-bordered moorland track was his own house—Moor Lodge! Facing as it did the front right-hand angle of the house, this strange peep-hole commanded a view which included the front entrance as well as the door at the side which gave access to the garden at the rear. It was impossible for anyone to enter or leave, or even to approach the house, without being observed by a concealed watcher in the little underground cave. A single glance satisfied him on this point, and he quickly turned to the detective by his side.

"Now I understand what you meant that night when you said that you had my place under constant observation. And it also explains how you and your men managed to be on the spot so quickly after Ronnie and I entered the house. Of course you were already posted here before we arrived."

Inspector Renshaw coughed modestly.

"Well, hardly that, sir," he hastened to disclaim. "You could hardly expect me to know just when somebody was going to turn up—we've had the place under observation for weeks previous to that—ever since the day following Marle's murder, in fact; and during that time not a soul has come near the place. We only keep one man at the 'observation hole'; the rest are quartered in a cottage about two miles down the coombe—a mere hut it is. If the man on watch sees anything suspicious, or needs help at any time, he just flashes an agreed signal from the mouth of the cave overlooking the valley. Of course, all this is in confidence, sir."

"You may rely on my discretion, Inspector," Hugh assured him. "I shan't mention your very ingenious arrangements to a soul—with the exception, maybe, of my close friend Dr. Brewster—"

"Not to *anybody*, if it's all the same to you, sir," said Renshaw quickly. "My experience teaches me that, no matter how clever an actor may be, he always acts most convincingly when he thinks he is speaking the truth, and it is of the utmost importance to my plans that everything should go on at Moor Lodge in exactly the same manner as if it were not under observation. That is most important."

"Very well, Inspector. I will keep my own counsel. By the way," Hugh added suddenly, "were you watching the house last night?"

"Naturally." The inspector smiled slightly. "I saw you come into the garden from the direction of the rear of the house and meet Miss Endean, and I saw you both enter by the front door. But I will admit that I didn't notice you leave the house in the first place."

"No, you wouldn't!" said Hugh grimly. "I made my exit head first through the back upstairs window!" And in a few words he told him of the attempted hold-up by Professor Felger.

"That must have been the shot I heard just before I saw you," Renshaw said musingly when he had finished. "I thought it sounded too faint to have come from the house itself. But I'll take my oath that nobody entered the house by either door."

Hugh Trenchard slapped his knee triumphantly.

"Just as I thought—there's a secret door somewhere!"

"Maybe," said the detective, slowly stroking his military moustache. "Maybe . . ."

"How about making a thorough exploration of this old mine to see if any of the side passages lead directly beneath the house?"

Inspector Renshaw hailed the suggestion with enthusiasm.

"That's a good idea, sir I'll signal for my men, and we'll make a search without delay. It'll be a longish job, for this mine is as complicated as a maze once you quit the main galleries. The only way you can find your way about is to take a ball of twine, and unwind it as you enter and follow the line back in order to get out again. You might wander for days if you lost your bearings. But you may rely on us to go over it with a fine-tooth comb." There was a short pause, during which Renshaw remained deep in thought. "Curious that you should have mentioned the possibility of someone else using the mine besides us," he remarked presently. "If it's true it explains something that has puzzled me more than a little."

"And what is that?"

"When we first found this place we saw signs that there had been swarms of rabbits here pretty recently—our observation-hole was one of their burrows—but since then we've not caught sight of a single, solitary one."

Hugh murmured a perfunctory agreement, although in his own mind he did not attach much importance to this sudden migration; it was, he thought, far more likely that the advent of Inspector Renshaw himself had caused the rabbits to seek fresh fields and pastures new. That, however, was an unimportant detail; the great outstanding fact was the comforting knowledge that Moor Lodge, instead of being lonely and isolated, was watched and guarded far better than the average suburban villa.

When, soon afterwards, Hugh took his departure, he had a much enhanced opinion of the capabilities of the man from Scotland Yard. That morning he had fully made up his mind to lose no time in transferring the precious sealed envelope to the vaults of a safe deposit company in London; now, however, he was quite content to allow it to remain in the ingenious chemical-guarded safe that had been devised by Silas Marle. His mind was pleasantly at ease when, after having eaten a solitary cold lunch, he locked the door of Moor Lodge and set off to walk to Excombe.

In passing he threw a keen glance in the direction of Renshaw's observation-post. It must lie, he decided, beneath that low grassy bank, overshadowed by the spreading branches of two dwarf oak trees. There were several rabbit-holes visible on the slope of the bank, but it was quite impossible to tell which one was being used by the hidden watcher. With a cheery but unobtrusive wave of his walking-stick, Hugh turned into the path which struck across the moor.

His first step was to call on Mr. Andrew Shale. Making his way along the straggling High Street, with its quaintly blended mixture of ancient and modern architecture, he halted before a double-fronted Georgian house whose rounded bay-windows were half covered with old-fashioned wire blinds bearing the legend, in letters of faded gilt, "Shale and Shale, Solicitors and Commissioners for Oaths". He presented his card to the clerk in the outer office, and was soon ushered into the inner sanctum. The lawyer advanced to meet him as he entered, and Hugh could not help being struck by the unusual warmth of the old man's greeting.

"Good morning, Dr. Trenchard. This is indeed an unexpected pleasure. Take a chair, my dear sir, take a chair. Your visit is most opportune—a most fortunate coincidence. I had intended to drive over and see you this very afternoon about a little matter that has cropped up with regard to Moor Lodge, but you have saved me that journey."

Hugh was conscious of a vague feeling of uneasiness.

"I hope there's no flaw in my inheritance," he questioned.

"Oh, not at all, not at all! Your title is sound enough in that respect—unless, of course, Silas Marle should suddenly turn up and claim his property." Andrew Shale gave the ghost of a dry smile, as though at some hidden joke. "No, sir, you may rest easy on that score; the business I had in mind will be to your advantage rather than otherwise. But that can wait for the moment, for I presume you have come here to consult me on business of your own."

At this hint, Hugh immediately plunged into the matter that had brought him there. The solicitor listened without speaking until he had finished, then nodded his grey head and again smiled genially.

"Of course, my dear sir, of course," he said. "You really need not have troubled to come personally about such a trifling matter. I intended to make it clear at our last meeting that you might draw on me for any reasonable amount of ready money. It is true that the legal formalities, which will result in the handing over to you of Mr. Marle's large bank balance, have not yet been completed, but to all intents and purposes it is at your disposal. But it would be advisable for you to regard me as your banker for the time being." He opened a drawer and produced an imposing cheque-book. "Just tell me how much you require."

"It's rather a large sum." Hugh hesitated. "You see, I must have a car if I'm to live in such an isolated place, and a car will mean a garage being built adjoining the house. I don't mean the ordinary type of garage, with brick walls and slate roof, but one specially planned to harmonize with the exterior of the old house—oak half-timbering, and weathered red tiles, and so forth. I shall have to consult an architect before I can tell you how much that will cost."

"H'm," purred the lawyer, thoughtfully stroking his grey sidewhisker. "You need have no fear about the money not being forthcoming, Dr. Trenchard, but you may not need that garage after all."

"What do you mean?"

Andrew Shale opened a box-file and selected a letter.

"This morning I received a communication from a firm which styles itself 'The Country Hotel Development Syndicate'. Apparently it is a company that has been newly formed with the object of acquiring genuine old houses situated amid pleasant and picturesque surroundings, and turning them into small residential hotels, while preserving their original old-world interest and comfort. You will perceive that they have made a very tempting offer for Moor Lodge."

He pushed the letter across the desk as he spoke. Hugh Trenchard looked at the figure and gasped. In his wildest dreams he had never imagined that the property could be worth one quarter of the huge sum which, quoted in figures and again in bracketed words to avoid the possibility of mistake, stared him in the face from the neatly typed sheet. As he looked, he felt an indefinite but profound suspicion forming in his mind.

"Do you know anything about this 'Country Development Syndicate'?" he asked, and the lawyer shrugged.

"I have already explained that it is a newly formed company, but their finances are sound enough. Their bankers' reference is unassailable. If I might venture to advise you, sir, I think it would be a sound policy to close with the offer at once. It is a very tempting proposition."

"It's far more than the place is worth," Hugh objected.

"That is their look-out; they have offered the money, and this signed letter constitutes a legal contract from which they cannot withdraw without your consent. After all, value in house property is a very elastic term. A residence which would have a merely nominal value to a private individual like yourself might appear very different to the directors of a syndicate anxious to develop it on novel and money-making lines."

"I'll think it over," said Hugh, rising to his feet.

Andrew Shale's grey brows flashed upward in an expression of deprecatory amazement.

"I don't see that it requires much thought, Dr. Trenchard. Most people would jump at such a tempting offer."

"It's a jolly sight too tempting, Mr. Shale, and that's what makes me suspicious."

The genial smile had vanished from Shale's face, and he was biting his under-lip in unconcealed disappointment.

"I am only an intermediary in this matter, and it concerns me very little whether you decide one way or the other," he said with a belated pretence of indifference. "But I really fail to see your motive in declining to sell. Is it that you have taken a fancy to living in the neighbourhood of the moor? If so, there are plots of land to be acquired on the outskirts of this town, and the proceeds of the sale of Moor Lodge would cover the cost of the erection of an up-to-date bungalow, complete with garage, and leave a very handsome balance into the bargain."

But Hugh shuddered inwardly. "An up-to-date bungalow!" he thought.

"I'll think it over," he said aloud, adding: "May I take this letter with me?"

"Certainly—I have already filed a copy for reference. But pray take care of it," he went on anxiously, "for it will come in useful if they try to back out of their offer."

There was rather a grim smile on Hugh Trenchard's face as he placed the letter in his wallet and crossed to the door.

"I don't anticipate any desire to back out on their part," he said quietly. "Good afternoon, Mr. Shale."

A brisk ten minutes' walk brought him to Ronnie's surgery, where he discovered that far from hard-worked young man indulging in an after-dinner siesta. He listened with lazy indifference while Hugh told him of the amazing offer he had received, and at the conclusion expressed his opinion of his chum's business capabilities in terms which left nothing to the imagination.

"Well, of all the unmitigated asses!" he exclaimed contemptuously. "Why, in the name of the Marble Arch, didn't you jump to it with both feet? I only wish some misguided philanthropist would offer a tenth of the money for this old shack, then my economizing days would be over for good! You surely don't mean to say that you're going to turn down the offer of this—this—what do they call themselves?"

Hugh drew the letter from his wallet.

"The Country Hotel Development Syndicate," he informed as he read the engraved heading. "And the offer is signed by a certain Clive Marchmount."

He had merely glanced casually at the signature as he spoke, but now a strange sense of familiarity about the neat writing thrust itself into his mind. He looked closer, and then, moved by a sudden impulse, drew from his wallet the letter of assignation which had led to his exciting adventure at the Devil's Cheesepress. Placing them side by side, he compared the writing, then sat back with a gasp, his heart hammering against his ribs, his eyes snapping with excitement.

Line for line, curve for curve, the handwriting was identical. The magnificent offer for the purchase of Moor Lodge had been signed by the same hand that had penned the note that had lured him to the midnight ambush in the Valley of Rocks!

Thrusting the two letters back in his wallet, he rose to his feet and faced his friend.

"Care to come and help me choose a car and see about the erection of a garage at Moor Lodge?" he queried of the astonished Ronnie. "I intend to stick to that house like a limpet, and to play the game through to the end!"

CHAPTER XXI

THE ARCHITECT on whom Hugh Trenchard's random choice alighted proved to be the very man for the job. He was young, enthusiastic, and energetic; moreover, he had made a hobby of the study of the domestic architecture of the past, and Hugh's unexpected commission came to him as a heaven-sent opportunity for the display of his specialized knowledge. He lost no time in visiting Moor Lodge and preparing a scale plan of the front elevation, and from this he succeeded in evolving a garage-annexe which so harmonized with the prevailing style that—on paper at any rate—it seemed part of the original structure.

By a lucky chance there happened to be a row of four sixteenth-century cottages in the little market-town, and these the landlord had allowed to fall into a state of dilapidation because the Town Council had failed to adopt the Town Planning scheme and had thus not been in a position to prevent him from selling the site to a firm of chain stores. Having netted so much profit, this landlord was willing to sell the building material for a very modest sum. Provided with this lucky windfall of antique oak beams, ready-weathered handmade bricks and tiles, to say nothing of the pick of the blown-glass leaded windows, the architect mobilized his brick-layers and labourers and set them to work.

Instead of inviting the usual tenders from building contractors, he superintended the job himself with the zest of a man whose heart was in his work. The result was a perfect gem of correct period craftsmanship, which subsequently figured in a supplementary coloured plate in one of the leading journals devoted to practical architecture, and was incidentally the means of introducing this budding genius to more ambitious things.

The question of the car was settled even more speedily, and the venerable bricks and timbers that had sheltered generations of ploughmen and farm labourers for four hundred years now found themselves sheltering a monster of shining enamel and gleaming metal. It was, in short, a six-cylinder sports model with a torpedo-pattern body, and capable of a speed that was never likely to be attained outside a racing-track.

During the two weeks when the solitude of his moorland home had been invaded by a gang of workmen, and its deep silence broken by the noise of saw and hammer and the ring of bricklayers' trowels, Hugh Trenchard had seen nothing of Joan Endean. In vain he hung about the empty house in Excombe, where he had talked with her when she had appeared so effectively disguised; he even took to calling at Ronnie's surgery, at such times as he knew his friend would be absent visiting his patients, and from the front windows ogling the windows of the mysterious house through a pair of field-glasses. But she might have completely vanished off the face of the earth for all he could see of her. Coming out of the vastness of the lonely waste of bog, bracken, and frowning crags of granite, passing through his life for a brief space like a storm-driven wraith, it seemed almost as if the desolate moor, which had brought her to him, had again taken her to its broad, mysterious bosom and had claimed her for its own.

As the weeks glided by, Hugh Trenchard, needless to say, kept his eyes and ears open for signs of fresh activity on the part of the horned apparition which Silas Marle had graphically dubbed "The Terror of the Moor"; but it was through the medium of the local Press that he received the first news of the elusive monster's reappearance. He was seated in the sitting-room of Moor Lodge, idly glancing through the pages of the weekly newspaper, which maintained a somewhat sluggish circulation through the district, when, wedged between the report of a local cattle sale and a description of a new type of reaping-machine, his eye lighted on a paragraph which brought him to his feet with tingling pulses. It bore a double heading:

STRANGE STORY FROM GUPWORTHY

WELL-KNOWN FARMER ATTACKED BY FEROCIOUS BEAST

An alarming and in some respects mysterious occurrence took place on the Excombe Road, near Gupworthy, at a late hour last night. Mr. John Thacker, of Uphill Farm, Gupworthy (a familiar and much-respected figure in local agricultural circles), was in the act of returning to his home after having attended Excombe market. Accompanied by one of his drovers, an elderly man named Amos Yokes, he set out from Excombe shortly after 10 p.m., and, whilst passing over the extensive stretch of uncultivated ground commonly known as Gallows

Heath, he was surprised to hear a voice, apparently coming from a dense clump of bushes, calling on him to halt. Thinking the cry emanated from some wayfarer who had met with an accident and was in need of assistance, Mr. Thacker immediately turned his horse in the direction of the voice.

We have been unable to ascertain with any degree of exactitude what subsequently transpired, but our representative gathered, from the brief statement that Mr. Thacker was able to give him, that he found himself confronted by the figure of a naked or half-naked man, who, he states, appeared to be riding on the back of a large stag. Mr. Amos Yokes, however, who seems to have had a better view of this unexpected sight, steadfastly adheres to his statement that the unclothed man was not riding on the back of the stag, but actually formed part of the animal itself; to quote his own expressive words, "the gashly thing were half-and-half".

While not committing ourselves by expressing an opinion as to the accuracy of the impression afforded by Mr. Vokes's admittedly hurried glimpse in the uncertain light, we regret to state that the injuries sustained by both men leave no doubt that the unknown made a violent and murderous attack on the two defenceless men, though happily the injuries of neither are likely to prove fatal.

Sergeant Jopling, our popular and energetic representative of the County Constabulary, was promptly on the scene, and we have been given to understand that there is every possibility of an early arrest being effected in connection with the matter.

Meanwhile the fact of such a thing being at large on the moor has given rise to a feeling of uneasiness among the dwellers in this sparsely populated district.

Although the local scribe had infused a fair amount of caution—not to say scepticism—into his work, Hugh Trenchard's own experience enabled him to supply the gaps fairly vividly. But he was determined to know more, and ten minutes after his eye had lighted on the headline he was seated at the wheel of his new car, speeding to the scene of the affray.

Gallows Heath was an undulating shoulder of ground covered for the most part in knee-high brake-fern and on slightly higher elevation than the rest of the moor. At a spot just before the narrow ribbon of road dipped out of sight over the farther slope, a few slabs of moss-grown stone still remained to mark the gallows themselves.

Hugh did not have a long search before finding the exact spot where Thacker and his drover had been attacked, for there was but one clump of bushes large enough to conceal a man. This was situated on the opposite side of the road to the site of the ancient gallows, and in the dense shade of the overhanging boughs the ground was as soft and plastic as the keenest amateur detective could desire. Footprints were there in plenty—but they were not the ones that Hugh Trenchard was anxious to see. The date of the paper had told him that four days had elapsed since the affray had taken place, and during that time the place had been overrun by scores of curious sightseers, and such tracks as may have been left by the Terror had been hopelessly obliterated.

Hugh gave one long, searching look at the ground, then, with a resigned shrug, turned and re-entered his car. He was scarcely surprised at drawing a blank; but he hoped to learn something from the two injured men, provided that they were sufficiently recovered to grant him an interview. He started the car and coasted down the inclined road which pointed straight to the distant cluster of houses which indicated Gupworthy.

He had fully expected to find the two victims in their beds, or at the best reclining in easy chairs; but his knock on the door of Uphill Farm brought a buxom, rosy-cheeked lass who, in the slow, burring dialect of the Devon and Somerset border, informed him that "Maister be up-along at poun-'ouse."

"And where may that be?" asked the frankly puzzled Hugh.

"The poun-'ouse be the wring-'ouse," she explained with the air of one imparting the fullest possible explanation.

"Wring-house? I fear I'm very ignorant, but—"

"That be the place weer they presses the apples for zider, zur."

A light broke on Hugh. "Oh, the cider-press? And how do I get there?"

"Coom wi' me and I'll show 'ee. Tain't var away, zur."

Hugh followed the girl through the house and out into a wide stone-paved yard lined on either side with thatched byres and stables, and having a large pump in the centre. Hugh could not help noticing the fact that the place appeared unusually silent and deserted, and he made a remark to that effect; but his guide explained that "it weer apple-harvest toime", and everybody except herself was either in the orchards helping to gather in the fruit, or in the wring-house engaged in turning the apples into cider.

The cider-house was an ancient and somewhat dilapidated structure standing about fifty yards from the farmhouse. Against one wall was heaped a very mountain of russet-hued fruit, a mountain whose bulk never diminished, in spite of the efforts of the two brawny labourers who were engaged in shovelling the apples through a square aperture which led to the hopper of the crushing-mill inside; for as fast as they shovelled, a constant stream of men, women, boys, and girls kept up the supply from their brimming baskets.

Stepping inside, Hugh Trenchard became aware of a scene of old-world rustic picturesqueness that would call for the brush of a Morland or Crome to do it justice. The greater part of the rambling building was wrapped in deep, umberous shadow, but here and there broad shafts of the mellow October sunshine slanted through the unglazed windows, throwing random splashes of light and colour which, however, only served to deepen the dusky mystery of the surrounding gloom. The air was fragrant with the sweet, penetrating odour which arose from the fermenting cider that was stored in the long row of shadowy vats which stood along one wall. In the centre was the grinding-mill, a huge, primitive contrivance with great iron cog-wheels, red with rust except on the actual working parts, and grinding-rollers of ponderous stone, beneath whose slow revolutions there seethed and squelched the pulpy mass which would eventually become the clear, sparkling beverage that has been termed, not inaptly, 'the champagne of England'. A little apart, a sober old cart-horse ceaselessly trudged his slow, circling path, communicating the necessary motion to the pulping-gear.

At Hugh's entry, a hale, weather-beaten old man glanced round from his task of lubricating the moving machinery.

"A ge'man to see 'ee, Varther," the girl announced, and immediately hurried back to her interrupted duties.

Farmer Thacker at once laid down the oil-can, wiped his hands on a wisp of straw, and advanced to Hugh.

"Good marnin', zur. What moight 'ee be wantin' wi' I?" he inquired with rough civility.

Hugh kept his eyes on the old man as he proceeded to explain the object of his visit. Save for the large patch of court plaster on his forehead, Farmer Thacker showed but little signs of his recent encounter with the Terror of the Moor. But the trained eye of the young doctor noticed an unusual sluggishness in his movements, and the eyes which were peering at him from beneath the shaggy grey brows were abnormally dull and vacant. When Hugh had finished speaking the old man stared at him for a few moments, then passed his hand across his brow in a bewildered and helpless manner.

"I dunno as how I can tell 'ee over-much, zur," he said slowly. "Ever since that night I feels all mazed and witless."

"What was it that attacked you?"

"Can't rightly zay, zur," replied Thacker, shaking his head.

"Was it a man?"

"Belike it weer—I couldn't rightly zee. Theer warn't no moon that night, zur, just a zort o' dimpsy-light from the stars."

"But you told Sergeant Jopling that you heard some words spoken," Hugh persisted, more than a little puzzled at the man's vague manner.

"Ay, you'm right theer, zur. I hears 'un, speakin' same's you or me. But when he coomed out from the clutter o' bushes I sees . . ."

Thacker stopped dead, and again passed his hand across his forehead.

"Yes?" Hugh prompted eagerly.

"I—I doan seem to mind what happened then. My brain seems dazed an' dead-loike."

Suddenly Hugh leant forward, his eyes fixed on the upper portion of the old man's arm which showed below his rolled-up shirtsleeve. Showing red and angry against the sun-tanned skin were several marks which Hugh immediately recognized as the punctures made by a recently used hypodermic syringe.

"Who has been giving you injections?" he asked sharply, all his vague suspicions crystallizing in an instant into one staggering fact. It was clear by the old man's expression that he did not understand; so Hugh repeated his question in a simpler form:

"What doctor attended to your injuries, Mr. Thacker?"

"Theer weer two on 'em as happened to be passin' a'most the same time as I got backalong home to the varm, and they weer kind enow to see to my hurts and those of my man Amos."

"Humph! Their arrival was very fortunate!" was Hugh's somewhat dry comment. "And did these kind gentlemen prick your arm?"

"Iss, fay," said the old man, nodding, "and they stucked needle into me every time they called since then. It tooked away the pain voine."

"I dare say it did," Hugh muttered, his eyes hardening to points of steel. "And what were the names of these good fellows?"

Thacker shook his head.

"They didn't zay, zur. But my gal said that she recognized one of 'em. She said he lived at the big house beyond Worplecombe and that his name was Dr. Felger."

"Felger?" Hugh jerked out the exclamation in a gasp. "The devil!"

"I fear you exaggerate, my dear Dr. Trenchard," said a smooth voice behind him, and, swinging round, he saw for the first time the face of his elusive enemy.

CHAPTER XXII

THE NEW-COMER had removed his hat with a sweeping bow as he had uttered his cynical greeting, and now stood bare-headed in the full glare of a shaft of sunlight which illumi-nated his face with the intensity of a theatrical spotlight, rendering each feature clear and distinct. There was no sign of furtiveness in Professor Felger's manner now; on the contrary, the position he had taken and the attitude he had assumed both seemed indicative of mocking defiance, as though he were inviting Hugh Trenchard to examine the features which he had till then kept carefully con-cealed.

Hugh, on his part, was not slow to take advantage of the oppor-tunity, and as he looked he realized, with secret satisfaction, that the personal appearance of the Austrian scientist was striking enough to be easily remembered. Slightly above the average height, his well-proportioned body hinted at the litheness of a pan-ther rather than the possession of great strength. His age was diffi-cult to guess, for the almost blue-black hue of his hair and beard was suggestive of the use of dye. His complexion was so sallow that Hugh mentally decided that he must either be in very poor health or else have a strong strain of Eastern blood in his veins. His hair, which was plentiful, was brushed straight back from a decided point in the centre of his forehead, and this, combined with his short pointed beard and upturned, waxed moustaches, gave him an aspect that was startlingly Mephistophelian. There was a look of sardonic amusement in the pale eyes which, keen as spear-points, challenged Hugh's from beneath the oblique brows.

There ensued a long pause, during which the eyes of the two men met, watchful and challenging as two duellists awaiting the first clash of steel. Then Professor Felger, replacing his hat with a slow, sweeping movement of his hand, broke the tense silence.

"It would seem that my presence here gives you some surprise, Dr. Trenchard," he murmured, and once again Hugh was aware of the note of mockery hidden in the silky tones.

"On the contrary," he returned steadily, looking the other full in the face, "considering the curious nature of Mr. Thacker's symptoms, your presence here seems the most natural thing in the world."

Professor Felger's jet-black brows flickered upward, and a slow smile curved his bearded lips.

"Symptoms?"—he repeated the word with an air of amiable tolerance. "You speak with the air of one who has discovered a— how do you call it?—a—a nest of a mare. So you have observed his symptoms, *hein?*"

"I have," Hugh said grimly, "all of them!"

"So?" Felger's manner expressed no more than a polite and gratified interest as he went on: "Truly it is touching to see a novice in medical science evince such an interest in an unfortunate sufferer—especially when that sufferer happens to be under the care of another medical man. But I have yet to learn that it is recognized English medical etiquette for one doctor to interfere with the patient of another. You see, I am but a stranger in your so-excellent country, and I should be obliged if you will be kind enough to enlighten my ignorance on that point, Dr. Trenchard."

"I will do more, sir," Hugh cried, stung into sudden anger by the scarcely veiled insult. "I will enlighten your ignorance on a point of law. It is an indictable offence for an alien doctor to practise in the so-excellent country of his adoption (as you term it), especially when such practice includes the injection of drugs which do not figure in the British Pharmacopoeia."

Hugh had expected his words to be greeted with an outburst of fury, but Felger merely laughed.

"Ah, that is a very wise provision on the part of your lawmakers," he said in a tone of hearty agreement, "but in this case their edicts have not been violated in the least degree. Mr. John Thacker is not *my* patient—I have no more interest in his case than, say, a friendly and disinterested inquirer like yourself. My excellent colleague, Dr. Nathaniel Mutley, is in sole charge of the case, and I feel sure that such an old and experienced practitioner would not inject anything except the recognized palliatives, or maybe a—ah—narcotic to soothe pain."

Before answering, Hugh glanced at the old farmer, who had been listening open-mouthed. Luckily the conversation had so far been as unintelligible as so much Greek to his simple understanding, but now Hugh had something to say that was for Felger's ears alone.

"I should like a word with you in private," he said to Felger.

"By all means—a thousand if you wish." The professor turned to the gaping farmer and gracefully raised his hat. "Good morning, Mr. Thacker. I am delighted to see you so hale and active. Allow me to congratulate you on such a rapid and complete recovery from your injuries. Good morning." And, after shaking the old man heartily by the hand, he followed Hugh out into the deserted farmyard. Once outside, however, he cast a keen, lightning glance at the young man's face.

"If you are so desirous of a private interview with me, why not call at the sanatorium?" he asked suavely. "There would be no risk there of our talk being overheard, and we would be quite safe from interruption."

"I dare say we should," Hugh commented, a hint of dryness in his voice, "but I prefer to say what I've got to say here and now."

"As you please," shrugged the other and waited.

And there, amid the drowsy peace of that old-world rustic scene, his voice accompanied by the country sounds of a sunny October afternoon, Hugh Trenchard spoke of life and death . . . and of a thing worse than death.

"Have you ever heard of the Apple of Lethe?" was his first question.

Felger repeated the question slowly, then shook his head.

"I am afraid my Greek mythology must be somewhat rusty," he said with an apologetic shrug. "I can only remember the *Waters* of Lethe, the river of forgetfulness in the classical Hades, of which the spirits drank before entering Elysium. But I certainly have no recollection of an *Apple* of Lethe."

"I will refresh your memory by calling it by its modern botanical name," said Hugh. "Does *Datura obliterare* suggest anything to you?"

"No!" Felger jerked out the denial with a cold, rasping ring.

"Then at the risk of boring you, I will explain," Hugh went on calmly. *"Datura obliterare* is a rare species of the genus of plants which are classed under the general name of *Solanaceae*. A very curious feature of this widely distributed order is that some varieties yield valuable food products, some have a recognized medicinal value, while others are powerful narcotic poisons. Stranger still, some varieties have certain parts with poisonous properties, while other parts of the same plant are innocuous."

"All this is very interesting, no doubt," interrupted the other impatiently. "And I congratulate you on your detailed knowledge, but—"

"You can cut out the congratulations for the present, and just listen. The peculiar properties of the *Datura* group have long been recognized. In India the seeds of the *Datura fastuosa* have been employed from time immemorial by thieves and other criminals; the Peruvians prepare a delirium-producing beverage from the seeds of *Datura sanguinea;* while in China a tincture of *Datura stramonium* is voluntarily swallowed by its devotees to induce erotic visions and hallucinations. All these, as I said, have long been known; but the most dangerous species of all was not known to scientific botanists until fairly recently. It was in 1913 that Rudolf Braüschütter—a fellow-countryman of yours, by the way—discovered a new variety growing wild on Lanzarote, a small island of the Canaries group, off the West Coast of Africa, and to this he gave the very appropriate name of *Datura obliterare.* Braüschütter, on returning to his native land, published a monograph on his find, a work that is now extremely rare owing to the amazing fact that he almost immediately suppressed it and forbade the publication of more copies. I was lucky enough to get hold of one, however, very recently, and it greatly interested me.

"The author, who seems to be an excellent all-round scientist, introduced his subject by a curious reference to the mythology of Ancient Greece. After remarking that the local name for the fruit of the newly discovered plant was a word meaning 'Apple of Lethe', he proceeded to propound the startling theory that Lanzarote, the only place where it grew, was the island described by Homer in the *Odyssey* under the name of the Island of Aeaea, where dwelt the enchantress Circe.

"Quoting from the original Greek of the ancient poem, Braüschütter went on to declare that Circe's 'charmed cup' in which were mixed 'infusing drugs' meant nothing else than an infusion of *Datura obliterate,* and the subsequent metamorphoses of the followers of the Greek hero into 'swine in head and voice, bristles and shape' was simply a poetical mode of expressing the brain-destroying properties of the drug, and the 'harmful venom' which made 'their country vanish from their thought' was but a naive way of describing the complete atrophy of the nerves of the anterior lobes of the brain which control the memory."

"Your little lecture may be very interesting to one interested in fairy-tales, ancient or modern, but I can scarcely see the point of your inflicting it on me," Felger burst out angrily.

"Wait! The point will soon be plain enough. Herr Braüschütter described the outward symptoms which follow the injection of his new drug, and those symptoms coincide in every respect with those of the men you and your partner have been attending! Dr. Felger, why have you gone to so much trouble to ensure the silence of the only men who could describe the appearance of the monster that is known as the Terror of the Moor?"

Felger had anticipated the accusation, and had braced himself to meet it. As Hugh's scathing words rang out, the Austrian turned and stared him full in the face, and in his cold grey eyes was the fixed, baleful glare of a snake about to strike. Only his lips were smiling as he replied:

"I really can't persuade myself that you intend me to take your accusation seriously, my dear Dr. Trenchard."

"Perhaps Scotland Yard will be able to persuade you!" Hugh suggested grimly.

The professor indulged in an elaborate shrug.

"The most that Scotland Yard would do would be to listen to your story with polite interest and then dismiss you with their renowned tact."

"What if I offered them something more than airy theories—the record of Silas Marle's experiments, and the description of the Apple of Lethe from Herr Braüschütter's book?"

There was a few seconds' pause.

"The latter might be somewhat difficult to offer," Felger then said slowly. "I understand that the publication is very rarely met with nowadays."

"But I happen to have a copy," Hugh cried in quick triumph.

Professor Lucien Felger raised his hand to the brim of his soft felt hat, at the same time bending his body in a low, ironical bow.

"In that case, allow me to compliment you on your forethought—and to bid you good day."

He raised his hat as he spoke, and Hugh glimpsed a tiny metal *nozzle* pointing straight at him from the inside of the crown. Instinctively he stepped backward. But, quick as he was, the professor was a fraction of a second quicker. His hand pressed the yielding crown and a dense spray of liquid drenched Hugh's face.

He fell back, reeling, gasping, righting madly against the clinging cloud of stupefying vapour that was like a palpable but invisible hand clutching his throat. Then a curtain of darkness seemed to descend on his mind, and like a man in a dream he heard the low purring of the swift car that was bearing his exultant foe . . . whither?

Then came a sensation of being borne dizzily downward in a lift that had no end, and then he remembered no more.

CHAPTER XXIII

HUGH TRENCHARD'S MIND was still spinning in a confused maelstrom when, after a space of utter blankness which seemed to have lasted ages, he again opened his eyes.

With a dull sense of wonder he realized that it was still day, but the light which greeted his eyes was the tempered sunshine that filtered through the drawn curtains of the window in his own bedroom at Moor Lodge. He was lying on his bed, and presently he began to speculate whether his encounter with the professor was nothing but an unpleasantly vivid dream. With a great effort of will, he reopened his eyes, and immediately came to the conclusion that he was still dreaming.

But now, he decided, his dream had taken a pleasing phase, and he devoutly hoped that it would continue. For there, seated by the table near the window, was the mystery-girl who had been ever present in his waking dreams—Joan Endean.

With a supine sense of contentment he allowed his eyes to rest on her slender girlish figure as she sat busily writing in a notebook. The sunshine behind her framed her head and threw her face into shadow so that all he could see was the nimbus of her hair and the deep surtees of contemplative eyes.

His heart swelled at the sight, but abruptly a phantasm much less pleasing to Hugh's idea of beauty intruded itself into his vision. It was his red-headed friend, Ronnie Brewster, with a medicine-glass in his hand and an anxious grin on his good-humoured but by no means handsome features.

"Behold, the wounded hero awakes!" he said dramatically. "And if the wounded hero aforesaid doesn't show more originality than to bleat out the usual 'Where am I?' as his first articulate speech, I will undo all Miss Endean's and my own good work by braining the wounded hero forthwith! Has that horrific threat trickled into your returning consciousness? Good! Then drink this."

He held the glass to Hugh's lips while he slowly sipped its contents.

"A simple prescription, and one not wholly unknown outside medical circles," Ronnie commented with another grin. "Did you like it?"

"It tasted like whisky," Hugh said slowly.

Ronnie gave a chuckle of delight and rubbed his hands.

"Capital! Capital! You haven't lost your memory, at any rate, since you are able to recognize your old friends so unerringly. Speaking of old friends—here is Miss Endean, who found you this morning roosting peacefully among the ducks and geese in old Thacker's farmyard."

He stood aside, and Joan came forward and laid her hand for an instant in Hugh's.

"You?" He looked up at her with unconcealed wonder in his eyes. "At last you have come to me?"

"Yes—and in the jolly old nick of time—just like a cinema film!" interpolated the irrepressible Ronnie. "By Jove, she must have arrived on the scene almost as if she knew that it was your turn to be sent down for the long count by that highly scientific thug—for I naturally assume it was either Felger or his amiable myrmidons who downed you."

Hugh struggled to rise as recollection came back.

"It was!" he muttered fiercely. "He squirted some fluid in my face—"

" 'And the subsequent proceedings interested you no more'?" quoted Ronnie. "But whatever made him do a thing like that? You—you didn't try to arrest him or anything?"

Hugh shook his head and immediately went on to give an outline of what had occurred. At the conclusion Ronnie's customary smile appeared a trifle twisted.

"Holy smoke! The mystery is getting more turbid and sticky than ever!" he exclaimed. "Gosh! I only wish to whiskers that I could get the chance to inject a little of that Apple-of-Lethe tincture into some of my creditors and make them forget what I owe 'em! That stuff would be worth a guinea a drop to me!"

"Oh, for goodness' sake try to be serious for once in your life," Hugh expostulated, but his friend only shook a grinning head at him.

"I couldn't, old bean. It 'ud take a major operation, to eradicate my sense of humour. But I will relieve you of my exhilarating presence by departing—I am sure you and your fair rescuer will have a lot of things to talk over, and I should not like to spoil the interview with my ribald comments. Ta-ta for the present. Just ring the bell when you feel you'd like the prescription repeated."

During the long silence which ensued after Ronnie had made his laughing exit, Hugh glanced at the girl once or twice out of the corner of his eye, and the look which he surprised in her eyes sent his pulses racing. Her eyes had only met his for the merest fraction of a second, but in that second a miracle seemed to have happened. Did she love him? The sudden realization that this might be so was like a breath of pure oxygen to a suffocating man; it inflamed him with an overwhelming longing to take her in his arms, to tell her of his own love; to leap, as it were, the dark gulf which stretched between them and force from those sweet lips the true explanation of the mystery that surrounded her life.

But he had the good sense to recognize that this was scarcely the time or place for such an avowal. He schooled his voice to a casual tone when at length he spoke:

"So you too paid a visit to Thacker's farm this morning? Was that due to mere curiosity on your part or—something else?"

"Idle curiosity is a luxury that is denied to such as I." The smile which accompanied her words held a suspicion of grimness. "To be quite frank, I went there for the same purpose as you did—to get Thacker's story of the Terror of the Moor. As I approached the side road which leads to the farm, a car was driven past me at full speed and I was forced to crouch into the hedge at the side of the lane to avoid being run down. I caught but a fleeting glance of the driver, but it was enough to enable me to recognize Professor Felger. He was crouched over the steering-wheel, his eyes glaring straight ahead, and the expression on his features was simply diabolical. I at once suspected that something was wrong, and hurried up the lane and went straight through to the yard—and there I found you. Two of the farmhands carried you to your car; I drove you back here, calling for Dr. Brewster on the way, and—and that's all there is to tell."

"Scarcely all," smiled Hugh, shaking his head. "There still seems to be quite a lot of things to explain."

She slowly raised her head, and he saw that her expression was almost defiant.

"What sort of things are they that need explaining?" she asked coldly.

"Oh, all sorts of things," he returned, endeavouring to speak lightly. "About yourself, for instance—"

"Please leave me out of it." She seemed to catch her breath as she spoke, uttering the words so low that he could scarcely hear them.

"I can't leave you out of it. As far as I'm concerned you are the central and most attractive figure in the whole of this ghastly business. Forgive me if I pursue the matter, but—is your name really Joan Endean?"

He saw the fingers of her clasped hands writhe together and a tinge of deeper red creep up her smooth throat and burn in her cheeks.

"My—my name is Joan."

"Endean?" He put the query in a low voice, at the same time taking her hand in his.

"That is an alias." The girl laughed with an assumption of defiant abandon which, however, did not for a moment deceive the keen-eyed Hugh Trenchard. "Oh, there's nothing to be surprised at in that. Every suspicious character, such as I, uses an alias."

She made to withdraw her hand, but he grasped it tighter as he went on.

"You may be mysterious, but not suspicious, at least not to me," he said tenderly. "I don't want you to talk, if you feel you can't, my dear. But—won't you trust me?"

It was several breathless seconds before she spoke, and in her voice was a wistful note that set his pulses racing anew.

"You're really rather a lamb." She sighed, her eyes still glistening and tender. "You see, I can't tell you anything yet. Who I am, what I am, and my mission are secrets which really are not mine to tell. I'm afraid I'm not giving candour for candour but"—she bent over him impulsively—"won't you be generous and trust me a little longer?"

Her lips hovered over his, and he strove to say something, but a huskiness rose in his throat instead. He reached out his arms and found himself holding her with her lips against his cheek. And thus they rested, scarcely breathing.

At length she disengaged herself and smoothed her ruffled hair.

"Am I to regard your extraordinary conduct as a symptom of relapse, or an indication of complete recovery?" she asked severely, though her eyes were dancing. "If your medical adviser—"

"If you mean Ronnie, you may tell my medical adviser to go to blazes," Hugh cried with a laugh. "Or—stop!—tell him that his patient never felt so blithe and gay in all his life, and that he'll be up and dressed in about three minutes from now."

A wild feeling of elation filled Hugh's mind when the girl had left the room. The memory of her so recently in his arms seemed to tinge his whole mental outlook with an alluring, rose-tinted hue, and if for an instant there obtruded through that rosy dream the vision of a horned head with baleful, leering eyes of luminous green, it was not sufficiently distinct to abate one jot of his new-found happiness. Joan was his! The unravelling of the mystery of the Terror could wait. Thus ran his thoughts as he hastily dressed, with the dark hand of impending catastrophe casting not the faintest shadow of its coming on his care-free mind.

"Well, old bean, what's the next jolly old move in your duel of wits with the professor?" drawled Ronnie as Hugh entered the library. "This affair reminds me of nothing so much as a game of blindfold chess—you know, the game where both players are unable to see the board and have to keep in mind both their own and their opponent's moves, as well as the position of every piece on the board. It's a nice, brainy pastime, but a trifle too slow for my liking. I prefer a game with a bit more dash in it."

"Before long there will be enough 'dash' in this particular game to satisfy your craving for excitement," said Hugh, "and it is not so much a blindfold game as you imagine. At least I have seen the face of Professor Felger, and after what happened this morning I have grounds on which to prefer a definite charge against him."

Ronnie Brewster indulged in a contemptuous grimace.

"Yes—a charge of assault and battery, with yourself as the only witness! Even if you proved your case, which is very doubtful, what good would it do to get Felger fined forty bob, or even a few days in gaol? No, old chap, you must wait till you have a bigger charge against him than that. You said just now that you had seen his face; well, I've gone one better than you. I've snapped his face."

"Snapped his face?" Hugh shook his head with a puzzled expression. "Is that a riddle?"

"Not on your life. I mean I've snapped his face with a camera." Ronnie lit a cigarette and puffed it with an air of supreme satisfaction. "It happened like this. I was passing the gates of the Excombe Sanatorium yesterday, when who should come out but a tall, black-bearded guy who looked like the Devil in mufti!"

"That was the professor!" Hugh burst out with some excitement.

"Just what I thought myself at the time, dear boy, and I thanked my lucky stars that I had my camera with me. I stepped up to him, raised my hat politely, and asked to be directed to a village on the farther side of the moor. I fear I must have appeared very dull, for he had to explain the route to me twice before I seemed to assimilate the information, and during that time I managed to press the button twice, and got two lovely photos—full-face and profile— without the professor being any the wiser. Here are the enlarged prints"; and he laid two unmounted photographs on the table.

Hugh seized on them eagerly.

"Excellent! The authorities at Scotland Yard will be delighted to get these."

"I dare say they will, but they're not going to get them," Ronnie responded dryly. "I didn't go to all that trouble to help some flat-footed copper get promotion; I intend to have some fun on my own before I let the police in on this. How would you say the professor's height compares with mine?" he asked, apparently going off at a tangent.

Hugh cast a critical eye over the proportions of his chum.

"About the same, as nearly as I can remember."

"Good! And the build?"

"Also about the same. But what is the idea?"

"See here," Ronnie took up the photographs and held them so that his fingers covered the hair and beard of each. "I'm not trying to shower bouquets on myself, but I think you'll agree that at a casual glance those features are not widely different from my own. With a cleverly made wig and beard and a touch of black grease-paint on my eyebrows, I wouldn't make a bad impersonation of Professor Lucien Felger. At any rate I intend to have a shot at it. I've been complimented on my amateur acting on more than one occasion, as you yourself will admit, and I flatter myself I could keep my end up as far as the voice and foreign accent were concerned. I'm going to start rehearsing as soon as I get back home, and I'll give you a dress rehearsal all to yourself before I make the great attempt."

Hugh looked doubtful.

"What, exactly, is your plan?"

"Haven't got more than the barest outline of one at present," Ronnie confessed with a grin. "But if I succeed in getting inside the Excombe Sanatorium without my real identity being discovered, it'll be a funny thing if I don't get hold of some evidence that will bring that infernal scoundrel's career to an abrupt termination."

Hard upon his words came a knock on the front door. Hugh glanced through the window and gave an exclamation of surprise.

"It's Inspector Renshaw of the C.I.D.," he muttered just loud enough for Ronnie to hear. "I wonder why he has taken it into his head to call."

"A Scotland Yard man?" Ronnie laid his hand on his friend's arm. "Don't breathe a word of my little stunt to him—it would spoil everything to have the police in this. They can come in afterwards to clear up the mess, but I want to have my bit of fun all to myself first."

Hugh nodded his head in token of agreement and went to admit his unexpected caller. Inspector Renshaw favoured him with a long, keen glance as he entered.

"You seem to have recovered pretty quickly from your nasty experience, sir," he observed. "What did he use—chloroform?"

"Something much more effective," Hugh returned with a rueful laugh. "But who told you of my experience?"

"Nobody." The inspector lowered his voice. "From my peep-hole I saw you being carried unconscious into the house, and I put two and two together, and surmised that you had gone to the farm to get details from the injured man. But you should have left that to us."

"Should I?" cried Hugh, with a pardonable feeling of pride. "Well, it may interest you to know that my medical knowledge has shown me something which would have escaped a layman. Thacker has been doped with a rare drug that acts on the nerve centres which control the memory. Come into the library and I will show you a monograph written by Herr Braüschütter, the scientist who discovered the rare plant from which it is prepared."

Hugh Trenchard led the way into the room as he spoke and halted opposite the shelves of books which covered one wall. He was in the act of running his eyes along the volumes, when he suddenly whirled round with a gasped question:

"Who entered this house to-day, Inspector?"

"Only Dr Brewster and yourself—and, of course, Miss Endean."

"You're sure of that?"

"Positive!"

"Then that proves my theory of the existence of a secret entry into the house," Hugh cried. "Some time within the past four hours Herr Braüschütter's monograph, which describes the action of the memory-stealing drug, has been stolen from that bookcase!"

CHAPTER XXIV

THE DETECTIVE STARED at Hugh Trenchard after he had made his startling discovery, stared at him so long and with such a curious expression on his face that Hugh felt compelled to ask for an explanation.

"What's the matter, Inspector? You look as though you only half believe me."

"Oh, I do not doubt your word in the least, sir. The book has gone—that's plain enough. But I rather think you're mistaken about there being a secret passage into this house. At any rate, if such a thing exists, I'll stake my reputation that it doesn't lead out into any of the galleries of the old mine where we have established our observation-post. Since I spoke to you last I have gone over every foot of the old workings, and I found that every passage ended up in a wall of solid rock. In future we must seek for an explanation of the mysterious happenings that go on in this house without falling back on sliding panels and suchlike romantic contraptions. And I don't think there is much hope of recovering that book. If it was stolen for the purpose you suggest, it's probably in ashes by this time. We mustn't lose sight of the main thread in this infernal tangle. We mustn't forget that Professor Felger is out to get hold of the formula of Silas Marle's secret method of causing living bodies to detonate, and that he has two ways of getting it. One is to read the contents of the sealed packet now in your safe; the other is to learn the formula from the madman who is masquerading as the Terror of the Moor."

"I see," nodded Hugh; "and your object is to prevent him accomplishing his purpose by either method?"

"Just so, sir, and I can assure you that I haven't been letting the grass grow under my feet. But the Terror has kept so quiet for the last two or three weeks that I was beginning to think he had quitted the neighbourhood until I heard of his attack on those two men on Gallows Heath. That gave me a new starting-point for the investigation, and I wasn't slow in following it up. Within an hour of receiving the news I had Nick Froude and his staghounds on the spot, and by the lively way they led off on the trail I thought we'd have an easy task in running him down. You can imagine my disgust and disappointment when the hounds finally led us to a travelling freak-show and menagerie."

"A menagerie? That was strange," Hugh mused.

"It was more unlucky than strange," said Renshaw. "Who could have anticipated meeting a wandering Noah's Ark on a place like Exmoor? Of course, no pack of hounds on earth could be trusted to run true in the face of such a variety of different scents—there were elephants, tigers, and lord knows what else in the show—maybe weasels and pole-cats, for all I know."

"To say nothing of the freaks," Hugh observed with a slight smile.

"Oh, they don't count. They're human—bearded women, living skeletons, armless wonders, and people like that. I thought the cinema had given the death-blow to enterprises of that sort, but Carl Magno's Colossal Congress of Wild Animals and Living Wonders of the World—to give the exhibition its complete title—was quite an imposing affair. It was on the road from one fair-ground to another when I saw it, and, judging by appearances, there is still a kick or two left in the old-fashioned show business. There were quite a dozen large vans, drawn by a couple of powerful traction engines, and a smart Pullman caravan belonging to the proprietor. It was like a little palace on wheels inside—electric cooker, silver-plated fittings, radio set connected with a telescopic aerial, and all the comforts of a bijou flat in town. But of course Carl Magno didn't know anything about the Terror of the Moor; his idea was that the hounds must have picked up the scent of one of his caged animals, and I think he was right. So that was *that!*"

"Hard luck, Inspector," condoled Hugh. "What's the next move to be?"

But the detective was not to be drawn.

"The next move will come from the other side—and I have a feeling that it won't be long in coming, either!"

The next morning Hugh drove into Excombe and called at Ronnie's surgery. Fully conversant with his chum's daily routine, he had timed himself to arrive soon after Ronnie's return from his round of morning visits; but to his surprise he found the place apparently deserted. He rang three times without getting an answer, and was on the point of turning away when, raising his eyes suddenly, he caught a glimpse of a figure in the act of drawing hastily back from one of the upstairs windows. Fleeting though the appearance was, it was enough to convince Hugh that there was a stranger in the house; for, while Ronnie had hair of a distinctly ruddy hue, that of the stealthy watcher was black as jet. The police-inspector's prediction of hovering peril was hammering at Hugh Trenchard's brain as he stood hesitating on the doorstep. A stranger was inside the house—a stranger who preferred to reconnoitre through the window rather than answer the door; and what had happened to Ronnie Brewster? As he asked himself the question all Hugh's vague misgivings crystallized into one great haunting fear for his friend's safety. He must enter the house and see for himself what was amiss.

Though he well knew the importance of haste, he was careful not to betray his intentions to the unseen watcher. He made a gesture of disappointment, glanced at his watch, shook his head, then turned and descended the steps and retraced his way to the garden gate. Here he again hesitated for a few moments, then, with the air of one whose patience is at an end, walked away briskly in the direction of the town.

But he went no farther than a few yards. The moment that he was sure his movements could not be observed from the windows of the house, he turned and forced his way through the hedge and, keeping in the shelter of the belt of evergreen shrubs with which the garden was planted, made his way with swift noiselessness toward the rear of the house. He raised the latch of the back door, and to his joy it yielded beneath his gentle push. Closing it behind him, he gently shot the bolts top and bottom and, pausing only long enough to slip off his shoes, crept through the house and fastened the front door in the same manner, taking the additional precaution of putting on the chain. He drew a long breath of satisfaction as he turned and slipped the revolver from his pocket and thumbed the safety-catch forward. Whatever might be the result of the coming encounter, he had at least made sure that the unknown intruder would have no swift and easy get-away.

With rapid, cat-like tread, planting his feet as near the wall as possible in order to lessen the risk of a betraying creak, he mounted the stairs. Arrived on the landing, he found himself confronted by three doors, all of which were shut. Putting his ear to each in turn, he listened intently, straining his ears with the knowledge that his life might hang upon their keenness. The right-hand door, which led to the room where he had seen the peering figure, yielded no result; neither did the middle one, which led to Ronnie's bedroom; but from the third door, that of a room where

Ronnie kept his private papers, he heard the faint sound of movements.

Over Hugh's set features there broke a smile of grim satisfaction. "Got him!" was his mental comment. Firmly grasping the butt of his revolver in his right hand and placing his forefinger ready on the trigger, he laid his left hand on the door-knob and slowly began to turn it; his nerves taut as harp-strings, his muscles tensed for swift action should the sudden click of the disengaged latch betray his presence. At last the handle was turned to its fullest extent, and then, a fraction of an inch at the time, Hugh began to open the door.

Through the slowly widening slit he eagerly scanned each section of the room as it presented itself to his arc of vision. At first he could see nothing but a foreshortened section of wall; then the view gradually widened until it embraced one window; then came another section of wall, facing him this time, then another window; then the edge of a bureau set in the farther angle of the room. But it was not until the door was half-way open that Hugh saw the face of the man who was seated at the bureau. One look was enough. He flung wide the door and advanced openly into the room, his revolver trained point-blank on the sallow, black-bearded countenance of the intruder.

"Good morning, Professor Felger! It is indeed an unexpected pleasure to find you here of all places!" Hugh's voice had an edge like chilled steel as he went on: "But you must not assume that I'm so overwhelmed with joy I cannot shoot straight."

The trapped man sat as though frozen into stone, his hands resting on the open desk before him, his eyes fixed on the unwavering muzzle of the revolver with an expression of unconcealed fear.

"Put up that gun, you fool!" he muttered thickly. "It might go off—"

"You bet it'll go off if you try any of your funny stunts," retorted Hugh, watching his every movement. "You made a complete ass of me the last time we met, but I think the last laugh is mine."

"Indeed?" A mirthless grin twisted the bearded lips. "And who do you think I am?"

Hugh Trenchard shook his head impatiently, determined to put an end to this trifling.

"It doesn't interest me what particular alias you are passing under at the moment, Professor. If there is such a thing as justice in this country you'll soon be identified by a number which it will not be so easy to change!"

Again the bearded man laughed, and this time there was a heartier ring in his mirth.

"Don't you realize who I am?" he cried. "Why, you purblind fool—"

"That's enough," Hugh interrupted curtly. "Put up your hands! You can't bluff me!"

"Indeed?" The slow smile still lingered about the bearded mouth as the other man slowly raised his hands, ostentatiously displaying their emptiness with the air of a stage conjurer demonstrating that, 'there is no deception'.

Keenly alert for the treachery which he felt sure was coming, Hugh followed his movement. Slowly the hands glided upward through the air until they were on a level with the captive's shoulders; then higher and slowly higher until his fingers touched his sleek black hair. Then came the climax like a bolt from the blue. Up shot the bearded man's hands above his head, stretched to the full extent of his arms, and with them rose his shock of jet-black hair. Beneath was a close-cropped head covered with hair of a shade that was strikingly familiar to Hugh's bulging eyes.

"Ronnie!" he almost shouted in his amazement. "Ronnie Brewster!"

The other coolly tossed the wig on to the desk and proceeded to peel off the short, pointed beard, cursing fluently at intervals when the spirit-gum refused to part company with the shaven skin underneath.

"Oh, hang it all!" he spluttered, fingering his chin tenderly. "I'll take jolly good care to have a smooth shave before I stick that wretched face-fungus on again. Getting it off was just like being flayed alive . . ." He broke off, unable to restrain a laugh at the look which still lingered on Hugh's face. "Well, was my impersonation a success?"

Hugh's echoing laugh was a trifle forced.

"It was a great success, Ronnie. So much so that you nearly paid for your cleverness with your life. If you had made the slightest suspicious movement I should have had no hesitation in shooting you down!"

"Thanks, old thing," drawled Ronnie. "I thought I'd work the wheeze on you first, but I'll confess it gave me a bit of a shock when I saw how ready you were to hand me an unsolicited testimonial in the shape of a bullet! But do you really think the make-up will pass muster?" he added anxiously.

"It was marvellous! I could have sworn that you were Professor Felger himself. If you act as cleverly as you acted just now you need have no fear of detection—unless, of course, you happen to meet the real professor."

"Ah, that would be dashed awkward. But I'll have to take jolly good care that he's safely out of the way before I attempt to enter the Excombe Sanatorium. Was my voice all right?"

"Splendid! You're a born actor," Hugh cried enthusiastically. "I really don't know what keeps you off the professional stage."

"Don't you?" Ronnie queried with a grin. "Then I'll tell you. Two things prevent me from exhibiting my shining talents before applauding multitudes—one is the 'talkies' and the other is my partiality for regular meals. Get me, Steve?"

Hugh Trenchard looked at his chum for a moment, then nodded his head.

"Yes, I think I've got you all right," was his laughing answer. "Gad, what a blind fool you must have thought me not to have seen through your disguise!"

Hugh was still smiling when he took his leave soon after and set out on his way back to Moor Lodge. Ronnie Brewster's ingenious plan had steered his thoughts into a new and more hopeful channel, and already a conviction was beginning to take shape in his mind that the next few days would witness the arrest of the elusive professor and the clearing up of the mystery which hung like a foul but invisible miasma over the girl he had grown to love.

CHAPTER XXV

T HE FOLLOWING EVENING the sun dipped to rest behind the
bare, rolling heights in a blaze of crimson and purple. Yet
the very vividness of its grandeur was an omen of coming
storm, an omen that was verified when the colours died out of the
heavens and the mantle of darkness descended on the moor; for
with the night came the unleashed wind in all its might and fury.
The moon rose like a storm-tossed galleon new-launched on a sea
of driving cloud. The voice of the gale dominated all other sounds,
now moaning and wailing like a living thing in torment, now buf-
feting the sturdy walls of the house with all the malignity of baffled human fury; denuding the lashing trees of the last vestiges of
their gorgeous autumn robes and flinging them in yellow tatters to
the sodden earth.

Hugh Trenchard sat in the library of Moor Lodge, with a pipe, a
book, and a blazing fire, and in spite of his comfortable surroundings he found himself shivering more than once as a blast fiercer
than the rest shook the fabric of the ancient house.

On such a cheerless night a bachelor feels his loneliness most
acutely, and it is scarcely to be wondered at that Hugh should find
his thoughts wandering from the printed message of the book before his eyes and journeying toward the girl who had come so
strangely into his life. Joan . . . where was that girl of mystery
now? Was she still hiding in that great deserted house in Excombe,
lonely, solitary, even as he was? Were her thoughts flying to him,
as his were to her? Or was she abroad on the moor, battling with
the winds in their furious revel, resolutely pursuing her mysterious
and perilous task?

A sudden sound, subtly differentiated from the natural voices of
the storm, snapped his train of thought. It was a footstep on the
gravel path outside, noisy in spite of its slow, deliberate stealth, as
though a heavily built man were endeavouring to approach the
house without betraying his presence. Hugh Trenchard sat motionless until the sound had been twice repeated, then laid down
his pipe and book and rose to his feet. Whether the unknown were

friend or foe, he must be bent on a mission that would brook no delay to have come to him on such a night as this.

Was it the Terror? As the thought flashed to Hugh Trenchard's mind the very atmosphere of the room seemed to grow suddenly fearful, with a thrill lurking in every shadowy nook and corner. Very softly, his feet making no noise on the carpeted floor, he crossed the room and took up a position against the wall, where, while his body was in some measure protected by the angle of the massive bookcase, he could watch the window of the room. It was, he reflected, the only illuminated window in the house, and if the stealthy visitant were indeed the cloven-footed Terror, it was from that direction that his attack would be launched.

There ensued a breathless, listening pause: then:

Tap . . . tap . . . tap!

Three knocks, slow and distinct, sounded on the leaded pane. Without a doubt it was a signal, and one intended to reach no other ears than his.

Tap . . . tap . . . tap!

Again it sounded. Instinct urged him to go to the window and ascertain the meaning of this summons; but caution whispered that it would be reckless folly to expose himself, silhouetted against the lamplight, to what might be waiting in the void of wind-swept blackness outside.

Tap . . . tap . . . tap!

At the first stroke of the repeated signal Hugh started to glide toward the window. Whipping out his revolver, and keeping well back to be out of range of a sudden shot, he stretched out his hand and unlatched the nearest casement.

"Who's there?" he challenged sharply.

"It's me, guv'nor," came a low, throaty whisper. "Jim Dawker."

Dawker—the giant gate-keeper of Professor Felger's so-called mental hospital! The information, though apparently frank and open, was far from reassuring. "Well, Dawker, what do you want here?"

"Only to 'ave a few words with you, guv'nor," said the unseen man in a tone that was very humble. "Just a few words—in private like."

"You've chosen a queer time for an interview," Hugh remarked dryly. "Come and see me in the morning."

"I can't—I must see you now"—the voice rose in a beseeching whine. "The morning will be too late—you'll regret it if you don't listen to me now."

For a few seconds Hugh stood with eyes narrowed in anxious thought. Remembering their previous encounter it was scarcely likely that the man bore him any great goodwill; he was, moreover, a paid servant of Professor Felger's. The most obvious explanation was that the whole thing was a carefully prepared trap. Yet its very obviousness made Hugh inclined to dismiss that theory. He felt sure that, when the professor struck, his keen brain would evolve something more subtle, and more deadly, than such a palpable ambuscade. First of all, however, he must make sure that Dawker was alone. "Wait a moment," he said, and immediately turned and made his way to a small window which, set in an angle of the passage, commanded a view of the back of the house. Peering through, Hugh saw the outline of Dawker's huge bulk as he crouched against the library window, but he could see no signs of any companions.

"I'll risk it," was his sudden decision. "After all, he may have something of importance to tell me."

He went to the back door and drew the bolts, purposely making enough noise to attract Dawker's attention to his action.

"I'm going to take you at your word, Dawker," he warned before he opened the door. "But if you intend trying any funny stunts it would be healthier for you to remain outside."

"Lor' love yer, guv'nor, I don't mean yer no 'arm. I'm on the square this time."

"Pleased to hear it," was Hugh's dry comment, as he allowed his visitor to catch a glimpse of the weapon he was fondling. "Come right in, Mr. Dawker, and may I trouble you to fasten those bolts behind you? Are they shot home? Thanks! Now be pleased to walk in front of me into that room on the left. Go right in, and don't be bashful—I have no young lady visitors here this time."

Dawker showed his yellow teeth in a grin at this oblique allusion to their last encounter.

"I don't blame yer for bein' a bit careful, Doctor, but you'll have no call ter use that gun on me. I've come to do you a service."

"Yes?" prompted Hugh as the other paused.

"I've come to put you wise to something that'll give you the shock o' yer life."

"Really?"

"Yus, reely an' truly," Dawker went on impressively. "I've managed to get hold of some valuable information—something that's worth big money. Un'erstand?"

"Yes, I understand," said Hugh in a tone that was far from encouraging. "I thought there was a catch in it somewhere."

Dawker scowled and stood silent, plucking nervously at his heavy jowl. It seemed plain that the man was ill at ease—was, in fact, already half regretting the step he had taken. He had expected his offer to meet with an eager and grateful acceptance, and Hugh Trenchard's undisguised scepticism filled him with a vague uneasiness. For a full minute he stood hesitating; then, with the air of one making a plunge into dangerous waters, he leant forward confidentially and came to the point.

"How much would it be worth to you to get hold of information as to who Professor Lucien Felger really is?" he asked in a husky whisper.

Hugh Trenchard lifted his shoulders in a careless shrug.

"If you are trying to sell me the information that Felger is Herr Rudolf Braüschütter, the Austrian scientist who discovered the so-called 'Apple of Lethe', I may tell you that you've come into the market a trifle late. I suspected as much the moment I detected the symptoms of the drug in Farmer Thacker."

For a moment Dawker was thrown off his balance by this unexpected avowal; but he quickly recovered.

"But that ain't all—not by a long chalk!" he went on eagerly. "The professor 'as been passing for somebody else—somebody you've met and talked with, and never suspected who he was. If you'll make it worth me while I'll put evidence into your hands that'll send him down for a lifer."

"If you really possess such evidence I should advise you to hand it to the police."

Dawker's lips twitched as he shook his head.

"The perlice!" he repeated contemptuously. " 'Ow much d'ye think the busies would give me if I went to 'em? Nuthin'—and maybe they'd jug me into the bargain! I'm risking my life in coming here, and I'm not doin' it for the fun of the thing, neither. See 'ere; I'll make you a fair offer, man to man. Give me five hundred pounds, and I'll spill enough to send Felger to the rope."

Hugh Trenchard shook his head.

"I hope to do that without your help," he said quietly.

Dawker showed his yellow teeth in a derisive grin.

"You'll never do that without my help, guv'nor—the professor is too fly for that! Why, even me, who's been workin' for him for years, never dreamt who he really was until yesterday—and then I only found out by accident. Don't you be afraid of not getting your money's worth if you hand over that five hundred pounds. Why, if you knew 'arf of the devil's work that's been going on in that sanatorium—s'help me!—yer blessed eyes 'ud drop out o' your head! You're a doctor, and I suppose yer thinks yer knows all about operations, but I bet you've never seen such operations as the professor has been performin'!"

"What on earth are you hinting at?" Hugh cried sharply.

Apparently Dawker realized that he was giving away too much. A gleam of cunning came into his narrow eyes as he shook his head.

"You'll get more than hints when yer pays the money. Five hundred pounds is my price, and it's worth every penny. Why, the newspapers 'ud give that to know what I know."

Hugh met this innocent assertion with a smile.

"The people who run newspapers have a very wholesome re-spect for the law of libel, and they generally prefer to wait until cases come into the courts before offering their comments. I should advise you to leave the newspapers alone and take your story to the police."

"Yus, and a fat lot I should get out o' *that!* I came 'ere thinking to 'ave a square deal with you—"

"Then I'm sorry to say you have wasted your time." Hugh's tone was final. "Even if I had that sum of money to throw away for information which may be of little or no real value, I should be compelled to inform the police authorities before any active steps could be taken in the matter."

"So the deal is off?" Dawker's face was a mask of ill-suppressed fury as he growled out the words.

Hugh Trenchard motioned to the door with the hand which still held the revolver.

"Absolutely, Mr. Dawker."

The would-be informer preserved a sullen silence as he allowed himself to be shepherded to the back door, but once he was outside his rage exploded in a savage oath.

"And it won't be long before you're sorry you turned down my offer!" he added darkly.

Disregarding the outburst, Hugh began to close the door, whereupon Dawker's fury got the better of his discretion.

"As you're so almighty clever, you'd better start lookin' after that gal o' yours!" he shouted recklessly. "When the professor gets hold of her, he'll serve her the same as he served Crazy Jake—"

"What's that?" Hugh flung wide the half-closed door as he jerked out the words. "Here, come back! I want to talk to you."

But Dawker was aware that he had said too much for his own safety. Swift as a hare, he darted into the shadow of the trees, and the next moment a succession of flashes and quick staccato reports of an automatic showed that he had not come on his errand unarmed.

Trenchard stepped smartly back into the cover of the porch as he heard the vicious smack of the bullets on the surrounding brickwork. He had no intention of playing a deadly game of hide-and-seek by attempting to follow the fugitive in the darkness. Dawker himself could wait, but his hint of hovering peril to Joan Endean filled Hugh's heart with a vague, intangible fear. Of course, the man's words might have been nothing but bluff; on the other hand . . .

A series of knocks on the front door, delivered with a peculiar rhythm, caused the young man's brow to clear with lightning-like rapidity, for it was the agreed signal by which the inspector from Scotland Yard had arranged to make his presence known.

"What was the shooting?" was Inspector Renshaw's first question after Hugh had admitted him.

"Oh, it was merely the gentle Dawker's mode of expressing his disapproval of my refusal to present him with a cool five hundred"; and Hugh gave the pith of the gate-keeper's offer. Long before he had finished, Renshaw was rubbing his hands together and showing other signs of intense satisfaction.

"So there's a split in the enemy camp? That's good news! When thieves fall out, you know, Doctor . . . I'll fix Mr. Dawker all right; once I get him in the cooler he'll be ready enough to talk—and without being presented with a five-hundred-pound memory-course, either! I'll get a warrant out and circulate his description first thing in the morning. In the meantime I should like to have a bit of a talk with you. You've seen as much of the queer happenings round here as anybody—in fact, they didn't make a start until you turned up here—and there may be one or two points which you may be able to assist with."

Nothing loth, Hugh led the way into the library, heaped some more logs on the fire, and sat down to listen as the police officer went over some of the knotty points. But it was not until some two hours later, when Renshaw was about to take his leave, that he let fall a remark which seemed to cast a new light on the baffling mystery.

"Don't you think it's rather funny that we have not found any trace of Silas Marle's body?" was the remark in question.

But Hugh merely shrugged. "You must bear in mind that Exmoor is an extensive tract of country, and second only to Dartmoor as the most sparsely inhabited district in the West Country. There are plenty of places in it that are never trodden by a human foot from one year's end to another."

"Supposing that the old man was still alive!" Inspector Renshaw went on in a speculative tone.

"Impossible!" The amazing theory almost took Hugh's breath away. "Sergeant Jopling saw him lying dead."

A faint smile deepened the lines about the inspector's mouth.

"I rather fancy the sergeant didn't stop long enough to make a cool and detailed examination of the body, and the next time he entered the room the alleged corpse had mysteriously vanished. Now, I've had plenty of time to think things over from various angles during my lonely watches in the dug-out over yonder, and I have come to the conclusion that old Marle had a very good reason for allowing certain people to assume that he was dead.

"On his own admission, the Terror of the Moor was on his track with the avowed intention of killing him at sight. The mere fact that he presented his house and fortune to you by means of a letter of attorney instead of the usual will argues that he anticipated disappearing in such a mysterious fashion that it would not be possible to prove his death to the satisfaction of the Probate Court. Moreover, he had very artfully contrived to saddle you with the responsibility, and the risk, of living here as his deputy; bribing you with a fortune to which you would have not the shadow of a legal claim the moment he turned up safe and sound. Taking into consideration all these things, you must admit that if the cunning old devil wanted to preserve the secret of his precious chemical formula, and at the same time save his skin, he could scarcely have put up a more convincing fade-out."

For a full minute Trenchard remained silent. The new aspect which had opened up before his eyes at the inspector's words was so unexpected, so full of sinister possibilities, that for the time being he was dazed. Almost unconsciously his mind groped for evidence to refute the unwelcome theory, which, if true, would prove him to be nothing but a too-confiding dupe of an unscrupulous schemer.

"You seem to have forgotten that the all-important formula has been left in my keeping," he said at length. "And it is still in its sealed envelope in the safe here."

"Have you opened that sealed envelope?" Renshaw asked quickly.

"Of course not. Marle left implicit instructions that I was not to break the seal."

"Then how on earth can you tell if the formula is really inside?" Trenchard could only answer by a helpless shrug, and the inspector went on, speaking with the air of a man who cannot relinquish a new and compelling theory: "Now I'm here, why not examine the contents of that envelope in my presence? I don't suppose you have forgotten that you have been fooled once with a sealed envelope that contained nothing but blank paper. What if this other envelope is but just such another fake?"

Trenchard started to his feet and faced the inspector squarely.

"There's more than guesswork in this," he declared. "Come, put your cards on the table. What do you know?

Inspector Renshaw shook his head.

"I know no more than you do, sir, but that doesn't prevent me suspecting a great deal more. I have a big opinion of Professor Felger's enterprise and daring, and I cannot square my opinion of him with the plain fact that he has allowed something like three months to pass without an attempt to break open that safe of yours. Something must have stopped him, and that something might have been the knowledge that the envelope was not worth the trouble of stealing."

"We'll soon see about that," cried Trenchard. "I'm going to see the inside of this envelope this very minute!"

Possessed with an impatience which demanded instant action, he hurried from the room and into the laboratory. The key was already in the lock of the safe, when a loud, strident voice, coming from the direction of the room they had just quitted, banished every other thought from his mind. "Hello, hello! Ronnie Brewster calling!" it said. "I'm in danger and I need your help along to my surgery at once!"

CHAPTER XXVI

T HE MAN FROM SCOTLAND YARD stopped dead and turned
an inquiring face to Hugh.

"What's that?"

"It's the radio set with which I keep in touch with my friend at
Excombe—I always keep it tuned in to our particular short wavelength—"

"The devil you do!" ejaculated the police-inspector, a look of
dismay mounting to his features. "And have you a transmitter your
end?"

"Of course."

"Well, you might have dropped me a hint before. When I was
talking to you just now I might have been broadcasting my private
theories all over Europe! For all I know, the very man I'm after
might have been listening to every word I uttered!"

"I don't think so," Hugh assured him. "Our wavelength is so
short that an ordinary radio set would be unable to pick it up
and—"

"Hello, hello!" interrupted Ronnie's voice from the loud-
speaker. "Wake up, Hugh, and get busy. I'm having a spot of
bother this end. Are you listening, Hugh?"

Trenchard made a flying jump for the transmitting microphone.

"Yes, yes. I'm here. What is happening?"

"Trouble. I was just about to turn in when I caught sight of a
couple of men skulking among the bushes of my back garden. One
was a great giant of a man—"

"Dawker?" gasped Hugh.

"I expect it's him," came the hurried reply. "But that's not the
worst. Those two birds have managed to break into the house, and
I, like a blithering idiot, haven't got so much as a pea-shooter on
the premises."

"You'd better look out, then! I know for a fact that Dawker is
armed. He had a good try to pot me about four hours since, but—"

"Just a moment—time is precious," interrupted Ronnie's voice.
"I have already rung up Sergeant Jopling at the local police sta-

tion—on the ordinary line telephone, of course—and he's answering now . . ."

There was a slight pause; then Hugh and Inspector Renshaw heard Ronnie speaking to the sergeant.

"That you, Sergeant?" they heard him say. "Dr. Brewster speaking. . . . Yes, from my surgery. Two strange men have entered my house . . . What's that? Burglars? Well, I suppose so, for *I* didn't invite 'em to call. They are outside the door of the room from which I am speaking now—trying to force the lock. You'd better rush your men round at once, for—"

The sound of a muffled pistol-shot cut into Ronnie's explanation. In an agony of fear for his friend's safety, Hugh Trenchard bent over the radio microphone and called repeatedly, asking what had happened. To his relief he heard his friend's voice continuing the conversation with Sergeant Jopling.

"Yes, that was a shot," it said, obviously in answer to a question from the other end of the line telephone. "But I'm all right—so far. The shot was fired by one of the burglars on the other side of the door. I fancy somebody was hit, for I distinctly heard a groan and a thud. Hurry along with your contingent of bobbies, for the love of Mike! . . . What? They're on their way? Good lads . . . I'll be mighty pleased to see 'em."

Hugh Trenchard waited to hear no more. With a hurried "Come along" to Renshaw, he flew to the garage, ran out the car, and in a few minutes the two were speeding over the deserted roads in the direction of the little market-town. It was not long before the swift machine drew up before the red lamp of Ronnie Brewster's surgery. Every window in the house was brightly illuminated, and the outline of a helmeted head against the stained-glass windows of the front entrance showed that the local police were already on the scene.

The constable who was guarding the door seemed inclined to dispute their entry, but a word from Inspector Renshaw made him stand aside with a respectful salute. Without further hindrance they stepped into the hall and shut the door. Before them stretched the hall and staircase, looking very spick and span with spotless white-enamelled woodwork and tapestry wallpaper of a rich but subdued shade. A low murmur of voices came from a room on the lower floor. Renshaw advanced to the door and knocked.

"Come in," invited the heavy voice of Sergeant Jopling.

There were three other men in the room when Inspector Renshaw and Hugh entered; two of them were constables in uni-

form, and their presence, combined with that of the man on duty
outside, showed that almost the whole personnel of the local force
had turned out in answer to Ronnie's call. The third occupant of
the room was Ronnie Brewster himself. He stood with his hands
thrust into his trousers pockets, puffing at a cigarette with an air of
nonchalance; but his white, drawn features seemed to hint that his
nerves were still at their tightest stretch. He greeted Hugh and his
companion with a smiling nod, but their reception by Sergeant
Jopling was not so friendly.

"Good evening, gentlemen," he said, adding in a dry tone: "It
seems as if ill news must travel mighty fast in your direction. May
I ask what made you call here at this time of night?"

Ronnie stepped forward and in a few words explained how he
had called up Moor Lodge at the same time as he had given the
alarm at the police station.

"Wireless, eh?" grunted Jopling. "Well, well, we do live in a
scientific age, and no mistake about it."

"What has happened?" It was Inspector Renshaw who spoke,
only to have his curt question met by a suspicious stare from Sergeant Jopling. But he anticipated the crushing effort that was
trembling on the sergeant's lips by adding quietly, "I am Detective-Inspector Renshaw of the C.I.D."

Jopling's manner underwent a remarkable change.

"I'm pleased to meet you, sir," he said affably, though it was
plain that he was completely mystified by the prompt appearance
of a representative of Scotland Yard. "Did you arrive by wireless
too?"

Inspector Renshaw ignored this piece of rustic wit.

"What has happened?" he repeated, somewhat impatiently.

"Murder, sir," was Jopling's brief response. Then, in a sepul-
chral tone, he supplemented his information with: "The body is
upstairs."

"Then let's have a look at it," said Renshaw briskly. "Come
with me, Dr. Trenchard. As a medical man your evidence may be
useful at the inquest, and," he added as an afterthought, "at the
trial too, when we get hold of the one who did it."

At the top of the first flight of stairs was a small landing; another, shorter flight led to a space which might be described either
as another landing or a passage, seeing that it ran almost the entire
depth of the house. Sprawled in the centre was the body of a man,
its legs toward the stairs, its head within a few inches of the door
of the room which Ronnie used as a study, and which contained

the radio set from which he had sent the message to Hugh. Evidently the body was lying where it had fallen after the fatal shot, for the knees were still flexed and the face still turned to the floor, just as a man sags and crumples forward when overtaken by instantaneous death. Hugh Trenchard had no need to look at the hidden face to identify that gigantic figure.

"Dawker!" he exclaimed. "He has been shot from behind, and at close quarters, too. See how his hair has been scorched by the discharge of the weapon!"

"How long has he been dead?" asked Renshaw. "That's the most important point for the time being."

With an effort the young doctor turned the huge body over; kneeling down, he opened the coat and vest.

"He has not been dead more than half an hour, at the most," he declared presently. "The flesh is still quite warm."

"I suppose he really *is* dead?" the sergeant put in suddenly.

Hugh Trenchard pointed to the film of grey which mingled with the crimson stream that had gushed from the wound.

"The bullet passed clean through the brain, causing instant death," he said in a tone of quiet decision. "He was shot from behind whilst standing on the same spot where he lies now."

"How can you tell that?" demanded Renshaw.

"There are several things which point to that conclusion. Take the general attitude in which the body was lying before I turned it over. When a man is shot in a vital spot, his knees immediately give way and he falls forward, crumpling up—'like an empty sack' is a rather crude but graphic way of describing it—and assuming a posture that it would be very difficult to imitate in a body that had once been shifted. Besides that, you will notice that the bloodstain on the carpet exactly corresponds with the spot where the head was resting. But the most convincing proofs are here."

Rising to his feet, Hugh pointed to the door of the study, indicating where a group of tiny red spots, clustered around a neatly-drilled bullet-hole, marred the whiteness of the enamelled surface.

"That hole could only have been made by the bullet after it had passed through Dawker's head; the spots of blood were thrown forward by the force of the discharged cartridge. Taken in conjunction, they prove conclusively that the fatal shot was fired *outside* the closed door."

Inspector Renshaw had listened throughout with his eyes fixed on the young doctor in an expression of undisguised admiration. At the conclusion he nodded his head slowly.

"Appears to me that there was a good detective lost when you decided to take up medicine," he remarked. "Your reconstruction of the crime lets your friend out completely."

"Ronnie!" cried Trenchard in surprise. "Surely you did not suspect that he committed the murder himself?"

There was a curious expression on Inspector Renshaw's face as he stood pinching his chin thoughtfully.

"This case is getting into such a glorious tangle that I'd be suspecting my own grandmother—if I had one. But I don't mind admitting to you, Doctor, that at first sight your friend's 'phone call, at the very time that the shot was fired, looked just a little bit like a ready-made, cast-iron, cut-and-dried alibi; for you must bear in mind the fact that it is quite possible for a man to talk into a telephone receiver and fire a pistol at the same time! But there is only one telephone instrument in the house, and only one radio microphone; so if Dr. Brewster was talking at the time, he must have been in his study. And if he was in his study, and Dawker was shot on the landing on the other side of the closed door—shot from behind, too—it follows that the murder must have been committed by the other man whom Brewster saw lurking in the garden before the house was entered." The detective paused for a moment, and his eyes narrowed. "Now I wonder who that other man was."

"Probably my friend will be able to furnish you with his description," Hugh suggested.

"Ah yes, perhaps so. I will question him on that point."

Together they descended the stairs to the room where Ronnie still sat smoking. But he shook his head dubiously at the inspector's query.

"I'm afraid I can't help you very much, for it was too dark to see details," he explained. "I recognized Dawker by his huge stature. All I noticed about the other chap was that he was of a very much slighter build. He appeared to be quite a young lad, in fact."

"Something like a girl would look if she were dressed in man's clothes?" interpolated Sergeant Jopling.

"A girl!" Ronnie's eyes widened. "By Jove, I never thought of that! Have you any special reason for asking that question, Sergeant?"

"Oh no," Jopling responded airily. "It's just a theory of mine—only a little theory. I've always had a great respect for the good old Italian proverb—or maybe it's French—which means 'Find the lady'."

"Reminds me of the three-card game that I've seen played in the race-trains," laughed Hugh Trenchard. "Speaking from my youthful experience in that direction, I can assure you that it's far easier to pick a blank than to put your hand on the elusive lady."

"I'll put my hand on her all right," asserted Sergeant Jopling, "and before long, too!"

Scarcely had the policeman uttered his confident boast when the sounds of scuffling footsteps, accompanied by a muffled scream, came from the direction of the front garden of the house. The whole party, headed by Inspector Renshaw, made a simultaneous dash for the front door. Tearing it open, they saw the burly constable who had been left on duty there grasping a dishevelled, struggling figure.

"Caught her crouching among the bushes, sir," gasped the almost breathless man. "She fought like a wild-cat."

As he spoke he swung his prisoner round so that she faced the group as they emerged from the front door. At the same moment another constable switched on his lamp, and by its white, merciless glare Hugh Trenchard saw a sight that turned his heart to ice.

The girl was Joan Endean, and in her right hand she held a heavy automatic pistol.

Renshaw darted forward and wrenched the weapon from her grasp.

"Here," he said, handing it to the sergeant, "this will be useful to compare with the bullet-hole in the door upstairs."

"But the girl . . .?"

"Leave her to me."

There was a sharp metallic click, and Hugh saw the girl he loved with a pair of regulation handcuffs fettering her slender wrists.

"I'll run her down to the station and be back in a few minutes," the inspector continued in a tone of brisk command. "Get inside the house, all of you. And nobody is to leave until I return."

Laying his hand on his prisoner's shoulder, he turned and strode rapidly into the darkness. Hugh, with one long, agonized look backward, turned and followed the others inside.

The period of waiting which ensued was one long torture to him. Although no accusation had been made against Joan, he well knew the construction that would be placed on her presence there armed with a weapon similar to that with which Dawker had been shot. Was she, in very truth, the second, slighter figure that had accompanied Dawker to the house?

As the minutes sped by, with no sign of Inspector Renshaw's return, his first feeling of dazed bewilderment began to give place to a sensation of vague, haunting dread. At last he could bear this suspense no longer. Springing to his feet, he made his way to Sergeant Jopling.

"That inspector seems to have been gone a mighty long time," he burst out impulsively. "He has had time to get to the station and back a dozen times by now."

Jopling looked up with an amused grin.

"What are you handing me?" he asked derisively.

"Good advice," snapped Hugh. "If you'll take it, you'll get on the 'phone to your station and find out what has happened to Renshaw—and his prisoner!"

Something in the young man's tone checked a grin that was spreading over the sergeant's broad features. He rose to his feet, took the stairs three at a time, and presently they heard his voice raised in a bellow like that of an angry bull.

"We've been sold—hoaxed—swindled!" he shouted as he re-entered the room. "That fellow Renshaw was no more a Scotland Yard man than you are! They haven't seen a sign of him at the station, but a fast car went by a few minutes after he had left here. What a danged fool I was to take him at his word!"

"But if he wasn't a C.I.D. man, why has he arrested Miss Endean?" cried Hugh.

Ronnie Brewster, who had been sitting with his brows creased in deep thought, now started to his feet with a sudden cry.

"Arrested? *Abducted,* you mean! I see it all now! Professor Felger was out to get that girl from the start, and now he has got her from under the very noses of all of you. Detective-Inspector Renshaw, the man you trusted in and confided with all your plans, was Professor Lucien Felger without his beard and make-up!"

CHAPTER XXVII

SOME FOUR HOURS LATER, when the last fitful gusts of the spent storm were fanning the dawn-tinged sky, a sports car wound upwards along the steep moorland road that led to the Excombe Sanatorium. In it crouched the muffled figures of Hugh Trenchard and Ronnie Brewster.

The disappearance of the girl he loved had forced Hugh to embark on an adventure which even his daring and sanguine spirit recognized as a forlorn hope. Alone and unaided, he and his friend were about to penetrate the defences of the sinister sanatorium and beard Professor Felger in his den.

It was not from choice that he had dispensed with the assistance of the police; on the contrary, he had wasted precious time in trying to induce the phlegmatic Sergeant Jopling to raid the place at once. But his pleadings had only met with a flat refusal. The worthy sergeant had too great a respect for the majesty of the law to act in such a sensible yet unprecedented manner. Information must be lodged, a warrant duly sworn, and heaven alone knows what other technicalities gone through before a single police-constable could violate the sanctity of a private dwelling by putting his foot across the threshold.

It was in vain that Hugh pointed out that every minute wasted lessened the chances of the girl's rescue. Sergeant Jopling was obdurate; the search must be conducted according to the rules set forth in the Police Code, be the consequences what they might. Finally, his heart filled with rage and despair, Hugh had flung caution to the winds and had openly proclaimed his intention of taking the matter into his own hands. That night, he had told the outraged Jopling, he would be a law unto himself.

They parked the car in the narrow coombe, thickly overgrown with bushes, some distance from the house, and proceeded on foot, avoiding the main gates and making for a section of the encircling wall that could not be overlooked from the house. Hugh's main endeavour was to make his approach without being observed by anyone who might be on the watch, and in this he had reason to think he was successful. The high wall offered scarcely any obsta-

cle to him and his equally athletic friend; after that, the dense undergrowth of the neglected grounds afforded them an ample screen
for their movements.

"So far, so good," Ronnie said in a low voice as the two
crouched in the shadow of the bushes on the inner fringe of planta-
tion. "And where do we go from here?"

For a moment Hugh Trenchard made no reply. His eyes were
scanning the outline of the house which loomed before them, silent—seemingly deserted—eerie in the ghostly grey light which
heralded the coming dawn. The two tiers of shuttered windows
stared blankly from its long, flat façade; if lights were burning
within, no unshrouded chink or crevice allowed an escaping gleam
to betray the fact. Hugh shook his head as he summed up the
chances of making a successful entry from that direction.

"Let's have a look at the other side," he whispered; and, retreating far enough to place a screen of vegetation between themselves
and the house, they made a rapid but stealthy circuit. Suddenly
Hugh stopped and pointed.

"Look!" he whispered.

But Ronnie had already caught sight of the oblong patch of
darker shadow which showed low down on the dark wall. It was a
window, set so near the ground that it could only belong to a sub-
terranean chamber. Silently as gliding shadows, they propelled
their bodies through the long rank grass. Their nearer approach
showed that the window was guarded with a heavy iron grating,
but no sooner had Hugh laid his hand on the interlaced bars before
he gave a low exclamation of satisfaction. The iron was deeply
corroded with rust more especially the lower part, where the ac-
cumulated rainwater in the stone sockets had so eaten away the
ends of the bars which were embedded in them that the large oxy-
dized flakes crumbled away beneath his fingers Grasping the grating with both hands and bracing their legs against the surrounding
masonry, the two men simultaneously pulled and pushed with the
same movements as a sculler urges his swift craft through the water. The iron creaked and groaned beneath the strain then with a
suddenness which sent them both sprawling on their backs, the
whole grating came away from the stonework.

Hugh was on his feet again in an instant, flashing his torch
through the now unprotected opening. Some ten feet below was
the stone-flagged floor of a cellar. Beyond the angle of the keen
white ray was a veil of blackness which looked almost solid.
Without pausing to allow his mind to dwell on the question of

what might be lurking beyond his range of vision, Hugh lowered himself through the window and dropped lightly on the flags beneath. A moment later Ronnie landed beside him.

Again Hugh brought his flashlight into use, and now he could see to the confines of the chamber in which they stood. But it contained nothing except rows of empty wine-bins ranged round the walls. Thick dust lay everywhere; festoons of black cobwebs hung from the vaulted roof; a dank, death-like odour clung to the weeping walls.

"This place hasn't been used for years," Hugh whispered. "We're not likely to discover much here."

The only exit from the cellar was a low but broad archway which, they found, led into another and even larger chamber. With its rows of massive pillars supporting its arched roof, it looked more like the crypt of some ancient church than the cellar of an ordinary country house. The same thought seemed to strike Hugh Trenchard, for he stepped close to one pillar and threw the beam of his torch on the carving of the capital.

"Look, Ronnie," he whispered. "If that is not Norman work I'll eat my hat! The sanatorium is a comparatively modern house, but it must have been built over the foundations of one much more ancient. Look at those semicircular arches—and that dog-tooth moulding—that massive stonework . . ." Abruptly he stopped speaking and sniffed the air. "Smells as if the place has recently been used as a stable."

Ronnie clutched his arm and pointed.

"By Jove, you're right! Look at that great heap of straw in that corner . . ."

But Hugh had stepped forward and was bending over something which sent forth a musical jangle as he lifted it from the ground.

"I've never seen a stable where they used a halter like this!" he said with a queer catch in his voice.

It was a heavy steel chain, about ten feet in length, having one end firmly riveted to a huge staple that was driven into one of the pillars; the other terminated in a leather-lined steel collar large enough to fit a Newfoundland dog. Near by was a jug of enamelled tinware containing the dregs of a liquid which looked and smelt like ale; a dish of the same material held several picked bones and a knife and fork. Thrown carelessly in the straw was a child's picture-book containing brightly coloured illustrations of different animals.

For a while the two examined these objects in silence; then their eyes met in a long, questioning look.

"It's a queer kind of horse that eats meat, drinks beer, uses a knife and fork, and looks at pictures!" was the remark with which Hugh broke the grim silence. "It strikes me that some creature has been kennelled here which had to be kept from the light of day."

Ronnie gave a low laugh and shook his head.

"Such things belong to melodrama, old thing," he said lightly. "Probably the man who looked after the gee-gee had his supper down here."

"And learnt his alphabet from a child's picture-book?" was Hugh's dry rejoinder.

"That?" Ronnie shrugged. "Oh, that was probably a bit of rubbish, thrown down here and forgotten."

Hugh Trenchard was far from convinced by this simple explanation, but he realized that nothing would be gained by pursuing the argument. He had already begun to move away, when Ronnie stopped him with a sudden question.

"I suppose you did not forget to bring your revolver with you?"

"Hardly!" he returned grimly.

"Is it loaded?" Ronnie went on anxiously.

"I should say it is!"

"You're sure of that—quite sure?"

"Of course I am," Hugh answered a trifle impatiently. "What are you getting jumpy about?"

"Nothing. Only I'd just like to make sure that your gun is in working order. Do you mind if I have a look at it before we go any farther?"

Without the slightest hesitation Hugh thrust his hand to his hip and handed his weapon to his friend.

"Well, are you satisfied now?" he asked, after Ronnie had squinted into the chambers.

"Oh, quite. By the way," Ronnie Brewster went on quickly and eagerly. "It has just struck me that you might have been right when you said that some strange animal had been housed in this cellar. This is a queer contrivance"—he stooped and picked up the chain and looked thoughtfully at the steel collar. "It almost looks as if it had been made to fit the neck of a human being. Do you mind if I try it on you for a moment?"

Hugh stared at him for a few seconds to make sure he was really serious. "We're wasting time—" he began to protest, but Ronnie cut him short.

"It'll only take a moment, and I'd like to make sure that my theory is correct."

"Oh—all right, then."

Ronnie bent forward and placed the hinged sections about Hugh Trenchard's neck. The steel of ring fitted him slightly more loosely than an ordinary linen collar.

"Do be careful not to fasten it," he said hastily, as he felt his friend fumble with the catch at the back.

"All right," said Ronnie easily.

But even as he gave the assurance his hands pressed the two ends of the collar together, and a faint but unmistakable click told that a spring-lock had engaged.

Filled with sudden dismay at his friend's clumsiness, Hugh grasped the collar and tried to pull the sections apart. They were as immovable as if they had been riveted about his throat.

"You silly fool!" he gasped. "I might not be able to get this thing off!"

Ronnie Brewster stepped back a few paces, and his features underwent a sudden change.

'No, Dr. Trenchard," he said calmly and deliberately. "It is yourself who is the silly fool, for you certainly will not be able to get it off!"

For a moment Hugh Trenchard thought that he had not heard aright.

"What do you mean?" he cried, still tugging at the encircling steel. "Is this some mad practical joke?"

"I hope you may find it so," was the other's cool response. "But you are at least right in thinking that the laugh is with me. Let me advise you not to waste your strength in trying to force open that collar. Before now it has defied the efforts of a creature of super-human strength—a creature, Dr. Trenchard, which you have long desired to meet. Soon, very soon maybe, your wish will be granted. You shall have the opportunity of a long and close—*very close*—interview with the Terror of the Moor!"

There was a pause, during which Hugh tried to fathom the other's meaning. Even then he could not bring himself to believe in the black treachery of the man whom he had trusted as a brother. The only construction he could place on his wild words and extraordinary behaviour was that he had suddenly gone mad.

"Come, Ronnie, this jest has gone far enough," he cried sharply. "I'm ready to allow that I was a goop to let myself be tricked into being fettered like this. But it was a silly trick for one friend to play on another at such a time."

"Did you say a *friend?*" The man whom he had known as Ronnie Brewster repeated the word with peculiar emphasis, his eyes lighting up with a baleful radiance, a cold, satiny smile playing about his lips.

"Of course. Are you not my friend?"

"Your friend? *Ewige Verdammung*—no! A thousand times no!" Gone were the drawling utterance and the vacuous smile of the erstwhile Ronnie; his face was contorted into a mask of fury, his voice like pent-up thunder bursting forth from a placid sky. "I am no friend of yours, Hugh Trenchard, and never was! My friendship was but a cloak so that I could use you as my tool, my catspaw, my foolish monkey who would pull the chestnuts out of the fire for me! But there is no need for me to fawn and truckle to you now, *Gott sei dank!* Now I can throw off the mask and tell you to your face that I hate both you and the whole of your accursed nation; tell you that my old name of Ronald Brewster was but an English-sounding form of 'Rudolf Braüschütter', the scientist who discovered the drug of oblivion, and the man who was known to you as Professor Lucien Felger!"

Hugh Trenchard listened aghast. His brain was dazed and numb, like that of a man who sees his world reeling into ruin about him.

"Then you—*you* are Professor Felger?" he could only stammer.

The other threw back his head and responded with a peal of guttural laughter.

"So at last you begin to see the obvious, *nicht wahr?* Now that I have revealed my secret, a glimmering of understanding lights up your dull English brain. *Himmel,* what a nation of trustful fools you are—you English! You will never learn your lesson—not even the experience of one great war will make you wise and wary. Do you imagine that an enemy will become a friend because you have beaten him? Don't you know that the only way to treat a fallen foe is to trample him down so that he can never rise again? *Lieber Gott,* it makes me ashamed of my victory when I see what arrant fools I have pitted my great skill against! Fooling you English is as easy as robbing a blind cat of a dead mouse!"

Hugh Trenchard's eyes flashed.

"It would be a better simile if you said it was as easy as blinding a man with vitriol whilst grasping his hand in friendship!" he cried in a voice of loathing and disgust. "But what is the use of wasting breath? Doubtless your code of honour would regard such an action as a crowning triumph of strategy."

"It would indeed be a waste of words to try to influence me with your sob-stuff"—there was a smouldering fanaticism in the cold, hard voice. "What are honour, and friendship but empty words weighing less than so many grains of dust when poised in the balance against the mighty prize for which I have been striving? Well enough I knew that the nation which held the secret of a gas, capable of rendering all living matter within its zone of influence self-exploding, would hold the means whereby the future domination of the world might be secured. That is the prize I strove for, and that is the prize I have won!"

"You have won?" Hugh ejaculated incredulously. "What do you mean?"

"I mean that my mission in England has ended—that Silas Marle's secret formula is now within my grasp. Within a few hours I shall have made enough of the detonating gas to annihilate a regiment." Professor Felger paused and allowed his eyes to rest on his shackled prisoner in a glare of implacable menace. "And you, Dr. Hugh Trenchard, shall have the honour of being my first victim!"

CHAPTER XXVIII

IN SPITE OF HIS IRON SELF-CONTROL, Hugh Trenchard's face grew a shade paler at the calmly uttered threat. He had not been deaf to the hiss of venomous hatred that had swept like a sinister undercurrent through the other's words. The man was in deadly earnest. Short of a miracle happening, he himself was doomed.

Yet he could have faced the adverse fortune of war with some greater degree of stoicism if it had been brought about by a fair duel of wits. His jaw tightened ominously as he recalled how his faith and trust in Ronnie's much-protested friendship had enabled his false comrade and ally to throw dust in his eyes with such ease and effectiveness. All unknowingly he had shown his opponent every card as soon as it had come into his hand. No wonder the game had gone against him!

"Well, Mr. Brewster—or Felger—or Braüschütter—or whichever of your crook aliases you prefer to be called by—I've had the misfortune to knock up against some pretty low-down skunks in my time, but I don't think there's one of them but wouldn't feel physically sick if he had to share the same gaol as you!"

Hugh was watching his man keenly as he spoke, and for an instant it seemed as if his tone of withering contempt had pierced the armour of his suave self-satisfaction. For the fraction of a second his scowling brows met on a forehead to which the hot blood had suddenly mounted; then he shrugged and laughed as though his humour had been tickled by an excellent joke.

"I suppose your temper is still a bit raw, so I will make some allowance, and for the present overlook the bad taste of your last remark," he said pleasantly. "But it seems to me, my dear Dr. Trenchard, that your quite natural irritation at finding yourself outwitted by a more subtle mind than your own is making you unappreciative of the delicate finesse by which that result has been achieved. For instance, take the method by which I eliminated Silas Marle—"

"Then it was *you* who murdered him?"

Professor Felger lifted his shoulders in a pitying shrug.

"That is a fact which you certainly should have discovered long before this. Why, I even went so far as to anticipate that you would suspect me, seeing that I was the only person in the upstairs floor of Moor Lodge at the time. The only precaution I took before striking the blow was to make sure that Miss Endean had already left the house, and I was pleasantly surprised at the readiness with which you assumed her to be the guilty party. Taking everything into consideration, I think you must admit it was a very neat piece of work."

"And so heroic!" Hugh cried in a tone of biting sarcasm. "I wonder that you are not ashamed to boast of the murder of a helpless old man!"

"Why should I have spared him? Why should I have shown him more mercy than he showed the halfwitted lad who had learnt his secret?" Felger retorted in swift defence. "The moment it suited Marle's purpose he doomed Crazy Jake to a horrible death, and exulted when he thought his secret was safe. But Jake did not perish in the explosion. I was awaiting his arrival here, and as soon as I heard the report I pretty well guessed what had happened, and hurried across the moor until I came to his body—or what remained of it. No wonder Marle was certain that his victim could not survive—he was a mere fragrant of a man. But, strangely enough, the head—the seat of the intellect and the memory—was but slightly injured. It seemed the very essence of madness even to dream of retaining life in such a mutilated torso; yet if I could do so I might still learn the secret that he was on his way to tell me that night.

"I was desperate, and I took a desperate chance. By a stroke of great good fortune I had at the time a large stag in my operating-room. I had been using the animal for a series of experiments which, though of great interest to me, would not have been appreciated by those who administer your narrow-minded vivisection laws. The animal was still living, though the man to all appearances was dead. I resolved to attempt what no other surgeon had attempted before . . ."

Professor Lucien Felger paused in his narrative, glanced at the watch on his wrist, and shook his head with an air of disappointment as he continued:

"I fear there is not sufficient time for me to give you a technical description of the operation, or rather the series of operations, which followed. Without undue egotism I can assure you that my daring and unprecedented conception deserves to rank as the

crowning triumph of reconstructive surgery. But do not imagine
that my triumph was lightly won. For the first three weeks after
the beginning of the experiment I did not snatch more than twenty
minutes' sleep at a stretch. By day and by night I watched my patients—or perhaps I should say my one composite patient—
tending, observing, taking notes and even photographs which,
when embodied in my forthcoming work, will electrify the whole
scientific world.

"In the end the result exceeded my most sanguine anticipations,
but I will not seek to hide the fact that at least some of my success
was due to the undoubted atavistic traits which existed in my human subject. Jake was, both mentally and physically, one of those
curious 'throw-backs'—reversions to ancestral type—which occur
now and then, subtle reminders (to those that have eyes to observe
and brains to understand) of the former lowly origin of the biped
race which now dominates the earth. Doubtless this accidental factor explains the readiness with which the tissues and sinews
united, and the almost perfect functioning which resulted in the
union. Be that as it may, I can claim some credit for the centaur-
like creature which at last emerged—a creature with the strength
and fleetness of a stag combined with the intelligence—naturally
small, unfortunately—of a man. The fictitious Frankenstein was
supposed to have created a monster: I, in sober truth, have evolved
from two distinct animal types the monstrosity that has become
celebrated as 'The Terror of the Moor'."

Hugh had listened in dumb, unbelieving amazement, so absorbed in the fate of the half-witted Jake that he had forgotten his
own perilous situation.

"You mean to stand there and tell me that you have linked a
four-footed beast to the body of a human being?"

"*Half* a body," Felger corrected gravely.

"And condemned him to an existence in that diabolical shape?"

The professor laughed.

"The shape is a mere accident due to the only material I had to
hand," he explained, soft-voiced and imperturbable. "My one object was to preserve the mind, the memory of the shattered frame,
so that I could learn the secret of that detonating-gas. But Jake in
his new form proved sadly intractable. He sulked and refused to
speak. I had to humour him by allowing him to roam the moors at
night, where, wearing a helmet made from the antlered skull of the
animal that had restored him to life, he indulged his crazy fancy by

proclaiming himself the King of the Moors. It was on one of his excursions that he met and fell in love with Joan Endean."

"He—*what?*" Hugh Trenchard cried thickly, a sudden surging fear almost choking his utterance.

"He happened to catch sight of her on the night on which he carried off Marle's body, and her wonderful beauty completely captivated his crazy desire. For whole weeks I couldn't get a word out of him except raving about her shining hair, her red lips, her smooth, rounded limbs—"

"Damn you!" shouted Trenchard, goaded beyond endurance by the mental picture which rose before his eyes. "Your swinish association of that girl and—"

Felger's lips parted in a slow smile as he saw the effect of his words.

"That is precisely what I told Jake at the time," he drawled. "But do you think I could make the poor sap change his tune? He got more goopy every day, and began to throw out hints that he was about tired of playing King-o'-the-castle all on his lonesome. He wanted a little playmate, and he told me flat that he wasn't going to talk about old Marle's chemical formula until he got one. But I humoured him a bit, and finally got him to promise that he would tell the secret of the gas to Joan Endean. Well, he's going to tell her to-night, and I'm going to be near enough to hear what it is."

"To-night?" ejaculated Trenchard. "It's you that's crazy—not Jake! Don't you remember that Miss Endean is far away beyond your reach by now?"

"True," Felger answered, and once again Hugh detected the note of mocking triumph hidden in the silk-smooth tones. "But a telephone message from your dear old pal Ronnie Brewster, telling her that you were waiting for her here, would soon bring her flying into the trap like a pretty little fluttering bird!"

Hugh Trenchard reeled under the shock as his mind plumbed the depths of the intended villainy against the girl he loved. His breathing became deep and rapid as that of an exhausted runner; queer flashes of red appeared before his staring eyes. He tore at the constricting chain with the fury of a maniac; his fingers itched to close about the throat of the man who had been his friend.

"Oh God! You foul, unspeakable swine!" In his fury Hugh hurled every scathing epithet which came into his seething brain. "I thought you had some dregs of honour and decency, but now I can see that you have never so much as understood the meaning of either word."

In an instant the suave demeanour dropped from Felger like a cloak, revealing the brute beneath. Clenching his fist, he drove it full in the face of his helpless captive, laughing like an exultant fiend as he saw him crash to the ground.

"You shall pay for each one of those words with an hour of exquisite agony, Hugh Trenchard! In imagination you shall die a thousand deaths before you gladly welcome the real thing at the finish. Wait till I return—then I'll show you something that will make the most devilish device of Chinese torture look like a toy to amuse a child. Wait—*just wait*—that's all!"

Abruptly Felger turned on his heel and strode away. Trenchard saw the reflection of his electric torch grow dimmer and dimmer; then came the dull clang of a distant door, and he was alone in the darkness, which, though pitch-like and impenetrable, was not blacker than his own despairing thoughts.

His situation was such as might have appalled the stoutest heart. Yet things might have been worse: at least his hands and feet were free, and the length of the chain permitted a certain radius of movement; his electric flashlight still remained with him, though he dared not avail himself of its light now in case the battery should fail later on, when he might need it badly. His revolver, of course, was in the professor's keeping, and he raged inwardly when he recalled how neatly he had been tricked into handing it over to his enemy. Never before had he so appreciated the inherent truth of the old American West adage: 'When you need a gun, you need it badly.'

But Hugh Trenchard was not one to waste time yearning for the unattainable. As soon as he was satisfied that his captor had really left him to himself, his first action was to make a thorough test of the chain and the staple which secured it to the stone pillar of his prison. But a very few minutes' strenuous exertion demonstrated the unwelcome fact that he could never hope to free himself without the aid of a file or a specially tempered saw.

Desisting from his vain attempt, he seated himself on the heap of straw and gave himself up to reflection. But his every thought was a torture in itself; every second the suspense became more intolerable; any certainty, however dreadful, was to be preferred to these dragging hours of haunting dread. His enforced inaction, while his Joan might, for all he knew, be even then hastening toward the cunning net spread by Felger, was harder to bear than the thought of his own approaching fate. Slowly but surely he felt that his nerve was leaving him—he was sure of it when the sudden scurry of a rat in the straw brought him to his feet tensed and trembling.

"Hugh," he said aloud, his eyes wet with a sudden nervous reaction, "this won't do at all."

Reseating himself on the bed of straw, he resolutely forced his thoughts into a different channel by reviewing the events that had happened since his first arrival on Exmoor. The revelation that had identified Professor Felger with Ronnie Brewster was like the beam of a searchlight focused on those hitherto dark and mysterious crimes.

Everything that had confused and bewildered him was now so clear that he marvelled how he had ever been baffled. The seemingly supernatural voice of the Terror, which he and Joan had heard in the library of Moor Lodge, had come from Ronnie himself. The letter making the assignation at the Devil's Cheesepress, which had so mysteriously appeared on the hallstand, had been left there by the same man, who, he remembered now, had been the last to leave the house. Ronnie, too, had been in the vicinity of the Cheesepress when Hugh had been attacked, and he had been careful to get rid of the inconvenient presence of Sergeant Jopling before the appointed hour; and now he could understand how his so-called friend had been able to appear on the scene so promptly after he, Hugh, had been felled senseless to the ground.

It was no mystery, now, how Ronnie had managed to find the hidden door leading to Marle's laboratory. And of course it was he who had held Hugh up at the pistol's point and demanded the key of the safe. Afterwards it would have been a simple thing for a man with Ronnie's medical training to fake a chloroform attack, feign unconsciousness, and thus divert suspicion from himself. But the most brilliant master-stroke of the whole elaborate plot was Ronnie's audacious plan of disguising himself as the professor—his real self, in fact—and pretending to enter the sanatorium. Even if the truth had been suspected, the fact of his acknowledged disguise (as the man he was really impersonating) would have completely baffled discovery and exposure.

The riddle of Dawker's strange words when he had paid his stealthy visit to Moor Lodge was now a riddle no longer. He had found out that Ronnie and the professor were one and the same, and he was trying to make capital out of his discovery. Having failed with Hugh, he had attempted to blackmail Ronnie, and had been silenced for ever with a bullet. But—Hugh saw it clearly now—the fatal shot had been fired *before* Ronnie had rung up the police, the report which had sounded while the conversation was in progress being merely that of a blank cartridge which had been fired by Ronnie for the purpose of establishing his own alibi. Afterwards he had thrown the weapon out of the window into the front garden, where it had been found by Joan just previous to her arrest. There never had been a third actor in that midnight drama, the story of a 'slightly built youth like a girl in man's clothes' being but a cunning attempt to cast suspicion on Joan. Nor had Ronnie's ingenuity ended there, for after Inspector Renshaw had pretended to arrest the girl, Ronnie had contrived to convince both Hugh and Sergeant Jopling that the detective was none other than Professor Felger in disguise.

Hugh Trenchard held the master-clue at last. But at what a price had his knowledge been bought! The readiness and completeness with which Professor Felger had thrown off his mask was in itself an ominous sign. Never would he have revealed his real identity unless he was sure that his secret would soon be buried in the grave. A man who had already taken two lives at least to attain his purpose, would he be likely to shrink from a third victim, when that victim knew as much as Hugh Trenchard?

Thus far proceeded Hugh's train of thought; then, like an over-strained harp-string, it snapped abruptly. Out of the surrounding blackness, with no sound of gliding footstep or rustling movement to herald its corning, Hugh felt the touch of cold steel on his bare, upturned throat.

CHAPTER XXIX

INSTINCTIVELY HE THREW UP HIS HAND and grabbed at the hovering weapon, but to his utter amazement it receded beneath his touch, as though it were floating in the air. Hugh wrenched his flashlight from his pocket, slid the switch, and the mystery was explained. The steel that had touched his throat was the blade of a file which dangled at the end of a long cord from a small round opening in the vaulted roof. Nor was this all. Looking down at him through the circular aperture was the familiar face of Detective-Inspector Renshaw of Scotland Yard.

"Snap off that light!" came the detective's urgent command in a whisper just loud enough to reach the ears of the shackled man; then, when Hugh had obeyed, he went on rapidly: "Get busy with that file, and work as you have never worked before. Felger may be in on you at any moment. If you can manage to saw through your chain before he comes, spring on him the moment he enters and take him by surprise. It's your only chance."

With unsteady fingers Hugh untied the cord, which Renshaw immediately pulled up.

"Can't you let me have a gun?" he begged.

"I'm afraid I can't," returned the detective. "I've loaned my shooter to Miss Endean—perhaps she'll be needing it even more than you."

"Joan! Surely she has not ventured into this place?"

"She surely has," came the whispered reply from above; "you'll never find that girl shirking her duty because of a bit of peril. Why, she's been carrying her life in her hand for the past three months."

"Her duty?" gasped Hugh. "Did you say her duty?"

"I did, and I'll say more. The girl you know as Joan Endean is really the daughter of Sir Arnold Edgeworth, the chief of the British Secret Service, and she's one of the smartest investigators on the job. She was sent down here not so much to secure the secret formula for our Government as to prevent its falling into the hands of a possible enemy. I thought you'd queer her game unless you kept away from her, so I pitched you the yarn that she was known to the police—which was quite true, though not in the usually understood sense. She's got nerve, has that girl—she even got herself certified as a lunatic in order to get inside that sanatorium of Felger's. But things got too warm and she was forced to make her escape with her task unfinished. She's back again now, though, and I'm willing to bet she'll put 'paid' to Felger's long overdue account before she quits the house."

"How did you find that trap-door in the roof there?"

"She discovered that when she was here last. They used it for the purpose of lowering food to the Terror when he was stabled down there. But there's no time for talk. Work at that chain of yours, and work as though you were working for your life."

Hugh Trenchard needed no further urging; any form of exercise was a positive relief after his long spell of enforced, nerve-sapping inaction. Making a swift circuit of the stone pillar, so that the tautened chain was forced against the masonry as immovably as if it were in the jaws of a vice, he plied the file with a fierce joy.

It was awkward at first, working in the dark, but as soon as the serrated edge of the tool had bitten the first slight groove the absence of light did not trouble him much. For a full hour he worked without pause, until the continuous friction of his fevered strokes had made the blade of the file too hot to be held by the naked hand. Yet the notch in the steel chain-link that was the result of his labour seemed disappointingly slight. Barely a quarter of the tough steel had been sawn through; at the same rate of progress it would take him another three hours to complete his task.

But he had no intention of giving up. Two minutes' rest was all he allowed himself as a respite for his cramped and aching arm. Then he once again seized the file and resumed his monotonous task. Backward and forward—backward and forward went the file, its short, sharp, grinding strokes sounding with the mechanical regularity of a steam-driven piston-rod, and at every stroke tiny grains of the disintegrated steel went to swell the little shining heap at the foot of the pillar. If it had not been for these indications he might have doubted whether he was making any progress at all. Hope and fear alternately possessed his mind as he worked at his task—seemingly as endless as the labours of Sisyphus.

Backward—forward . . . backward—forward. Backward—though his cramped muscles felt as though they were constricted by iron bands. Forward—though the handle of the tool felt like a searing-iron against his blistered palm. Backward—forward. Backward . . .

Above the low, rhythmical grind of steel against steel, another and different sound came to Hugh Trenchard's ears. It was the noise of heavy bolts being drawn, and only too well he knew that it heralded the return of Professor Felger. Desperately he exerted his whole strength on the chain, but the half-severed link still held firmly. His labour had been in vain!

Hastily thrusting the file into his pocket and throwing the straw over the tell-tale heap of filings, he seated himself in such a position as to conceal with his body the portion of the chain on which he had been working, resting his bowed head on his hand in an attitude of dejection that was not wholly assumed. The knowledge that he had been so near to freedom made his failure all the harder to bear. Yet, even in the bitterness of heart which that knowledge brought, Trenchard's keen ears did not fail to note that the man who had entered had not refastened the door behind him. Oh, if only he could convey that intelligence to Inspector Renshaw or Joan! She, at least, was armed, and . . .

"Good evening, Dr. Trenchard," the smooth accents of Professor Felger cut into his thoughts. Standing well beyond the limit of the chain, his captor was regarding him with a mocking smile. "So our noble hero is growing despondent? Curious, is it not, what an inferiority complex can be induced in a naturally rebellious spirit by such a simple thing as a chain? I fancy those Norman barons of bygone ages possessed a much greater insight into psychology than we give them credit for, when they compelled their serfs to wear a collar as the symbol of servitude. It is a fascinating study, this strange influence which a few steel links has over the mental outlook of the man on whom they are riveted, and I can but regret that I cannot demonstrate it more fully just now. For one thing there will not be time; for another, it would be profitless to enlighten a mind which will soon be incapable of appreciating any knowledge. Still, I can accommodate you with some light of a more material nature."

Professor Felger raised his hand to a switch that had hitherto escaped Hugh's notice, and immediately a single electric globe in the vaulted roof burst into radiance, flooding the prison with its white glare.

"Presently you will understand my motive in providing you with such an excellent illumination," Felger went on, "though it is extremely doubtful whether you will thank me for it. But it is necessary for the success of the coming entertainment that you should have the fullest use of your eyes."

Hugh Trenchard made no reply, but his observant eyes did not fail to note every one of the professor's subsequent actions. And these were extraordinary enough to have merited attention, even if they had been enacted under less dramatic conditions.

Crossing to the centre of the floor, he stooped and lifted up a hinged circular slab of stone, revealing a sunken, funnel-shaped basin, in the middle of which was a very bright and new-looking brass nozzle. The professor reached down and turned a tap, and immediately a fine jet of water sprang from the nozzle, ascending about a yard into the air before curving outwards like a glittering plume and falling in a shower of tiny drops into the surrounding basin. Professor Felger straightened himself up and stood with his hands in his pockets watching it with an expression of placid satisfaction.

"A pretty contrivance, is it not?" he remarked at length. "I fear, however, that you do not appreciate its full beauty—yet! Wait until the basin is full of water, then I'll show you something. Nothing alarming, my dear sir, nothing alarming—merely a little demonstration of centrifugal force."

When the water had reached the brim of the shallow basin and was beginning to escape through the drainage holes which had evidently been placed near the rim to prevent its overflowing, Felger withdrew his hand from his pocket, and Hugh saw, with a sense of puzzled astonishment, that it was grasping a globe of greenish glass about the same size as an ordinary cricket-ball.

Without a word, Felger leant over and carefully placed the transparent sphere in the centre of the tiny fountain, where it remained dancing up and down in the grip of the continuous stream, in precisely the same manner as the coloured balls which form elusive targets in some shooting-galleries.

"At first sight it seems impossible that such an unstable force as a rapidly moving column of water should be capable of neutralizing the weight of the ball, but such a condition is only maintained so long as the ball is accurately balanced, as it were, in the centre of the stream. When the erratic movements of the ball carry it sufficiently to one side, it topples over—as it is about to do now."

As he spoke, the ball's downward path failed to bring it within the power of the jet, and it fell with a little splash into the water in the basin. Professor Felger chuckled softly as he saw the bewilderment reflected on Hugh Trenchard's face. Rack his brains as he might, he failed to grasp the meaning of this seemingly senseless piece of child's-play.

"Oh, our little game is not finished by any means," Felger went on. "Having fallen into the water, the centrifugal force once more comes into play, bringing the little ball nearer and ever nearer the jet in the centre, until at last the upward stream catches it and once more sends it merrily aloft. So . . . ."

Again the gleaming sphere began its mazy dance in the air; again it escaped from the stream and fell, only to be again caught and whirled upward. Not a word was spoken by either of the men as they watched the process repeated time after time, until, a chance spurt of the fountain having sent the ball a trifle higher than usual, it rebounded, not into the water-filled basin, but on to the stone floor, where it was shattered in pieces.

"And that, my dear Dr. Trenchard, is the whole point of this little demonstration. Ninety-nine times out of a hundred the glass ball will be precipitated into the basin, where the water will break its fall and enable it to reach the jet again. But the hundredth time it will be projected beyond the rim of the basin and shatter itself on the stone. On this particular occasion it has taken exactly nineteen and one quarter minutes before the smash came; but my previous experiments have shown that there is a great divergence in the various times which elapsed before the end came. Sometimes the ball would dance uninjured for over an hour; sometimes it would be shattered in a few minutes. It is pure chance whether it takes seconds or hours; it is, in vulgar parlance, just a gamble. *As far as you are concerned, Hugh Trenchard, it's going to be a gamble with death!"*

A cold sweat broke out on the forehead of the fettered captive. There was a suave and devilish malignancy in the coldly precise voice of Professor Felger that was more terrifying than any blustering threat.

"Speak out like a man—if you call yourself one!" cried Hugh. "Why don't you kill me now, and end this torture?"

Felger's eyebrows flickered upward in an expression of mild surprise.

"My dear sir, your—er—your little ordeal has not so much as begun so far. As for my taking you at your word, and killing you offhand, that—considering the novel means I intend to employ— would be far too risky to my own life. When at last you quit this earthly vale of tears—that is the nicest way of putting it that I can call to mind on the spur of the moment—I shall be far away from here. Knowing how completely I have succeeded in fooling everybody connected with this case, you may well believe that I have

not overlooked the obvious precaution of securing for myself what
is vulgarly termed 'a slick get-away'. Long before the little ball
has finished its last gavotte, I shall be beyond the coasts of England. Nor will I travel alone, for I shall have a very beautiful and
interesting companion in the lady whom you have hitherto known
as Miss Joan Endean."

"You'll find your science is at fault there!" Hugh cried with a
ringing laugh. "Joan would rather die a thousand deaths than allow
you to lay your filthy hands on her. She knows you for what you
really are."

"Indeed?" The Professor's tone expressed no more than the tolerance with which one may explain an obvious thing to an unruly
child. "But have you stopped to ask yourself how long she will
continue to know me for what I am? An injection of a few drops of
the memory-stealing *Datura obliterare,* and both my past mis-
deeds, as well as the all-important formula of the detonating-gas,
will be wiped from her mind. As for yourself, she will be utterly
unconscious that such a person as Hugh Trenchard has ever existed."

"You devil!" raged Hugh, vainly straining at his chain. "You
fiendish devil!"

"Spare your mouthings," said Felger in a voice of cold contempt. "I have the same dislike that every possessor of a scientific
mind has of mere empty forms of speech. Be silent and listen to
me! The glass ball with which I conducted the last experiment
was, of course, empty. But this—" he carefully drew another from
his pocket and held it aloft for Hugh's inspection—"this one, I
say, though to all intents and purposes its very counterpart, contains a concentrated liquid solution of the detonating-gas invented
by the late Silas Marle. Before I leave this room I shall place this
glass sphere on the jet of the fountain—and you shall stand there,
chained, and watch it dance. And when it ceases to dance you will
cease to live! For, the moment the glass is shattered, the gas will
envelop you, changing your living tissues into a deadly explosive,
converting you into a human grenade that will blow your soul to
eternity!"

With a swift but precise movement he placed the gas-filled
sphere on the leaping fountain, then swiftly crossed the floor in the
direction whence he had entered. At the door he paused and
looked round.

"Farewell, Hugh Trenchard!" he cried with a mocking salute.
"Let me wish you a swift and pleasant journey into the Great Un-

known. My forthcoming journey with your sweetheart will not be so swift as yours, but it will be more pleasant, and there will be more certainty as to the destination. Any last message for the fair Joan? No? Then it only remains for me to give you my parting benediction. *Requiescat in pace!"*

The door slammed. Hugh Trenchard was alone with the dancing globe of death.

CHAPTER XXX

FOR SEVERAL MINUTES Hugh Trenchard stood rigid and motionless, staring as if hypnotized at the tiny sphere of glass that leaped and gyrated under the impulse of the glittering stream which issued from the nozzle of the fountain. Suddenly he bit his lip to restrain a cry of horror. The ball had missed the propelling jet of water. With widened eyes he followed its downward plunge, and a gasp of relief escaped him as he saw it fall into the water which bubbled in the basin below. Yet it had missed the stone margin by less than an inch. The narrowness of his escape from death roused him to the necessity of immediate action, for only too well did he know that the slightest impact of the glass ball against a solid substance would mean the shattering of the frail envelope, the release of the imprisoned gas, and then . . .

He felt no inclination to follow his speculations any further, nor was there anything to be gained by so doing. While life remained to him he must try his best to circumvent the deep-laid plot of the scientist whose misapplied genius had evolved that elaborate and diabolical apparatus of death. Henceforward 'work' must be his watchword. Now or never must he exert his wits and muscles, or before long they would be stilled for ever by the fate which must inevitably overtake him if he delayed.

With an effort of will he tore his gaze from the glittering ball which had just recommenced its mazy dance in the air, and, pulling the file from his pocket, he applied it to the stubborn steel of his chain. He had worked hard before, but now he plied the tool with the frenzy of a madman, for now he knew that he was striving for something that was even more precious than life itself. Joan—his Joan!—was in the clutch of that scheming villain. Even now she might be vainly calling on him for the aid that he would willingly have sacrificed his life to give.

The maddening thought nerved his flagging muscles to even greater effort. The blade of the file grew hot beneath the continued friction of his frenzied strokes; its handle became moist and slippery with the blood which oozed unheeded from his raw and blistered palm. But the steady grind of steel on steel continued without pause or falter, and accompanying it—a grim, reminding spur to his efforts—was the musical purling of the fountain which, like a pretty child innocently playing with a deadly bomb, alternately tossed and caught the gleaming ball of death.

Suddenly another sound came to Hugh Trenchard's ears. From the direction of the hidden door came the slow, stealthy creaking of ponderous bolts being withdrawn. Again he whipped the file back into his pocket and threw himself on the straw at the base of the column. A thousand wild thoughts seethed in his brain. Was it the professor returning? Scarcely that, for he would have no need to exercise caution in his approach. He thrust the idea of Felger's return from him and knitted his brows in thought. The next instant he was on his feet, his heart beating a wild tattoo, his brain humming with the reaction as despair gave place to returning hope.

Until that moment he had completely forgotten that Inspector Renshaw was inside that house of mystery.

The second bolt was drawn, the heavy door opened, and Renshaw appeared from out of the gloom.

"Thank God you've come!"

"All right, sir. Just a moment."

With the utmost coolness he stepped forward and deftly caught the spinning ball. Hugh slipped back on the straw and closed his eyes.

"Near thing." The inspector dropped to his knees and gave the prisoner something from a flask. "Takes it out of you—mental strain. Take a good swig and lie close for a spell, as the saying goes. Feel a bit that way myself. Seen things a few minutes ago—never dreamed . . ."

Renshaw was himself badly out of breath. The neat, harsh habit that denotes a plain-clothes policeman looked a sorry affair; it was torn and muddy as if the wearer had been worming through undergrowth on his stomach.

"Feel like the old lady who saw a giraffe and said, 'I don't believe it.' "

"What?" said Hugh, past humour and fearful of the implication of the words. "What have you seen?"

"The Terror of the Moor!"

Hugh rose unsteadily to his feet. The chain jangled a little, and the dank odour of decay seemed to surge back, not to the nostrils, but to the brain.

"Inspector," he said, and his voice was—he thanked God for it—quite calm, "I've got to get the safe side of this dog-collar.

While we file away we can think. Can I rely on you to do each damned hard?"

He picked up the file and laid it to the niche.

"Five minutes each; my go first and you can tell me about the 'apparition'."

Renshaw held the chain while Hugh worked feverishly, pausing only for an odd split second to query the extraordinary narrative.

"It was roaming about the grounds, sir. We've got a cordon round the building, and I was watching with one of my men; dammit if it didn't crash out of the bushes. *It was the upper portion of a man's body united to the body of a large stag!* Terrified? I'll say that, if it's only admitting it to you, sir. But after a second or so it wasn't sheer funk but wonder. The co-ordination of movement between the muscles of the beast and man was perfect, perfect."

Hugh handed over the file.

"Your turn, Inspector. Yes, I secretly doubted the operation until five minutes ago, when Felger explained it all; and now I remember seeing it through the window at Moor Lodge—the space of time that's elapsed has served to clear the confused picture. I realize now exactly what I saw then, for the man—Jake's—torso was bare and I could almost see where the human skin merged into the reddish-brown hide of the deer."

He paused and watched the file rasping deeper into the link.

"I don't know what's happened above, but it looks as if we're completely sunk!" He took the file and noted with a stab of hope that it was almost wholly embedded in the groove.

"We don't need to fear the Terror, sir. When it saw us it started bleating for the 'pretty lady', like a sick lamb who's lost its shepherd. It certainly wasn't going to attack anybody—unless they were attempting to harm his 'pretty lady'."

"Wha-up!"

Renshaw was peering at the chain. Hugh's heart missed a beat. In a few moments he would be free, free to grapple with his enemies, if it were not already too late! Where was Felger and his beautiful captive? Had they succeeded in eluding the police net, or were they hiding out among the honeycomb of vaults under the sanatorium?

"Steady, sir."

Renshaw's calm warning served to master the premonition of evil that had been mocking his impotence. In another second the link had been forced apart and Hugh was free. Free!

"Inspector, for the love of St. George and the Dragon, give me a cigarette. No, don't give me a cigarette. Give me air! I'll feel better in God's fresh air."

"Best see what Regan's got to report," said the inspector, leading Hugh by the arm up through the dank passage and a flight of steps. "I hope you'll forgive me, sir, not coming to your assistance when I saw you first. I hadn't brought my men up then, and I thought that if Felger returned to gloat over you before he made his escape he'd take alarm at not seeing you there. It's only by posting men all round that we can hope to catch him."

Hugh gasped as the cold air smote him, and drew several deep breaths. The night was like wine! They were standing beneath a short flight of steps flanked by ancient clipped yews. The ground-level—probably a stone terrace—was only a few feet above them.

"Down!" whispered Renshaw. "A man can be seen against the stars."

His low whistle brought the crouching figure of Regan out of the hedge on their right.

"Must have got clear, sir," the detective-sergeant said huskily. "We've combed the house and the garden. No sense in their waiting in the crypt, neither. It 'ud only be a waiting game, and the bloke who runs this place is certainly not playing that."

Renshaw pursed his lips.

"What about the stag?"

"That's gone too, sir."

Hugh gripped the detective's arm with a sudden intensity.

"We're in a hell of a quandary, but I'm going to make a damn' good guess of a way out. Follow that stag, or centaur, or whatever it is. You said it was moping for the girl, Miss Endean. Isn't it possible it picked up the scent somewhere and is trailing them?"

"What if they got away on the road?" said Renshaw sceptically, "If Felger got away before I moved my men up, what about the scent on a tarmac road? Pretty feeble, I think you'll agree." He turned to Regan as a sudden thought struck him. "What time were Jenkins and Soffley posted on the Excombe road?"

"About ten, sir."

"And the lane to Worplescombe?"

"Same time, sir."

"No message through?"

"No, sir."

"What time did you last see your late host, Doctor?"

"Heaven alone knows. It must have been well after ten, though."

A flush of triumph lighted Renshaw's dull features.

"Good enough. Felger hasn't got away on the road. I think we can assume he's not still here because he's bound to show his face sooner or later, and my men can wait till Domesday, if necessary. He can do many things with his infernal surgery, but he can't make wings for himself or Miss Endean. Ergo, he's escaped across the moor. Regan, call the men up and tell 'em to scout about for a promising-looking stag's trail. Doesn't matter about showing themselves—we'll take a risk on that. And tell 'em to work quick."

Hugh shrugged as the detective-sergeant dived up the flat stone steps. To him a definite trail of slots was a very slender possibility. The Terror had been ranging the moor for months, and there was bound to be an awful confusion of hoof-marks, especially in the vicinity of the sanatorium. And every second Joan was being dragged farther from him! It was now almost three o'clock, and Felger could easily have had four hours' start. Renshaw's men had probably arrived at least an hour late, although the roads had been patrolled at a much earlier stage.

"Find any papers, Inspector?" he said suddenly. "Or hasn't there been time for a proper search?"

"Nothing much. He was too cunning a bird to leave incriminating evidence about. Regan went through his desk."

They moved out on to an open space of lawn flanked by shrubs and tall conifers. Accustomed now to the starlight, Hugh stared glumly at the dim silhouette of the beacon. Dark figures were moving about flashing torches. There were pinpricks of light winking from the hillsides—the moor was virtually alive with men. But what use were they? It was closing the stable door after the horses had bolted. Horses? Now what had made him fasten on to *that* idea with such eagerness, with hope resurging into the empty caves so long unwashed by the great seas wherefrom man drew his greatest strength?

"Inspector, I want a map, as large a scale as possible, of the country between here and the sea. And I want one of your men who knows the district inside out. He's got to tell me, say within a radius of two or three miles, which are the farms and houses *not on the roads* that have stables."

"What line have you got, sir?"

"Get the map and the man, and I'll tell you."

Jopling himself produced the map about three minutes later. It had been reposing in his tunic pocket ever since the proud moment the previous evening at which Renshaw had given him the responsibility of patrolling the roads.

"Good man, Jopling," said Hugh. "Let's have a light while I quiz." A trembling finger traced out the Excombe Sanatorium and then jerked northward. "My idea is Felger was prepared to leave at a moment's notice and he had plans well laid. By road was best, but it also suffered the disability of being the obvious way. And if he was going to make off across the moor he wouldn't be able to get far on foot. The inference is he had a horse or horses stabled within striking distance—probably paid the farmer a lump sum to keep quiet, and said it was a champion steeplechaser or something. Felger knows he's only got to get to the nearest large town, Minehead for instance, where he can drug Miss Endean and disguise himself as a holiday-maker. Once he gets to civilization, so to speak, we're dished. You know what he is in the matter of disguises."

"Gorbooger!" said Jopling, instinctively using an expression of his boyhood's farm days. "You could count the hacking stables in these parts on two fingers. There's Trentiscombe Farm four mile up the coombe—"

"Too far west," exclaimed Hugh, studying the map intently. "And the motor-road separates it from us. They'd have to cross it to strike north. What's the other?"

"Lank Farm, over by Wootton."

"Good enough." Hugh swung away, and he and Renshaw and three other men were packed in the police car and a hundred yards down the road before the worthy Jopling recollected himself sufficiently to fold the map.

The driver of the police car knew his business. In a few moments they struck the Excombe road, narrow but well surfaced, and swung north. Although it was a shot in the dark each man felt happier for doing something. The night was windless, but their speed roused an icy gale and bit into their faces. The rolling upland moors, covered in their last glory of purple heather, rising to their beacons and falling away into tree-filled coombes, were but faintly scarified by the starlight, unseen by man, and unconscious of the grim drama that might so soon reach its climax.

Hugh groaned. If only—if only their inference was valid, then the six miles between the sanatorium and Lank Farm would be a wonderful start along the trail of the kidnapper. Six miles on foot across difficult country would take Felger at least two hours. And they were nearly there already!

In about twelve minutes' time the car had passed the police patrol and was backed against a gateway. Led by a local policeman who knew the farmer, Hugh and Renshaw sprinted up a cart-track. Lank Farm stood just across an ancient clapper bridge, dark and eerie in the trees, with the coombe-side rising steeply behind. Were Hugh's hopes to be dashed utterly by following a false trail? He did not know. Renshaw's leathery face was set and grim; he was past thinking of the possible results of failure, to his country—or what would happen to his career within the ponderously enriched room of the Whitehall oligarchs! There was a certain irony in those two desperate men trusting to Providence or to the boldness that Providence is supposed to favour.

Call it what they would, Providence or Fate did favour them. The farmer, a God-fearing man, was startled out of his life when he was knocked up a second time that night and faced with three dishevelled men carrying guns who inquired tersely for the dark gentleman who occasionally hired out his hacks.

"Did he come here to-night?" shot out Hugh, his eyes like slits.

"Surenuff, mister. Said he liked a little moonlight scamper wi' the maid. A gennulman, I reckon. Plenty of money, must have."

"How long ago?"

"About ha'f-anur since."

"Which way did he go?"

"Took the path over the barrow. Come you here an' I show 'ee." Thoroughly cowed, he led the three men to the clapper bridge and pointed downstream.

Within the next hour Hugh spoke only once, and that was to say: "I can't imagine even now how 'Brewster' managed to fool me. I knew him so well in my early days."

"Easy enough, sir. When Felger realized you were well in on the game he had to find somebody you knew in order to impersonate him. Perhaps you don't know the real Brewster went out to East Africa with the Expeditionary Force and was killed."

It was the country policeman, Copplestone, who first espied the runaway horse. Towards the east, where the moor falls away to pastureland before it rises again for the Brendon Hills, the sky was faintly luminous. The farmer had set them on the river-path, too tortuous for a horse, as half the time it meant climbing over rocks. It halved the distance, however, of the moorland track that led over the barrow. As they climbed, nearing the summit, the Devonian clutched at Renshaw's arm.

"Look!"

Against the sky a riderless horse galloped away and disappeared over the brow of the hill.

"Come on!" shouted Hugh a few yards ahead.

It would be very difficult to detail the events of the next few minutes, because even to-day there is a certain muzziness in Hugh's mind due to extreme physical exhaustion and the powerfully induced suggestion that early morning holds over the imaginations of people who visit the camps of early man.

Running forward, he saw three fire-pricks in rapid succession, followed by reports that echoed and re-echoed over the hills.

For the first time Hugh had full sight of the monstrous beast known as the Terror of the Moor; it was rearing up against a fast-brightening dawn, a creature not of this world but of nightmare, resembling nothing so much as the centaurs of the Greek Parthenon. As it dropped out of sight he heard a horrible scream, the scream of a man who sees death face to face. And then he tripped and fell, hitting his head on an outcropped rock, and knew no more.

The Terror had trailed the fleeing man and girl, and, swifter than horses, had overtaken them while Felger was resting on one of the narrow stones. Seeing the 'pretty lady' bound to her mount, it had attacked Felger, who, turning at bay, had shot it through the breast. The Austrian was horribly mauled when Renshaw found him, and quite dead. The Terror apparently had enough reserve of strength to batter out Felger's life with its hoofs before it breathed no more. Thus had creator and created vanquished each other at the end of the trail.

Hugh opened his eyes to find his head pillowed on Joan's lap. He raised his hand to touch her cheek, and saw that her eyes were strangely luminous.

Detective-Inspector Renshaw of the Special Branch of the Criminal Investigation Department raised his brows and went to examine the cicatriced stone of the prehistoric encampment. The formula was safe, and he was smoking his pipe in peace.

But Copplestone, who had been brought up in these hills, knew that all the birds in the universe seem to trill at this hour of the morning, and, seeing what he saw, had to blow his nose.

THE END

RAMBLE HOUSE's
HARRY STEPHEN KEELER WEBWORK MYSTERIES
(RH) indicates the title is available ONLY in the RAMBLE HOUSE edition

The Ace of Spades Murder
The Affair of the Bottled Deuce (RH)
The Amazing Web
The Barking Clock
Behind That Mask
The Book with the Orange Leaves
The Bottle with the Green Wax Seal
The Box from Japan
The Case of the Canny Killer
The Case of the Crazy Corpse (RH)
The Case of the Flying Hands (RH)
The Case of the Ivory Arrow
The Case of the Jeweled Ragpicker
The Case of the Lavender Gripsack
The Case of the Mysterious Moll
The Case of the 16 Beans
The Case of the Transparent Nude (RH)
The Case of the Transposed Legs
The Case of the Two-Headed Idiot (RH)
The Case of the Two Strange Ladies
The Circus Stealers (RH)
Cleopatra's Tears
A Copy of Beowulf (RH)
The Crimson Cube (RH)
The Face of the Man From Saturn
Find the Clock
The Five Silver Buddhas
The 4th King
The Gallows Waits, My Lord! (RH)
The Green Jade Hand
Finger! Finger!
Hangman's Nights (RH)
I, Chameleon (RH)
I Killed Lincoln at 10:13! (RH)
The Iron Ring
The Man Who Changed His Skin (RH)
The Man with the Crimson Box
The Man with the Magic Eardrums
The Man with the Wooden Spectacles
The Marceau Case
The Matilda Hunter Murder
The Monocled Monster

The Murder of London Lew
The Murdered Mathematician
The Mysterious Card (RH)
The Mysterious Ivory Ball of Wong Shing Li (RH)
The Mystery of the Fiddling Cracksman
The Peacock Fan
The Photo of Lady X (RH)
The Portrait of Jirjohn Cobb
Report on Vanessa Hewstone (RH)
Riddle of the Travelling Skull
Riddle of the Wooden Parrakeet (RH)
The Scarlet Mummy (RH)
The Search for X-Y-Z
The Sharkskin Book
Sing Sing Nights
The Six From Nowhere (RH)
The Skull of the Waltzing Clown
The Spectacles of Mr. Cagliostro
Stand By—London Calling!
The Steeltown Strangler
The Stolen Gravestone (RH)
Strange Journey (RH)
The Strange Will
The Straw Hat Murders (RH)
The Street of 1000 Eyes (RH)
Thieves' Nights
Three Novellos (RH)
The Tiger Snake
The Trap (RH)
Vagabond Nights (Defrauded Yeggman)
Vagabond Nights 2 (10 Hours)
The Vanishing Gold Truck
The Voice of the Seven Sparrows
The Washington Square Enigma
When Thief Meets Thief
The White Circle (RH)
The Wonderful Scheme of Mr. Christopher Thorne
X. Jones—of Scotland Yard
Y. Cheung, Business Detective

Keeler Related Works

A To Izzard: A Harry Stephen Keeler Companion by Fender Tucker — Articles and stories about Harry, by Harry, and in his style. Included is a compleat bibliography.

Wild About Harry: Reviews of Keeler Novels — Edited by Richard Polt & Fender Tucker — 22 reviews of works by Harry Stephen Keeler from *Keeler News*. A perfect introduction to the author.

The Keeler Keyhole Collection: Annotated newsletter rants from Harry Stephen Keeler, edited by Francis M. Nevins. Over 400 pages of incredibly personal Keeleriana.

Fakealoo — Pastiches of the style of Harry Stephen Keeler by selected demented members of the HSK Society. Updated every year with the new winner.

RAMBLE HOUSE's OTHER LOONS

The End of It All and Other Stories — Ed Gorman's latest short story collection

Four Dancing Tuatara Press Books — *Beast or Man?* By Sean M'Guire; *The Whistling Ancestors* by Richard E. Goddard; *The Shadow on the House* and *Sorcerer's Chessmen* by Mark Hansom. With introductions by John Pelan

The Dumpling — Political murder from 1907 by Coulson Kernahan

Victims & Villains — Intriguing Sherlockiana from Derham Groves

Evidence in Blue — 1938 mystery by E. Charles Vivian

The Case of the Little Green Men — Mack Reynolds wrote this love song to sci-fi fans back in 1951 and it's now back in print.

Hell Fire — A new hard-boiled novel by Jack Moskovitz about an arsonist, an arson cop and a Nazi hooker. It isn't pretty.

Researching American-Made Toy Soldiers — A 276-page collection of a lifetime of articles by toy soldier expert Richard O'Brien

Strands of the Web: Short Stories of Harry Stephen Keeler — Edited and Introduced by Fred Cleaver

The Sam McCain Novels — Ed Gorman's terrific series includes *The Day the Music Died, Wake Up Little Susie* and *Will You Still Love Me Tomorrow?*

A Shot Rang Out — Three decades of reviews from Jon Breen

Mysterious Martin, the Master of Murder — Two versions of a strange 1912 novel by Tod Robbins about a man who writes books that can kill.

Dago Red — 22 tales of dark suspense by Bill Pronzini

The Night Remembers — A 1991 Jack Walsh mystery from Ed Gorman

Rough Cut & New, Improved Murder — Ed Gorman's first two novels

Hollywood Dreams — A novel of the Depression by Richard O'Brien

Seven Gelett Burgess Novels — *The Master of Mysteries, The White Cat, Two O'Clock Courage, Ladies in Boxes, Find the Woman, The Heart Line, The Picaroons*

The Organ Reader — A huge compilation of just about everything published in the 1971-1972 radical bay-area newspaper, *THE ORGAN*.

A Clear Path to Cross — Sharon Knowles short mystery stories by Ed Lynskey

Old Times' Sake — Short stories by James Reasoner from Mike Shayne Magazine

Freaks and Fantasies — Eerie tales by Tod Robbins, collaborator of Tod Browning on the film FREAKS.

Seven Jim Harmon Double Novels — *Vixen Hollow/Celluloid Scandal, The Man Who Made Maniacs/Silent Siren, Ape Rape/Wanton Witch, Sex Burns Like Fire/Twist Session, Sudden Lust/Passion Strip, Sin Unlimited/Harlot Master, Twilight Girls/Sex Institution*. Written in the early 60s.

Marblehead: A Novel of H.P. Lovecraft — A long-lost masterpiece from Richard A. Lupoff. Published for the first time!

The Compleat Ova Hamlet — Parodies of SF authors by Richard A. Lupoff – A brand new edition with more stories and more illustrations by Trina Robbins.

The Secret Adventures of Sherlock Holmes — Three Sherlockian pastiches by the Brooklyn author/publisher, Gary Lovisi.

The Universal Holmes — Richard A. Lupoff's 2007 collection of five Holmesian pastiches and a recipe for giant rat stew.

Four Joel Townsley Rogers Novels — By the author of *The Red Right Hand: Once In a Red Moon, Lady With the Dice, The Stopped Clock, Never Leave My Bed*

Two Joel Townsley Rogers Story Collections — Night of Horror and Killing Time

Twenty Norman Berrow Novels — *The Bishop's Sword, Ghost House, Don't Go Out After Dark, Claws of the Cougar, The Smokers of Hashish, The Secret Dancer, Don't Jump Mr. Boland!, The Footprints of Satan, Fingers for Ransom, The Three Tiers of Fantasy, The Spaniard's Thumb, The Eleventh Plague, Words Have Wings, One Thrilling Night, The Lady's in Danger, It Howls at Night, The Terror in the Fog, Oil Under the Window, Murder in the Melody, The Singing Room*

The N. R. De Mexico Novels — Robert Bragg presents *Marijuana Girl, Madman on a Drum, Private Chauffeur* in one volume.

Four Chelsea Quinn Yarbro Novels featuring Charlie Moon — *Ogilvie, Tallant and Moon, Music When the Sweet Voice Dies, Poisonous Fruit* and *Dead Mice*

Five Walter S. Masterman Mysteries — *The Green Toad, The Flying Beast, The Yellow Mistletoe, The Wrong Verdict* and *The Perjured Alibi*. Fantastic impossible plots.

Two Hake Talbot Novels — *Rim of the Pit, The Hangman's Handyman*. Classic locked room mysteries.

Two Alexander Laing Novels — *The Motives of Nicholas Holtz* and *Dr. Scarlett*, stories of medical mayhem and intrigue from the 30s.

Four David Hume Novels — *Corpses Never Argue, Cemetery First Stop, Make Way for the Mourners, Eternity Here I Come*, and more to come.

Three Wade Wright Novels — *Echo of Fear, Death At Nostalgia Street* and *It Leads to Murder*, with more to come!

Eight Rupert Penny Novels — *Policeman's Holiday, Policeman's Evidence, Lucky Policeman, Policeman in Armour, Sealed Room Murder, Sweet Poison, The Talkative Policeman, She had to Have Gas* and *Cut and Run* (by Martin Tanner.)

Five Jack Mann Novels — Strange murder in the English countryside. *Gees' First Case, Nightmare Farm, Grey Shapes, The Ninth Life, The Glass Too Many.*

Seven Max Afford Novels — *Owl of Darkness, Death's Mannikins, Blood on His Hands, The Dead Are Blind, The Sheep and the Wolves, Sinners in Paradise* and *Two Locked Room Mysteries and a Ripping Yarn* by one of Australia's finest novelists.

Five Joseph Shallit Novels — *The Case of the Billion Dollar Body, Lady Don't Die on My Doorstep, Kiss the Killer, Yell Bloody Murder, Take Your Last Look.* One of America's best 50's authors.

Two Crimson Clown Novels — By Johnston McCulley, author of the Zorro novels, *The Crimson Clown* and *The Crimson Clown Again.*

The Best of 10-Story Book — edited by Chris Mikul, over 35 stories from the literary magazine Harry Stephen Keeler edited.

A Young Man's Heart — A forgotten early classic by Cornell Woolrich

The Anthony Boucher Chronicles — edited by Francis M. Nevins
Book reviews by Anthony Boucher written for the *San Francisco Chronicle,* 1942 – 1947. Essential and fascinating reading.

Muddled Mind: Complete Works of Ed Wood, Jr. — David Hayes and Hayden Davis deconstruct the life and works of a mad genius.

Gadsby — A lipogram (a novel without the letter E). Ernest Vincent Wright's last work, published in 1939 right before his death.

My First Time: The One Experience You Never Forget — Michael Birchwood — 64 true first-person narratives of how they lost it.

A Roland Daniel Double: The Signal and The Return of Wu Fang — Classic thrillers from the 30s

Murder in Shawnee — Two novels of the Alleghenies by John Douglas: *Shawnee Alley Fire* and *Haunts*.

Deep Space and other Stories — A collection of SF gems by Richard A. Lupoff

Blood Moon — The first of the Robert Payne series by Ed Gorman

The Time Armada — Fox B. Holden's 1953 SF gem.

Black River Falls — Suspense from the master, Ed Gorman

Sideslip — 1968 SF masterpiece by Ted White and Dave Van Arnam

The Triune Man — Mindscrambling science fiction from Richard A. Lupoff

Detective Duff Unravels It — Episodic mysteries by Harvey O'Higgins

Automaton — Brilliant treatise on robotics: 1928-style! By H. Stafford Hatfield

The Incredible Adventures of Rowland Hern — Rousing 1928 impossible crimes by Nicholas Olde.

Slammer Days — Two full-length prison memoirs: *Men into Beasts* (1952) by George Sylvester Viereck and *Home Away From Home* (1962) by Jack Woodford

Murder in Black and White — 1931 classic tennis whodunit by Evelyn Elder

Killer's Caress — Cary Moran's 1936 hardboiled thriller

The Golden Dagger — 1951 Scotland Yard yarn by E. R. Punshon

A Smell of Smoke — 1951 English countryside thriller by Miles Burton

Ruled By Radio — 1925 futuristic novel by Robert L. Hadfield & Frank E. Farncombe

Murder in Silk — A 1937 Yellow Peril novel of the silk trade by Ralph Trevor

The Case of the Withered Hand — 1936 potboiler by John G. Brandon

Finger-prints Never Lie — A 1939 classic detective novel by John G. Brandon

Inclination to Murder — 1966 thriller by New Zealand's Harriet Hunter

Invaders from the Dark — Classic werewolf tale from Greye La Spina

Fatal Accident — Murder by automobile, a 1936 mystery by Cecil M. Wills

The Devil Drives — A prison and lost treasure novel by Virgil Markham

Dr. Odin — Douglas Newton's 1933 potboiler comes back to life.

The Chinese Jar Mystery — Murder in the manor by John Stephen Strange, 1934

The Julius Caesar Murder Case — A classic 1935 re-telling of the assassination by Wallace Irwin that's much more fun than the Shakespeare version

West Texas War and Other Western Stories — by Gary Lovisi

The Contested Earth and Other SF Stories — A never-before published space opera and seven short stories by Jim Harmon.

Tales of the Macabre and Ordinary — Modern twisted horror by Chris Mikul, author of the *Bizarrism* series.

The Gold Star Line — Seaboard adventure from L.T. Reade and Robert Eustace.

The Werewolf vs the Vampire Woman — Hard to believe ultraviolence by either Arthur M. Scarm or Arthur M. Scram.

Black Hogan Strikes Again — Australia's Peter Renwick pens a tale of the outback.

Don Diablo: Book of a Lost Film — Two-volume treatment of a western by Paul Landres, with diagrams. Intro by Francis M. Nevins.

The Charlie Chaplin Murder Mystery — Movie hijinks by Wes D. Gehring

The Koky Comics — A collection of all of the 1978-1981 Sunday and daily comic strips by Richard O'Brien and Mort Gerberg, in two volumes.

Suzy — Another collection of comic strips from Richard O'Brien and Bob Vojtko

Dime Novels: Ramble House's 10-Cent Books — *Knife in the Dark* by Robert Leslie Bellem, *Hot Lead* and *Song of Death* by Ed Earl Repp, *A Hashish House in New York* by H.H. Kane, and five more.

Blood in a Snap — The *Finnegan's Wake* of the 21ˢᵗ century, by Jim Weiler

Stakeout on Millennium Drive — Award-winning Indianapolis Noir — Ian Woollen.

Dope Tales #1 — Two dope-riddled classics; *Dope Runners* by Gerald Grantham and *Death Takes the Joystick* by Phillip Condé.

Dope Tales #2 — Two more narco-classics; *The Invisible Hand* by Rex Dark and *The Smokers of Hashish* by Norman Berrow.

Dope Tales #3 — Two enchanting novels of opium by the master, Sax Rohmer. *Dope* and *The Yellow Claw*.

Tenebrae — Ernest G. Henham's 1898 horror tale brought back.

The Singular Problem of the Stygian House-Boat — Two classic tales by John Kendrick Bangs about the denizens of Hades.

Tiresias — Psychotic modern horror novel by Jonathan M. Sweet.

The One After Snelling — Kickass modern noir from Richard O'Brien.

The Sign of the Scorpion — 1935 Edmund Snell tale of oriental evil.

The House of the Vampire — 1907 poetic thriller by George S. Viereck.

An Angel in the Street — Modern hardboiled noir by Peter Genovese.

The Devil's Mistress — Scottish gothic tale by J. W. Brodie-Innes.

The Lord of Terror — 1925 mystery with master-criminal, Fantômas.

The Lady of the Terraces — 1925 adventure by E. Charles Vivian.

My Deadly Angel — 1955 Cold War drama by John Chelton

Prose Bowl — Futuristic satire — Bill Pronzini & Barry N. Malzberg .

Satan's Den Exposed — True crime in Truth or Consequences New Mexico — Award-winning journalism by the *Desert Journal*.

The Amorous Intrigues & Adventures of Aaron Burr — by Anonymous — Hot historical action.

I Stole $16,000,000 — A true story by cracksman Herbert E. Wilson.

The Black Dark Murders — Vintage 50s college murder yarn by Milt Ozaki, writing as Robert O. Saber.

Sex Slave — Potboiler of lust in the days of Cleopatra — Dion Leclerq.

You'll Die Laughing — Bruce Elliott's 1945 novel of murder at a practical joker's English countryside manor.

The Private Journal & Diary of John H. Surratt — The memoirs of the man who conspired to assassinate President Lincoln.

Dead Man Talks Too Much — Hollywood boozer by Weed Dickenson

Red Light — History of legal prostitution in Shreveport Louisiana by Eric Brock. Includes wonderful photos of the houses and the ladies.

A Snark Selection — Lewis Carroll's *The Hunting of the Snark* with two Snarkian chapters by Harry Stephen Keeler — Illustrated by Gavin L. O'Keefe.

Ripped from the Headlines! — The Jack the Ripper story as told in the newspaper articles in the *New York* and *London Times*.

Geronimo — S. M. Barrett's 1905 autobiography of a noble American.

The White Peril in the Far East — Sidney Lewis Gulick's 1905 indictment of the West and assurance that Japan would never attack the U.S.

The Compleat Calhoon — All of Fender Tucker's works: Includes *Totah Six-Pack*, *Weed, Women and Song* and *Tales from the Tower*, plus a CD of all of his songs.

Totah Six-Pack — Just Fender Tucker's six tales about Farmington in one sleek volume.

RAMBLE HOUSE
Fender Tucker, Prop.
www.ramblehouse.com   fender@ramblehouse.com
228-826-1783   10329 Sheephead Drive, Vancleave MS 39565

www.ingramcontent.com/pod-product-compliance
Lightning Source LLC
Chambersburg PA
CBHW030516020726
47494CB00004B/1115